Bruce

Murder by Magic

Detective Inspector Skelgill Investigates

LUCiUS

Text copyright 2015 Bruce Beckham

All rights reserved. Bruce Beckham asserts his right always to be identified as the author of this work. No part may be copied or transmitted without written permission from the publisher.

This is a work of fiction. Names, characters, places and incidents either are the product of the author's imagination or are used fictitiously. Any resemblance to actual persons, living or dead, events and locales is entirely coincidental.

Kindle edition first published by Lucius 2015

Paperback edition first published by Lucius 2015

For more details and rights enquiries contact:
Lucius-ebooks@live.com

Cover design by Moira Kay Nicol

EDITOR'S NOTE

Murder by Magic is a stand-alone crime mystery, the fifth in the series 'Detective Inspector Skelgill Investigates'. It is set primarily in the English Lake District, although for the purposes of storytelling some minor liberties have been taken with the geography of the Langdales.

Absolutely no AI (Artificial Intelligence) is used in the writing of the DI Skelgill novels.

THE DI SKELGILL SERIES

Murder in Adland
Murder in School
Murder on the Edge
Murder on the Lake
Murder by Magic
Murder in the Mind
Murder at the Wake
Murder in the Woods
Murder at the Flood
Murder at Dead Crags
Murder Mystery Weekend
Murder on the Run
Murder at Shake Holes
Murder at the Meet
Murder on the Moor
Murder Unseen
Murder in our Midst
Murder Unsolved
Murder in the Fells
Murder at the Bridge
Murder on the Farm

1. YOWES

Walking in the Lake District, it is not unusual to come across the carcass of a sheep. With an ovine population that outnumbers the human residents of the National Park by more than ten to one – put bluntly – they have to die somewhere. Desiccated by wind, bleached by sun, bones and fleece scattered by scavengers, sometimes all that remains is a skull, its empty sockets staring out from the bracken like a stranded spirit. Since early medieval times sheep have been reared in the Lakes, and breeding flocks of Herdwicks have lived – and died – upon the same 'heaf' for countless generations. Their husbandry is woven into the fabric of a landscape that has dry stone enclosures bent like ribs through the heather. High above, the hardy creatures speckle the open fells, scrambling down 'in bye' to lamb only upon the insistence of crafty dogs and their whistling masters. These shepherds still count using ancient Cumbric, a relict language that tells of a Celtic ancestry, and varies even by dale, with *yaena, taena, teddera* (one, two, three) in Eskdale becoming *yan, tyan, tethera* in neighbouring Borrowdale.

Most closely associated with the latter, and thus familiar with both the rhythmical pattern of life and death, and the vernacular, it is only when Skelgill's morning tally of fellside casualties reaches *tethera* that he begins to take note. That, and the absence of the sheep's head.

This particular corpse is what might be described as 'Raven fresh' – and, indeed, it is an unruly unkindness of these sinister corvids that calls his attention to the site of excoriation, high on the northern flank of the Scafell Pikes. "Fighting for the eyes," is Skelgill's muttered observation, as he hears a battering of wings and sees the jousting of great beaks. Upon his cautious approach, one by one the birds launch themselves reluctantly, their protests of *brok* resonant about the silent comb. He pauses to watch them glide to a crag below Round How, and crowd into a surly committee that conspires to vote him off the mountain.

Having parked his motorbike before dawn at Hope's Farm in Borrowdale, this April Sunday sees Skelgill trailblazing a running route that packs in some of Lakeland's most famous peaks. He is calling it 'The Mammoth', for its outline upon the map looks like two flapping ears and a flared trunk. In brief, it skims south over Glaramara and Allen Crags; from Esk Hause due east upon Rossett Pike and the Langdales; south to Pike of Blisco, with its epic cairn; west along the roller coaster of Crinkle Crags, Bow Fell and Esk Pike; down into Eskdale, whence to scale Sca Fell via Foxes Tarn; a hair-raising scramble to Mickledore through the boulder-choke that is the Lord's Rake; then 'home' over the small matter of Scafell Pike, Broad Crag, Great End, Great Gable and Green Gable. Thirty-five miles, fifteen thousand feet of ascent, and Gladis Hope's legendary Cumberland Fry – and make that a large one.

It is upon Broad Crag that Skelgill has encountered his third dead sheep since sunrise. The first two comprised little more than weathered remains, encrusted like lichen upon the splintered rocks, with scant form but clumps of fleece and strands of sinew. Now, as he pensively regards *tethera*, he might be wondering whether *yan* and *tyan* were similarly lacking in essential parts of their anatomy – for it is not just the head that is absent. Ravens might be equipped with bills capable of tearing the exposed hide of a sheep's belly, but this animal has been savagely butchered, its thoracic cavity cleaved apart, a gaping red wound that has so aroused the winged opportunists.

Skelgill is travelling light. There was a good forecast and the weather has lived up to its billing. A cloudless dawn has given rise to a crisp and bright early morn, and only now are the first few cumuli beginning to bubble up on the south-westerly drift that bears the fresh itch of birch pollen. A water bottle and two *Wainwrights* (books four and seven) contribute the majority of weight to his small backpack, but there is also his mobile phone, and he employs it now to take a series of photographs of the unfortunate animal. Sheep can ordinarily be recognised by *lug* marks – though not this one; given the deficiency of ears Skelgill captures the coloured *smit* marks on the fleece, which ought to identify the owner. The image of the underbelly has him narrowing his eyes – an onlooker might say in anger – for this yowe was ready to lamb.

*

'Aye – thon's one o' George Dixon's yowes – frae ower Wasdale.'

Skelgill nods, grim faced.

'Who'd do that, Arthur?'

The farmer is a big man; he'd seemed a giant once, when Skelgill was a boy, unofficially apprenticed on Arthur Hope's farm, being a classmate of his son. Now his frame is bowed, by age and the dipping of ten thousand yowes – but he can still cart a vintage motorbike about his workshop that would take two ordinary folk to heft. He shakes his large head, chiselled like a boulder taken off the side of the fell that rises above the slate-built farmstead.

'Offcomers.'

This single word conveys his feelings on the matter – no man of the fells could commit such an act.

'You've not had any problems?'

'Ourn are all in-bye since Wednesday – but we've lost a couple o'er the winter. Might have strayed. I'll 'ave a word wi' our Jud case 'e's sin owt.'

Skelgill takes a deep breath and exhales slowly. The air is still cool and wraithlike condensation drifts across the yard.

'Lambing yet, Arthur?'

'Any day, lad.' The farmer grins, wry lips covering his teeth. 'Thou volunteering?'

Skelgill, appropriately, looks sheepish.

'As I recall, you put me on tea duty last time, Art – that's how much use I was.'

Arthur Hope winks.

'Jud tells me tha's got a fighting dog.'

Skelgill grins; the farmer is ribbing him.

'Aye – she'll just about fight the cat for your dinner if you turn your back.'

There comes a sharp rapping on a small pane of glass, a steamed-up side window of the kitchen. It is a signal that Skelgill's breakfast is ready.

'Get the'sen fed, lad – I heard thee come.'

Skelgill looks a little alarmed. Earlier he had wheeled his motorbike the last hundred yards so as not to disturb the family.

'Sorry if I woke you.'

'I were up, lad – thought it wo' sound o' your bike – it's only thee that's touched enough to be ont' fells int' dark.'

Skelgill shrugs apologetically.

'Aye, well – I like the place to myself, Arthur. How come you were awake?'

'If t'yowes start ter lamb it's at four int' mornin' – and Jud's away for a sale – yowes and hoggs wi' lambs at foot.'

Skelgill nods appreciatively – it is a positive sign that the farm is seeking to add to its flock. The knocking comes again, more insistently now, and Arthur Hope inclines his head towards the planked door that displays a tilted hand-lettered notice marked 'café'.

'Gan an get that fry, lad – afore Gladis gives it t'cur dogs.'

*

In a condition allied to drunkenness, Skelgill staggers under the burden of his Cumberland Fry, his saturated fat levels soaring like the surrounding fells. His *Triumph* motorcycle is parked a short distance down the farm track, and ahead of him the first swallow of the summer – though by tradition an oxymoron – dips and dives for clegs attracted by the dung. A yellow splash of *Forsythia* spills from a little walled-off garden, and along the lane whitebeam are budding, their clusters of leaves exploding in a display of mock *Magnolia*. From their midst a chiffchaff, just landed from Africa, imperfectly announces its presence. Spring has arrived in the Lakes.

Approaching Rosthwaite Skelgill has to slow for a flock of Herdwicks, perhaps two hundred that have been gathered from the fells and now are being walked up by their shepherd and two hands. There is no need for the dogs – their work done, they balance improbably on the back of a quad; the village walls provide all the necessary curbs. The ewes graze as they go, bellies swaying, eager to trim the lush verges, remembering the taste of fresh green couch after a winter of austerity. Their fleeces are stained by peat and rock and bracken, like the greatcoats of a ragtag rebel army that has been holding out in the hills, now under truce and trading grass for little black lambs. Thus, the wheel of life takes another turn.

2. MR LEONARD

'Morning, Guvnor.'

Skelgill glances up from his computer without tempering his scowl. DS Leyton has arrived bearing mugs of tea from the canteen, but this softener has little apparent impact upon his superior's mood. If DS Leyton were able to see the map on his screen and the scribbled calculations on his pad, he might deduce that Skelgill is dissatisfied with some aspect of his run yesterday morning. Alternatively, had he observed Skelgill's arrival a few minutes earlier, prising himself from his car and hobbling across to the rear entrance, thence to seek out drugs from a reliable dealer in the shape of a cleaning lady, he might form another theory for the cause of his boss's displeasure. More profound sleuthing would reveal that Skelgill had 'dined out' rather well on his latest exploit and, frankly – at 37 – is no longer able to treat either real ale or fell running with the casual indifference he once could. He might now be wishing he had spent his Sunday fishing, which would have avoided at least one of his present ailments.

DS Leyton, having seated himself, and given Skelgill a reasonable window in which to voice either a complaint or – less likely – an acknowledgement for his provision of the tea, and receiving neither, leans forward and places a forearm across one knee.

'Just received a report of a missing person, Guv – young chap never came back to his B&B in Keswick last night.'

Skelgill takes a long draught of tea and regards his colleague thoughtfully across the rim of his mug.

'We've probably arrested him.'

DS Leyton grins, but shakes his head.

'I checked, Guv – nobody matching the name or description.'

Skelgill appears largely disinterested, and his gaze drifts back to his screen.

'Landlady thinks he was hillwalking, Guv.'

The word *hillwalking* seems to ignite a tiny spark of interest in Skelgill's otherwise unenthusiastic demeanour.

'Where?'

'She doesn't know, Guv – want me to shoot over and have a natter?'

Skelgill swallows the remainder of his tea, seemingly inured to its incipient heat. He bangs down the mug and pushes himself to his feet by the arms of his chair, grimacing through bared teeth.

'Pity our mob closed down that burger van, Leyton.'

*

'Grisedale Vista' is a tall, narrow end-of-terrace guesthouse that – despite its promising designation – overlooks the public cark park in the centre of Keswick. True, leaning on tiptoes from the loft dormer, the summit of Grisedale Pike is just about visible, but this is not the most auspicious view, and certainly does not do justice to the mountain that defines the small town's splendid western horizon.

The entire row is given over to B&Bs and, efficient landladies having promptly fed and shooed away their overnight guests, there are vacant parking spaces outside most of the properties. The front doors are reached by a stiff climb up a zigzag of stone steps – perhaps a cunning defence against undesirable oversized suitcases – and this banked frontage is adorned in such a way that it also presents a considerable challenge to the eye. It is rather as if a local garden centre has gone bankrupt and all the unwanted stock from the fire sale has ended up here. Not only does a plethora of 'Vacancies' signs and Tourist Board rosettes compete for the attention of the prospective lodger, but also a battle of paraphernalia is being fought. There are birdbaths, windmills, classical sculptures with noses and fingers missing, solar-powered lanterns, pots with dwarf conifers and hanging baskets that trail ivy and withered remnants of last year's *Lobelia*. Grisedale Vista appears to specialise in gnomes.

'That one looks like you, Leyton.'

Skelgill has picked out a chubby – though cheerful – character waving a trowel and what might be a cauliflower. However, DS Leyton gives as good as he gets.

'Well – that's you then, Guv – with the fishing rod – and the big hooter.'

Skelgill, scaling the steps ahead of his more ponderous colleague, surreptitiously runs a finger and thumb from the bridge to the end of his nose; he scowls and reaches for the bell push. However, he hesitates for a moment as he reads a series of notices that have been taped to the inner door of the porch:

"No arrivals before 5pm."
"No muddy walking boots or wet clothing."
"No smoking or dogs."
"No admission or noise after 10pm."
"No alcohol on the premises."

Skelgill folds his arms as he considers these directives – perhaps contemplating the futility of his ever applying here for a night's bed and breakfast.

'Why not keep it simple and say, "No visitors", Guv?'

Skelgill nods as he thumbs the bell. It is the sort that keeps ringing when depressed, and he holds it down with a certain determination. He starts, however, when the figure of a woman suddenly pops up from beneath the wood-panelled lower section of the door and glares at them through the glass. She is probably in her late fifties, thin and angular, with a long pointed nose and deep-set eyes ringed by dark shadows, short mousy hair and pale skin, most notable on her bare arms, which droop limply before her. A meerkat is called to mind. Evidently she is in the process of cleaning the hall floor, for she holds a scrubbing brush, and wears yellow rubber gloves and a faded sky-blue overall. Peeling off the gloves, and setting her jaw ominously, she unfastens the latch. Skelgill steps back and quips out of the side of his mouth.

'Over to you, Leyton.'

DS Leyton hurriedly engages the defensive shield of his warrant card.

'Mrs Robinson?'

'Yes?'

'I'm DS Leyton and this is DI Skelgill, from Cumbria CID, madam – you spoke with one of our colleagues earlier – about your missing guest – Mr Leonard?'

'He isn't here.'

'Yes madam – that's why we've called.'

The woman glowers disapprovingly, although she is already scrutinising their shoes as if she is resigned to having to admit them.

'We'd like to know a little bit about him for our files.'

'Well, I don't see how I can help.'

'Perhaps – if we could see his room – you told the duty officer he'd left some belongings?'

'There's no wallet – he hasn't paid, you know.'

The woman appears quite unabashed by her revelation of this knowledge.

'Well – maybe if we can track him down, madam – we can get that sorted out.'

This suggestion seems to win a modicum of approval, and rather grudgingly she moves aside and allows the detectives to enter. A loud electronic alert sounds as the door closes behind them. The hallway is narrow and tiled in a chequered Victorian style; there is a smell of disinfectant, and from beneath knitted brows the woman frowns at their footprints. They pass a doorway on the right marked 'Residents' Lounge' (subtitled, "Locked at 9pm"). Skelgill catches a glimpse of a firm-looking sofa that has clear plastic stretched over the seat cushions, and the shade of a table lamp with its pleated cellophane wrap still in place. Ahead on the left is a staircase, and beyond doors of what might be a breakfast room ("Wait to be seated") and the kitchen ("Keep out"). Beneath the stairs is an austere upright chair and beside it on a stand a telephone and a gnome piggy bank – the latter labelled "Honesty box" with the word honesty underlined twice.

They are led to a small single bedroom on the second floor, in the eaves at the rear of the house. The air is stuffy and Skelgill automatically gravitates to the window; it faces north and has pleasing views to Skiddaw. He raises the sash and leans out, as if to satisfy himself that the browbeaten lodger has not made some escape bid and is hiding on a flat roof – but there is a sharp drop, perhaps thirty feet, to a paved courtyard. When he turns back, DS Leyton is unzipping a worn black sports holdall that sits at the foot of the apparently undisturbed bed. The landlady is in close attendance, gnawing at a fingernail.

'Mrs Robinson?'

The woman twitches. Skelgill gestures to a mahogany wardrobe.

'Could you show me inside, please?'

He is perfectly capable of looking for himself; it seems he wishes to divert her attention away from DS Leyton.

'It is quite empty, Inspector.'

She tugs at one of the doors, causing its ill-fitting twin to swing open at the same time. Other than half-a-dozen odd coat hangers the cupboard is bare.

'How about the dresser?'

One by one she pulls open the drawers. Like the wardrobe this item is warped by age; it has lost its original shape and each action is met with a shriek of protest.

'And there was nothing left in the bathroom – if he even went in there. Everything is in the bag, Inspector.'

Skelgill nods. DS Leyton, perhaps fearing sharp objects, is gingerly working his way through its contents.

'So, when did you last see Mr Leonard, madam?'

The woman reverts to her meerkat pose – as if she believes she will be held responsible for his disappearance.

'Actually, it was when he arrived.'

'What time was that?'

'Four fifty-eight.'

Skelgill nods implacably. She would have noticed exactly.

'And when did he go out?'

'I thought he had stayed in his room until bedtime. I don't understand how I did not hear the exit alarm.' She wrings her hands in self-reproach. 'And this morning I cooked his breakfast – a complete waste.'

For a moment Skelgill appears as though he might beg to differ – but he overcomes his instinct for food and deals with the matter in hand.

'There's a back entrance?'

The woman's scowl suggests she would not let someone give her the slip so easily.

'Through the kitchen – but I was there most of the time.'

'Where are your quarters, madam?'

'I have a bed-sitting arrangement – in the basement.'

'Perhaps you were down there?'

'But the bells are also wired to my rooms.'

'Is it possible he left at the same time as some other folk?'

'My only additional guests last night were an elderly couple – and they watched television in the lounge until nine – after which they went directly to their room on the first floor – at the front. Before they left I asked them if they had seen Mr Leonard, and they said not.'

Skelgill rubs his chin with a knuckle. The stubble makes a rasping sound and the landlady narrows her eyes disapprovingly.

'Did he suggest he might want to go somewhere in particular – you mentioned hillwalking when you called us?'

She folds her arms, as though offended that her report is being called into question.

'There was a map sticking out of the side pocket of his jacket.'

'Did you see the title or the sheet number?'

'It just said, "Derwentwater" it looked like an old one, a *Bartholomew*.'

Skelgill nods.

'It was observant of you to notice, madam.'

The woman looks away, and bends down to straighten the corner of a rug that Skelgill has inadvertently scuffed. It seems that she has shied away from the compliment, unaccustomed to such. Meticulously, she arranges the little carpet tassels. Skelgill, meanwhile, is watching DS Leyton, who has discovered a concealed zip on the base of the holdall: it is in fact a flat compartment housing straps that enable the bag to convert into a rucksack. He slides his hand inside and, after a second or two of exploration, pulls out a small rectangular plastic wallet. The two detectives exchange glances, and DS Leyton hands the item to Skelgill.

'You said he was called Mr Leonard, madam?'

Skelgill has opened the wallet and is squinting at the contents. Then he folds it and places his hands casually behind his back as the woman rises and straightens her overall. Her features have regained their pained aspect, and constrict further as she is asked to repeat this particular fact.

'That is correct, Inspector.'

'Did he have a reservation?'

She shakes her head.

'Until the Bank Holiday, most of my trade is walk-up. It falls late this year.'

'Did he sign in?'

'I don't have a visitors' book, Inspector – I found it was being abused.'

Skelgill nods grimly. Out of the woman's line of sight DS Leyton is smirking.

'What else did he say to you?'

She compresses her thin lips.

'Very little, Inspector – he was somewhat taciturn. He just asked if I had a room available for one night, and listened in silence when I explained the house rules. He probably paid no attention. I left him here and that was the last time I saw him.'

'Where was he from?'

'I have no idea.'

Now the woman appears nonplussed – that she should be expected to know this. Evidently she dispensed with the regular pleasantries in greeting the new guest.

'What about his accent?'

'I couldn't say, Inspector.'

'Well – did he sound British?'

She folds her arms and gives them a little shake of what might be frustration.

'These days it is quite frankly impossible to tell – I understand there are thousands of British people in the country who barely speak a word of English.'

Skelgill does not respond to this observation but instead he produces and holds open the passport – for that is what it is.

'Is this the man, madam?'

*

'So much for "Mr Leonard", Guv.'

'I suppose it was near enough.'

'Think he didn't want to let on he's a foreigner, Guv?'

Skelgill takes a sip from his cup and grimaces – he has commandeered the residents' lounge, perhaps hoping that Mrs Robinson would feel obliged to extend her hospitality to the second of the two *B's* – but all that has been forthcoming is a rather stewed and tepid concoction masquerading as tea. He shrugs in response to DS Leyton's question. He is carefully perusing the pages of the passport. Its owner – identified by the landlady as a look-alike for the pixelated image – is in fact a twenty-four-year-old Ukrainian citizen by the name of Leonid Pavlenko, birthplace Donetsk. Superficially, he could pass as British – his longish wavy brown hair and blue eyes would blend in – and perhaps only critical analysis of his mildly Slavic brows would raise any doubt. Skelgill hands the passport to his sergeant.

'Leyton unless my eyes deceive me, there's no UK visa in here.'

'So he's an *illegal*, Guv?'

DS Leyton begins to thumb through the passport, however his stout fingers lack Skelgill's fisherman's dexterity and he finds it difficult to separate the pages. He pulls off the plastic cover to make the job easier. As he does so, a photograph flutters onto the surface of the table. It lands face up – and a striking portrait it presents: a girl, early twenties, with long combed blonde hair centre-parted, a tanned complexion, immaculate make up, and – beneath curving pencilled brows – penetrating pale-blue irises with distinct black borders. It is a model shot, taken professionally, and its subject could be naked, for she poses provocatively, her delicate chin resting upon a bare shoulder, an enigmatic smile creasing her full pink lips, and in her eyes just the hint of an invitation.

'Girlfriend, Guv?'

'He's a lucky lad if she is.'

Skelgill picks up the photograph and flips it over. He frowns: there is some handwritten lettering – two words – but it is written in Cyrillic script and makes no sense. He rotates it so DS Leyton can see.

'Maybe her name, Guv?' DS Leyton puffs out his cheeks as though he is defeated by the prospect, but then holds up a forefinger to indicate an idea has struck him. 'DS Jones might know.'

'What?'

'DS Jones, Guv – ain't her old granny from the Ukraine?'

Skelgill looks irked.

'News to me, Leyton.'

DS Leyton appears a little uncomfortable – that he should know this ahead of his superior.

'We were discussing it the other day, Guv – in the canteen. What with all this independence malarkey –I was saying I've got ancestors from Scotland, Wales, Ireland – in years gone by they flocked from all over to work on the docks – and DS Jones reckons she's a quarter Ukrainian – *and* a quarter Welsh.' He scratches his head absently. 'And two quarters English, Guv.'

Skelgill looks perplexed, as if he has hitherto assumed his sergeants Leyton and Jones are one hundred per cent pure Cockney and Cumbrian respectively.

'I mean, Guv – it's a Welsh name, ain't it, *Jones*?'

Skelgill does not respond, but instead he pulls out his mobile phone and uses it to take a photograph of the inscription on the back of the picture. He taps in a short message and transmits the image.

'Let's see if you're right, Leyton.'

It can only be a matter of two or three minutes before his phone rings. It is lying on the coffee table and he engages the loudspeaker function.

'Jones – got you on speaker so Leyton can hear.'

'Sure, Guv.'

'Make any sense? Leyton here tells me you're fluent in Ukrainian.'

DS Jones chuckles.

'*Trokhy*.'

'Come again?'

'It means a little, Guv.'

'You've kept that quiet.'

'It's not often it comes up in conversation.'

'Aye, well – maybe now's your chance.'

'Don't expect too much, Guv.'

'So what about this name?'

'It's not a name – it's not even Ukrainian.'

'What do you mean?'

'I've been checking it online – it doesn't make sense – the letters are random.'

'It must mean something, Jones.'

'I can tell you what it sounds like, Guv – in case it's phonetic.'

Skelgill hesitates for a moment.

'Aye?'

'The first word could be *block* or *black*, and the second *back* or *beck*.'

DS Leyton leans forward.

'A black-back's a seagull, ain't it?'

Skelgill stares at him rather disparagingly. He speaks to DS Jones.

'What makes you think it could be phonetic?'

'If you wanted to ask for something in a foreign country, Guv – you'd write it down so you could pronounce it – so the locals would understand.' She makes a tentative cough. 'Or if someone had told you a name over the phone – you'd write it the way it sounded.'

Skelgill is staring out of the window, his eyes narrowed.

'So it could be *black beck*?'

'It could be, Guv.'

'There is such a place.'

There is a silence while Skelgill's subordinates wait for him to elaborate. In fact he rises and stalks across to a bookshelf. He extracts a folded map from among a section of dated visitors' guides and discarded paperbacks. Efficiently he locates what he is looking for and scrutinises it for a moment or two. Then he returns to the sofa and lays the quartered map on the coffee table.

'There's a thousand becks in the Lakes and more than one Black Beck – but the best known's a bit of an unofficial attraction – Blackbeck copper and slate mines over in Little Langdale. The beck joins the Brathay and runs into Elter Water.'

He indicates with a finger so that DS Leyton can see the locale. DS Leyton does not have Skelgill's lifelong relationship with the Ordnance Survey and frowns with consternation.

'It says *Blackbeck Castle*, Guv.'

'Aye – that's a private estate – the abandoned mine workings are up the valley towards Coniston Old Man.'

DS Jones now chips in.

'Do you think he might have gone there, Guv?'

Skelgill hesitates.

'It's that or we're talking needles and haystacks.'

Skelgill suddenly chuckles to himself – for he has just named two specific topographic features of the Lakeland fells – but he does not elucidate for the benefit of his colleagues.

'Jones – you head over this way – rendezvous at Threlkeld in half an hour. We'll go down through St John's in the Vale. My car keys are on my desk – grab my boots, will you – and there's a torch in the driver's door pocket.'

'Sure, Guv.'

Skelgill terminates the call and scoops up the handset. Then he picks his jacket from the arm of the settee.

'Er, Guv –' DS Leyton lifts a leg rather forsakenly. 'I've just got ordinary shoes.'

'Leyton – which one of you two speaks Ukrainian?'

'Well – not me, Guv – obviously.'

Skelgill holds out his hands in a gesture of the obvious.

'So drop me at Threlkeld and get back to your desk – see what you can find out from Immigration.'

DS Leyton glowers disapprovingly as he falls in behind his superior. They exit the B&B unannounced. As they descend the steep steps DS Leyton holds back for a second and, with the tip of a toe, delivers a gentle prod to the big-nosed gnome with the fishing rod, despatching it into a small ornamental pond.

3. BLACKBECK MINES

Although Cumbria is England's third largest ceremonial county, by area the Lake District is only slightly larger than medium-sized counties like Leicestershire, Nottinghamshire or Warwickshire. Indeed, at 885 square miles, it would fit within a grid of sides just 30 miles long. That said, journeys in the Lakes are measured not by distance, but by time. Arthur Hope's farm at Seathwaite is a little over three miles as the crow flies from the inn at Wasdale Head – but it is an hour-and-a-half's drive on a good day. It is a topography that could never have endeared itself to Roman road-builders, though they left their mark with a string of forts across the region. And travel times will soar in a few days, when the Easter vacation brings a tenfold increase in traffic, choking Cumbria's winding lanes and white-knuckle passes.

In a similar vein, to reach Little Langdale from Penrith – DS Jones's journey, via Threlkeld to collect Skelgill – takes a good hour, despite the modest mileage. And that does not allow for Skelgill's impromptu halt in order to solicit a takeaway lunch from his chef cousin at the kitchen door of a Grasmere hotel. By the time they reach the nadir known as Fell Foot, at the bottom of Wrynose Pass, the clock has ticked over to one p.m. – high noon according to recently inaugurated British Summer Time. Skelgill directs his colleague to park on a rather rocky verge beside a dry stone wall, in the shade of a mixed wood of budding native oak and introduced Sitka.

'I expected there to be some information signs, Guv – I looked up Blackbeck mines before I left – they're obviously popular with climbers and cavers.'

'Aye, well – you might say this is the trade entrance.'

DS Jones is lacing her trail shoes, an amused smile forming on her lips.

'Guv, I don't see *any* entrance.'

'It's a mile yet – but this is the quickest way on foot. There's a cart track winds up at the old workings, but it's kept locked.'

Skelgill places his torch on the ridge of the wall and swarms over, dropping down silently and reappearing as a head and shoulders. He offers a hand to DS Jones and they grasp one another's wrists. She finds a foothold and levers herself up, though her tight jeans restrict her movement, and Skelgill has to grab her waistband to haul her past the tipping point. He rather overdoes this and she is obliged to spring in hope – but the woodland floor is a carpet of mulch and moss and makes for a soft if undignified landing. She rises, brushing pine needles from her knees and perhaps unaware that Skelgill is critically scrutinising the small round damp patches on her buttocks.

'I'm in a mess already, Guv.'

'You look fine to me, Jones.'

As they set off there is no obvious path, and Skelgill appears to be navigating by the sun, keeping it just a few degrees to their left, thus heading a touch west of south. While the wood is dense, the going is relatively straightforward – beneath the mature conifers there is no shrub layer to impede them, and the oaks are in flower but not yet in leaf, affording plenty of light amidst the dappled shade. Although it is too early for most summer migrants, residents such as great tits, blackbirds and chaffinches are filling the resonant ether with robust birdsong. Here and there purple dog violets and little constellations of wood sorrel hint at the forest's antiquity. In a small clearing they pass a gnarled hawthorn – Skelgill snatches a pinch of fresh green foliage, and to his colleague's evident surprise stuffs it into his mouth.

'Aw – Guv!'

'What?'

'How can you do that?'

Skelgill is chewing approvingly.

'First salad of the year, Jones – you must have heard of *bread-and-cheese?*'

'I'm a townie really, Guv – albeit a small-townie.'

Skelgill grins.

'You don't know what you're missing.'

'Grubs, probably, Guv.'

'It's all good protein.'

DS Jones shakes her head, but before she can reply, ahead a white notice with printed black lettering catches her eye. It warns that *'Trespassers Will Be Prosecuted'*, and is fastened onto a wall that gradually takes shape through the trees, and which must tower a good eight feet above the ground.

'What's this, Guv?'

'Blackbeck Castle. We need to circle round to the right to break out onto the fell.'

'I thought this was all Access Land, Guv?'

Skelgill scowls.

'It doesn't apply to the castle grounds.'

DS Jones nods.

'I suppose they have to draw the line somewhere.'

Skelgill regards the sign pensively and does not reply. The issue of to whom land morally belongs is a controversy that rumbles on in his own thoughts – never mind in many a pub argument – and his opinion depends upon which hat he might be wearing at any one time. Public access in the Lake District falls somewhere between Scotland's more or less unfettered 'right to roam' and England's general policy that restricts ramblers to marked rights of way. As a fisherman and fell-runner Skelgill is often frustrated by the limitations the landed classes are able to place upon his freedom; but as a police officer and member of a mountain rescue team there has been many an occasion when he has cursed the temptations that draw unqualified or delinquent citizens into his ambit. At this moment, while his ideal route would take a beeline more or less due south, the high stone barrier forces a detour.

Although the ground now begins to rise quite steeply, beside the wall there is easier going underfoot. In its shadow grows little vegetation – just decurved ferns that spill from crevices, and creeping liverworts glistening like seaweed exposed by the ebb tide. After some ten minutes they reach a grey-painted gate set into the stonework. Skelgill stops to stare at the construction.

'What is it, Guv?'

'Don't remember this.' He reaches to give it a push; but there is no ironmongery on the outside and nothing yields. 'It's a year or two since I've been this way, mind.'

The door is in good repair, and it fits flush with the stone jambs and lintel. Despite his best efforts to find a crack Skelgill is defeated, and he is unable to see what lies beyond. He sizes up the wall, as if he is thinking about scaling it to peer over. But then he examines the ground below the step – there is no indication of wear, just an even scattering of rotting leaves and twigs.

'Doesn't look like it's used.' He shrugs and turns in the direction of their travel. 'Come on – I'll show you something more interesting.'

Still in woodland they continue for another minute or so to a point where the hillside on their right climbs into a vertical cliff. There is perhaps the semblance of a path along the foot of this miniature escarpment, and after maybe thirty yards it abruptly angles left into a great fissure: a gorge about ten feet wide, its walls as high as a house. Upon first impression this appears to be a natural feature, for a stream trickles out from its shingled floor, and mosses and creepers trail down the damp rock faces; the atmosphere is thick with the peaty humidity of a botanical hothouse. But, as the eye follows the tiny beck to its source some fifty feet into the crevice, the jagged black mouth of a cave reveals man's hand in this creation. Skelgill purposefully splashes the sole of his left boot into the rippling water.

'Some folk consider this to be the original Black Beck – it comes right through the mines and joins another tributary further down the valley.'

He sets off into the gully, watching the ground ahead of him as he goes. But the stony surface is unforgiving, and if he seeks tracks he is disappointed – only near the entrance is there a trace of life, and that is an indistinct cloven hoof print in a patch of silvery sand.

'What would it be, Guv?'

Skelgill ponders for a moment and shakes his head.

'Roe deer, most likely – coming to this pool to drink where it's deeper.'

'I hope they can't read, Guv.'

'Come again?'

DS Jones indicates towards the entrance of the cave. Set back by a couple of yards, and thus invisible to their approach, the tunnel is blocked by half a dozen planks wedged diagonally across the passage. On these is hung a notice, *"Danger Keep Out"* – but DS Jones refers to additional graffiti – a more curt Anglo-Saxon exhortation to go away (although this might equally be directed rebelliously at the official sign writer). Skelgill smiles grimly and shakes his head.

'The places folk bring marker pens never ceases to amaze me.'

DS Jones grins.

'So, what is this, Guv?'

'The lowest outlet of the copper mine. This part was closed over a hundred-and-fifty years ago. There's shafts coming down seven hundred feet, chasing the veins through the rock.'

DS Jones takes a couple of tentative steps inside the mouth of the adit.

'Here.' Skelgill hands her his torch. It is small – about the size of a *Churchill* cigar – but when she switches it on it floods the recess with its brilliant light. She approaches the makeshift barrier, finding a gap through which to shine the flashlight. 'Slide the hood – it focuses the beam. You'll be able to see further down the tunnel.'

She does as directed – and immediately recoils with a shriek and a grimace of revulsion.

'Oh, no – what is *that?*'

Skelgill takes the torch from her and pokes it between two of the planks, holding its base against his left cheek. In the slick wet darkness of the cave, seemingly hovering just beneath the arch of the roof, a demonic visage gleams bone-white, the ebony hollows of its eye sockets staring ghoulishly from beneath great curled horns. It is the skull of a Herdwick ram.

'Bloody kids.'

DS Jones shudders and backs out into the half-light of the fissure.

'That's more than enough to keep me away, Guv – never mind the danger of falling down a pit.'

Skelgill grins. He clicks off the torch and slides it into his back pocket. Then he takes hold of one of the planks in both hands and gives it a hard shake, but it refuses to budge. He tries a couple of others, but they appear to be firmly wedged, and nailed together where they overlap.

'I don't reckon our Leonid came this way.'

He bows his head and ducks out into the fresh air. DS Jones's complexion appears pale, despite their brisk walk up through the forest; Skelgill seems to notice, for he leans sideways and pulls a half-eaten packet of glucose sweets from the map pocket of his trousers.

'Here – the best I can do in lieu of brandy.'

She grins self-consciously.

'Sorry, Guv – I wasn't expecting that – it really spooked me.'

Skelgill shrugs and steps past her.

'Come on – let's get up to the top. They mined the slate up there as well – there's some big chambers – that's where folk tend to knock around if they're exploring.'

*

'This is like being in a secret Covenanters' chapel, Guv.'

Skelgill glances about proprietorially.

'Aye, well – you're not so far wrong – they call this the *Apse*.'

DS Jones nods appreciatively. They are speaking in whispers, and have halted at an aperture that leads into a huge domed chamber. Skelgill has switched off his torch, for there is a fracture in the roof through which a shaft of sunlight illuminates a rockfall of gigantic flakes of slate. The biggest of these points back skyward like a jagged standing stone, and in front of it one great slab the size of a bed lies flat – together they give the impression of a primitive altar and reredos, mysteriously floodlit amidst the crowding shadows. Beyond, the darkness gathers, even blacker for the light that streams down into the centre of the cavity. But before the shadows consume all, it is evident that a large pool of water stretches from behind the rock formation to the back of the cave, and the constant timpani of drips and plops make an eerily echoing fugue.

'This is as far as you can go – or you can abseil in and walk out the way we've come.'

Skelgill directs his flashlight so that its beam reflects off the black water and highlights the naturally vaulted ceiling, a succession of arched ribs like the interior of a great pharynx, taking a greenish hue from the once sought-after slate. At either side of the chamber are horizontal shafts, known as drifts, but these are blocked with rubble – whether by accident or design it is impossible to know. As they begin to retrace their steps other side-passages beckon, and Skelgill inspects them as far as is possible. In due course he leads them along one such corridor; killing the torch reveals a bend some seventy-five yards ahead, with daylight filtering from just beyond.

When they emerge DS Jones stretches with relief, turning her face up to the sun.

'I'm not good with the dark, Guv – these tunnels give me the creeps.'

'Aye, well – I'm no big fan of caving myself – though we have mock rescue exercises in these places – I've done them right here in days gone by.'

DS Jones, despite the ambient warmth of the fine day, visibly shivers.

'Imagine being trapped underground – I think I'd die of claustrophobia – if you can do such a thing.'

Skelgill grimaces.

'The worst scenario is when someone gets stuck roof-sniffing and then it rains – and the water level rises.'

DS Jones seems to understand his caving slang; she winces and brings her palms together in prayer fashion. Skelgill waves a hand to indicate that she should follow him. They walk across the smooth bedrock of an opencast section of former quarry, to the entrance they had originally taken. There is an official notice warning members of the public that they enter at their own risk, and that group activities require prior permission of the National Trust.

'Why would he have come up here, Guv?'

'Same reason as we did.'

DS Jones looks perplexed – but perhaps as she considers her superior's answer she comprehends his logic: armed with similar information, Leonid Pavlenko might naturally have reached an identical conclusion.

'I suppose so, Guv.'

'Maybe he didn't – but I think it made sense to look first. If that wording means Black Beck, it's not such a long shot.'

'Why stay at Keswick though, Guv – why not Ambleside or Coniston?'

Skelgill shrugs.

'Keswick's easy to get to – handy stopping-off point – he only took the room for one night. He might have a contact in the town – someone who could have given him a lift.'

DS Jones begins to read the small print on the information board. There is mention of helmets, head-torches, ropes and harnesses.

'Guv, it's hardly a regular tourist attraction and by the sound of it he was wearing ordinary clothes.'

Jeans, t-shirt, leather jacket and trainers had been the description provided by his landlady; none of these items were among the possessions left in the holdall. Skelgill nods, and casts about with a rather dejected air.

'There's a couple of properties we can ask at on the way down. If he came here looking for something – or someone – then he might have knocked on doors.'

'When do you think he left the B&B?'

Skelgill exhales somewhat resignedly.

'It could have been any time between five yesterday afternoon and eight this morning – but there's no indication he hung about – yesterday seems more likely.'

'What time would it have got dark, Guv?'

Skelgill folds his arms and looks to the heavens.

'Sunset last night was more or less bang on seven. But it was clear – it was light until about eight.'

DS Jones is pulling down her lower lip with her middle finger.

'Still, he wouldn't have had a lot of daylight, Guv.'

'Maybe not. Look – he might turn up yet, Jones, wanting his bag – for all we know he went out in Keswick, met someone, got lucky –' Skelgill hesitates as he gauges his colleague's reaction. 'It's not unknown.'

DS Jones turns away and takes a few steps towards the rock face. She puts her hands on her hips and leans back to look up the cliff.

'Or unlucky.'

Skelgill stoops and picks up a rhombus of slate. He regards it for a moment before skimming it left-handed into the opening of the mine. There is a hollow echo as it skips over the floor of the stone passageway and comes to a silent halt. His arms drop down by his sides, and for a moment he seems lost for what to do next. But DS Jones has gathered her thoughts and pirouettes to face him.

'The thing is, Guv – if he has done a runner from the B&B, why would he leave his passport?'

4. BLACKBECK CASTLE

'This is private property.'
'It's mainly Access Land.'
'It 'int where tha' be standing.'
'Aye, well, maybe I've got a reason for that.'

Skelgill fishes his warrant card from his hip pocket and pushes it close to the man's face.

'I take it you've got a licence to use *Larsen* traps?'

The man eyes Skelgill suspiciously. A couple of inches the shorter, he is nevertheless of a muscular build, shaven headed, his demeanour hostile. Though probably in his mid-forties he wears faded combat fatigues and a soiled olive t-shirt with dark patches of perspiration at the armpits, army surplus boots in need of polish, and an oily bandana around his forehead. His complexion is swarthy, and an ugly scar beneath his left eye combines with features – nose, lips, teeth and ears – that are too big for his face, suggestive of a caricatured goblin from fantasy fiction. He still wields the hammer with which he was crossly knocking in staples, as the two detectives rounded the side of his stone-built gamekeeper's cottage. There is a stack of ten or so traps – rough wooden frames about the size of a rabbit hutch, covered in wire mesh. The property itself sits on the eastern fringe of the expanse of woodland through which they earlier climbed, perhaps a furlong from the rough track that connects the mine workings with the winding Langdale-to-Eskdale road. From a rickety pen set between ramshackle sheds two dogs stare hungrily – a black Labrador and a piebald Working Cocker; perhaps surprisingly they do not bark. Neither does the man reply immediately, but transfers his gaze from Skelgill to DS Jones, his narrow black eyes feeding upon her figure. She does not like this attention and is reaching for her own ID when he turns back to Skelgill.

'The estate's got a licence, aye.'

'Blackbeck Castle?'

The man nods.

'And you are?'

'Jed Tarr.'

'Gamekeeper?'

The man looks over his shoulder and holds the pose, as if he means Skelgill to follow his line of sight. Strung upon a wire fence are the rotting carcasses of crows, rats and a couple of stoats. It has not been the most auspicious of introductions, but Skelgill is inherently allergic to unjustified aggression. Now, however he requires the man's cooperation. He gestures casually to DS Jones.

'My sergeant has a couple of questions.'

DS Jones has the passport and photograph in the zip pocket of her gilet. The gamekeeper is watchful as she extracts them, both contained inside clear polythene bags.

'We're looking for this man – he's aged twenty-four, five feet nine, wearing a black leather jacket and jeans with trainers. We believe he may have been in this area yesterday evening, or possibly this morning.'

Jed Tarr's scowl is unchanging as he squints at the passport. DS Jones keeps the printed details covered, and when he reaches as if to take it from her she withdraws it. He meets her eyes, and then smirks, as if to say *touché*. Then he shakes his head.

'Never sin 'im.'

DS Jones waits for a moment, but he appears to have nothing to add. She brings the photograph of the girl to the front and displays it. Now the man betrays the semblance of a reaction – not in his facial expression – but his grip seems to tighten on the hickory handle of his hammer, suggested by the knotting of the muscles on his forearm. He stares at the image, and then shifts his gaze to DS Jones, and back again, as if he is comparing the two females.

'We're also looking for this woman – the two of them may have been together.'

There is now just the hint of a leer, the uneven yellowed teeth more exposed than before.

'Nope.'

He turns back to the trap at his feet and digs into his pocket. He pulls out half a dozen staples and jams them between his lips, picking one back out and recommencing the job the detectives have interrupted. DS Jones glances at Skelgill; he indicates with a flick of his head that they will leave. He directs a final salvo at the disobliging gamekeeper.

'Contact the police if you see either of them.' (The man perhaps grunts an acknowledgement, although it could be the effort of hammering, much harder than is necessary.) 'And remember – those traps are only legal for small corvids.'

This latter remark attracts a contemptuous glance. Indeed, as Skelgill and DS Jones depart towards the main track, he breaks off from his task and watches them from the corner of the building. Then, first checking the frontage of his cottage, he returns to the rear and unlocks the door and enters within.

*

'Did you notice, Guv – all the windows were shuttered?'

Skelgill nods grimly.

'Aye – I'd like to know what he's got in there – a freezer full of dead goshawks and hen harriers, like as not.'

'Are you going to ask at the castle to see the licence for the traps?'

Skelgill shakes his head.

'Much as I'd like to – but they don't need one – it's a General Licence to take or kill birds to prevent damage.' He scoffs at his use of the ironic formal terminology. 'Anyone can download it from the government website – all you have to do is comply with the requirements.'

'He didn't seem to know that, Guv.'

'He probably knows enough to know he's covered – so long as we don't catch him with a hawk in one of the traps.'

'How do they work, Guv?'

Skelgill contracts his lips in an expression of distaste.

'You bait one half with a live magpie. Stick the trap in a clearing in another bird's territory – ten minutes later and it'll come to investigate – when it lands it falls into the other section through a trapdoor. Then you put your twelve bore through it – unless you want the new magpie as bait for a second trap.'

DS Jones appears appalled at the prospect.

'He had a ruthless look in his eyes, Guv – I shouldn't like to be caught accidentally trespassing by him.'

Skelgill frowns as though he begs to differ, and would happily prompt such a situation.

'He wasn't about to go out of his way to help us, that's for sure.'

'No, Guv.'

They stride downhill, the gradient still quite steep; the track has now entered the forest. The mid-afternoon birdsong is subdued, although a buzzard mews persistently above, lording over its realm. At one point they glimpse the flashing white rear of a roebuck as it bounds into the undergrowth, and at intervals clumps of primroses rejoice in the spring sunshine. In due course they encounter the locked gate that restricts vehicular access to Blackbeck mines. A notice similar to that at the quarry warns visitors of the perils that lie ahead. By turning left onto the 'trunk' road (a narrow lane that accommodates two cars only with extreme care), another mile will return them to their parking spot. About halfway, however, an unmarked track cuts back into the woodland: it is the inconspicuous driveway of Blackbeck Castle.

'Must be fun being the postie around here, Guv.'

'Aye – you'd want a Land Rover and plenty of emergency supplies in winter.' For a moment Skelgill becomes contemplative. 'I'd quite fancy that – having to camp out for a couple of nights in the snow – maybe trek to the nearest inn – log fire and unlimited real ale.'

'So long as they'd got their delivery, Guv.'

'I'd make do with bottled, at a push.'

DS Jones grins and shakes her head. But if she is forming a reply she adapts it to accommodate the sight that greets them as they round a bend in the track.

'Wow, Guv – this place looks about as scary as the mines.'

While Blackbeck Castle might disappoint the visitor hoping for an authentic medieval fortress, it would almost certainly find favour among *Hammer Horror* aficionados. Not that it is open to the public as an attraction. Indeed, the towering wall yields only to wooden gates of an equivalent height, leaving visible solely the upper storeys of the castle – with its towers, turrets and battlements. Built in the early Victorian era for an heiress whose dubious fortune was built upon the 'sanitised' leg of a despicable triangular trade that shipped rum from the West Indies to Whitehaven, its mock Gothic Revivalist architecture would equally dismay today's architect or archaeologist. As it is, surrounded by dense forest, supplemented with a preponderance of large ornamental conifers in its immediate grounds, the unsightly edifice generally goes unseen by tourists and hillwalkers alike.

The large gates appear well maintained and are painted in the same shade of grey as the portal they came across earlier. Indeed, to their right is a similar door, with an electronic panel cemented into the wall at head height. Skelgill presses a button marked "Call." Immediately there is a sound – but it emanates not from the loudspeaker in the control panel, but from the smaller gate itself. The noise sounds like the lifting of a bar, and then the door swings open – inwards – and the tall figure of a man steps out. He has on leads a pair of large German Shepherds. The door appears to be sprung, and closes behind him. The man, whose eyes have been on his animals, looks up in apparent surprise to see the two detectives standing so close by. The dogs, when they might be expected to exhibit some territorial reaction, in fact are simply watchful.

'Ah – may I direct you good people?'

The man's accent and clipped enunciation betrays little provenance other than British public school – though there may be the hint of a foreign brogue beneath, perhaps Dutch or German. Aged in his late fifties, he is well over six feet, and attired in sturdy leather brogues, beige moleskin trousers and a green quilted shooting jacket with stitched suede shoulder patches – these garments, in contrast to those of the gamekeeper – are in pristine condition. His bearing is very upright, a naval impression that is emphasised by short-cropped grizzled hair and a matching anchor beard. His wide-set eyes stare unblinking astride an aquiline nose. Though his opening words are friendly enough, his underlying demeanour – rather akin to that of the dogs – is entirely neutral, as though he is gauging the status of these interlopers. Skelgill produces his warrant card.

'DI Skelgill – and this is DS Jones – Cumbria Police.'

Skelgill says no more – but the man merely returns his gaze, thus obliging him to elaborate or face a silent standoff.

'We're trying to locate a person who may have been in this area – yesterday evening or this morning.'

DS Jones has the passport ready, and holds it up to the man, again covering the identification details. He narrows his eyes and retracts his head by a couple of inches, as though he would prefer to be wearing reading glasses. However, he scrutinises the image for several seconds, before allowing his gaze to trace a path from DS Jones's neatly manicured nails and along her bare forearm to her face. His eyes are a disconcertingly pale blue and she appears uncomfortable beneath his interrogative stare.

'Does the picture ring any bells, sir?'

It is Skelgill that breaks in, perhaps detecting his sergeant's discomfort. The man turns back to face him. His expression remains implacable.

'Neither I nor any of my staff have been outwith the grounds since yesterday lunchtime, Inspector – apart from my gamekeeper who is based up towards the quarry.'

'I believe we met him on our way down, sir.'

The landowner inclines his head in acknowledgement.

'This man didn't call here, sir – asking for somebody?'

'You are our first visitors since a delivery of wine on Saturday, Inspector. I have been at home the whole time myself and I would know.'

Skelgill gestures with an open palm towards the gates.

'Is it remotely possible that he could have wandered into your grounds, sir?'

'I think Hansel and Gretel would have soon found him and let me know.'

'I'm sorry, sir?'

'My Alsatians, Inspector. They have the run of the place – they tend to be rather more assertive when they are not under my command.'

Skelgill glances down. Unobtrusively, one of the creatures has stepped closer and is sniffing at his trouser leg. He looks away, and at the same time casually lowers the back of a hand. The dog transfers its attention to his wrist, but then seems content as Skelgill rubs a knuckle against its mastoid process. The man is watching keenly.

'You perhaps have been a dog handler, Inspector?'

Skelgill appears surprised by this remark. He places his palm gently on the top of the Alsatian's head.

'My own dog is best of pals with one of these, sir.'

The man regards the animal with a detached stare.

'They make good friends – and bad enemies.'

'That might be why our chaps use them, sir.'

The man nods, though his expression remains inscrutable.

'I am about to walk around the perimeter – it is a route I take some days – precisely five kilometres. If I see anything I shall contact you.'

Skelgill nods. There is little they can do to detain him – even should they have more questions. His responses have been perfectly adequate, if economical.

'I didn't catch your name, sir?'

The man has already begun to move off. He hesitates, and then turns back to face the two officers. He contrives a perfunctory smile.

'It is Wolfstein – Doctor.'

*

'I was surprised you didn't ask him about the girl, Guv.'

Skelgill holds up his pint against the light of the pub window.

'Aye – I didn't feel inclined for some reason.' He takes a sup of the golden ale. 'He was as tight-lipped as the gamekeeper.'

DS Jones swirls the cubes of ice and sliver of lemon around her glass of mineral water.

'It seemed a bit of a coincidence that he was just coming out as we arrived.'

Skelgill nods over the rim of his glass.

'Certainly saved us a trip inside.'

'That guy Tarr could have tipped him off that we were on our way, Guv.'

Now Skelgill shrugs.

'We shouldn't make too much of a conspiracy out of this – it's only because we're quiet at the moment that we've followed it up this far.'

'Is there something wrong, sir?'

Skelgill and DS Jones turn simultaneously towards the bar. The landlord, a portly chap in his mid forties, has raised the serving hatch and is lumbering across the stone-flagged floor of the old inn.

'I'm sorry?'

'I noticed you were checking the beer, sir – I wondered if it were cloudy? Would you prefer something else – the guest IPA's pulling well? I'm afraid Eva the new barmaid hasn't quite got the hang of the cask ales yet.'

Skelgill looks wide-eyed – that the landlord has been so attentive. He takes another swig and holds up the now half-empty glass.

'The only thing wrong with this is that I can probably only have two pints.'

The landlord glances at DS Jones's water.

'You seem to have a driver, sir?'

Skelgill grins.

'Unfortunately Sergeant Jones here will be taking me back to my car later.'

Skelgill flashes his ID in a non-threatening sort of way.

'Ooh.' The landlord holds up his hands in apology. 'To what do we owe the honour?'

Skelgill shakes his head.

'Just thirsty after a bit of a hike, sir – although you may be able to help us.'

The man rather awkwardly straddles the stool at the head of their table.

'I'd be pleased to make your acquaintance, er – Inspector. I'm new around here myself – as you can probably guess from my accent.'

Skelgill nods. The *Langdale Arms* is a favourite watering hole, though occasional given its distance from his regular North Lakes stamping ground. It is one he patronises more often on foot than by road. However, since his last visit the previous autumn, the long-standing elderly local couple who ran the place appear to have moved on, and the tenancy to have been taken up by the self-confessed 'offcomer' – who sounds like he hails from the Black Country, pronouncing you as *yow* and your as *yower*. Skelgill indicates to DS Jones that she should go ahead and show him the photographs.

'We believe this man has gone missing – he could have been in the vicinity within the last twenty-four hours.'

The landlord leans over, breathing wheezily as he examines the picture. DS Jones slides the photograph of the girl beside it.

'He may have some connection to this girl.'

Now the man glances from one to the other. Then he shakes his head and puffs out his cheeks.

'We were dead quiet last night – closed early – what with it being a Sunday and the holidays coming late this year – and today we've just had three or four elderly couples in for lunch.'

DS Jones nods.

'Were you here in the bar the whole time?'

The man seems a little worried by this question, as if he is unwilling to admit that he abandoned his post at any point.

'Well – I've got Eva, you see?'

'Perhaps we could ask her, sir?'

Rather reluctantly he rises and pads across to the bar. The young barmaid appears to be humouring an overweight duo of middle-aged commercial travellers who are perched on stools at the counter; they give the impression of settling in to make a night of it. She is about to pull them fresh pints, but the landlord moves in to take over, and mutters a few words of instruction. She looks anxiously in the direction of Skelgill and DS Jones, before rather self-consciously parading around the bar and across to their table.

'Have a seat, miss.'

The girl does as DS Jones bids. She is tall and slim, perhaps five feet ten, with short dark hair and blue eyes – attractive despite a nose that some would cruelly call *beaky*. She appears braless in a low-cut vest top, and wears faded hipster jeans and ankle boots with cut-away toes. She could still be late teenage, and the low stool only serves to emphasise her height, as she contrives to fold her gangly limbs into a comfortable position.

'It's just a quick word – we were wondering if you have noticed either of these two people come into the pub – within the last day or so?'

The girl's eyes flick from one photograph to the other, though they seem to pay more attention to the blonde female. However, it only takes her a couple of seconds to respond.

'I have not seen them.'

Skelgill leans forward with an arm on the table.

'How long have you been here, Eva?'

'I come in March.'

Although she has spoken little, it is evident from her accent that she is Eastern European.

'Where are you from?'

'Lublin.'

Skelgill frowns in an endearing manner. The girl elaborates.

'It is city in Poland.'

'You're a long way from home.'

'It is very poor region.'

Skelgill nods. He sighs and casts around the place – it is a quaint enough old hostelry – but the isolated mountain hamlet of Little Langdale is a far cry even from the bright lights of Penrith, let alone some distant Slavic metropolis.

'How's it going?'

'Is okay.'

'Can't be much social life?'

'I like outdoors – is different from my city.'

Skelgill nods.

'Well – if you happen to see either of these people – in here or out – your boss will know how to contact us – Penrith CID.'

The girl inhales as though she is about to speak – then she glances over to the bar and notices that the landlord is watching her – instead she holds in the breath for a moment. She lowers her eyes and folds her long slender hands upon her lap.

'Is all?'

Skelgill stares at her for a moment. Then he too exhales and reclines against his spindle-back chair.

'Aye, that's all. Apart from what time do you start serving food?'

The girl begins to rise from the stool.

'Chef arrive at seven.'

Skelgill checks his wristwatch. The time is five-thirty. Beyond the window the light has subtly deepened, the sun has dropped behind the fells, creating a premature sense of evening in the Langdales. He nods.

'Thanks but we'll love you and leave you.'

As the girl returns to her station Skelgill rises and wanders across to a noticeboard fixed on the wall to the right of the bar. Its main feature is an out-of-date promotional poster from one of the beer companies, offering a free inflatable leprechaun's hat with four pints of their gassy stout. Skelgill scowls disapprovingly and mutters, "Handy to be sick into," and then realises he has said this out loud and winces in the direction of DS Jones. She chuckles and joins him in perusing the various postcards, faded photographs and local newspaper clippings – many of which date back to the time of the previous tenants.

43

Skelgill points out a blurred image of an elderly bearded tramp, beneath the headline, *"Ticker Thymer Clocks Up 25 Years In The Woods."*

'What is it, Guv?'

'I've heard of this guy, "Ticker" – supposedly lives up in Blackbeck Wood – never come across him, though.'

DS Jones is reading the article.

'It says it's a mystery how he feeds himself – all he would tell this journalist is that "Mother Nature is bountiful" – but it's rumoured that some of the older locals conceal tins in regular hiding places and he exchanges them for prophesies written on charms carved from oak. And he does character readings and predictions at local fairs and shepherds' meets.'

Skelgill gives an ironic laugh.

'I must find out where and ask him when England are going to win the World Cup again.'

DS Jones raises her eyebrows, acknowledging the improbability.

'It's hard to envisage, though, Guv – how anyone could survive like that.'

Skelgill shrugs.

'If he's got folk helping him – plus think of all the food that's dumped in bins in laybys and picnic spots, most of the year round – and he could probably scavenge round the back of the shops and restaurants in Coniston.'

'Imagine being ill, Guv – getting the flu and being stuck on your own in a camp in the woods in winter.'

'If he keeps to himself he probably avoids most bugs – there was a famous hermit lived over in Dodd Wood above Bass Lake – this is going back to the eighteen hundreds – they say he subsisted on tea and sugar and never got sick – aside from a liking for the local ale.' Skelgill shrugs and turns to move away. 'I can see the appeal of the simple life.'

DS Jones grins knowingly and follows her superior. She checks the time on her mobile. They have already overrun their official shift, but one of the perils of working with Skelgill is that he operates to his own timetable – or, rather, to no particular timetable at all, and will continue apparently 'on duty' without reference to formal hours, and equally undertake what are apparently 'off duty' activities (including fell walking and fishing) during his shifts, if challenged claiming 'thinking time'. Now, with the clock approaching six p.m. and a good hour's drive to Penrith ahead, there is no guarantee he will not be distracted by some whim – perhaps to seek out the local 'Prophet of the Woods'. As they pass the bar and make for the timbered door, the landlord breaks off from the hushed conversation he is having with the suited sales reps; he raises a hand of farewell.

'Thanks for *yower* custom.'

The two men facing the bar turn disinterested stares upon the departing couple – although perhaps slightly less so in the case of DS Jones. Skelgill glowers in return as he passes, and nods to the landlord. The girl, Eva, has already moved out to collect their empty glasses, and casts a rather forlorn glance at their backs as they leave. By the time she returns to the sink behind the counter, the landlord has the pub's telephone handset to his ear, and seems to be awaiting a response.

5. NEEDLES & HAYSTACKS

'By all accounts, Guv, the border between the Ukraine and Poland leaks like a sieve – Customs reckon ten billion contraband cigarettes get smuggled through every year. A quarter of a million Ukrainians work in Poland in low-wage jobs the Poles have left behind. Immigration quoted me an annual figure of twelve million border crossings. Once you're in Poland you're in the Schengen Area.'

Skelgill is shaking his head.

'Leyton, you'll be on *Mastermind* at this rate.'

DS Leyton grins and taps his notepad with his knuckles.

'I'd never remember all this, Guv – blimey, I struggle with my own date of birth.'

A mug of tea sits on the desk and Skelgill tastes it. He has allowed it to get cold. He swallows the lot in one gulp and pulls a face of disgust.

'We're not in Schengen.'

'I know, Guv – but say you've got a couple of Polish pals living in Britain. They drive over to Poland for a few days – then only one of them returns – you come in place of the other geezer, using his passport.'

Skelgill nods.

'I imagine there's plenty just take their chance in the boot of a car.'

'That as well, Guv.'

'So what about Pavlenko?'

DS Leyton shakes his head.

'No record of him entering Britain – or leaving the Ukraine. The border authorities in Kyiv are investigating – but our boys are saying don't hold your breath.' He puts down his pad and folds his arms. 'On the plus side, they've confirmed it's a genuine passport, and it hasn't been reported stolen – so it's a fair bet that it's him as came to Keswick and not some lookalike.'

Skelgill shrugs indifferently – he appears to need no convincing on this particular point.

'We need a mobile number or a bank account – something we can trace.'

'I've asked for all the usual details, Guv.' DS Leyton looks a bit ruffled. 'Want me to organise some door-to-door inquiries in Keswick – shops and cafés and other guest houses?'

Now Skelgill rather rounds on his subordinate.

'Leyton, he's not even officially missing – technically he's the one who's committed an offence – doing a runner from his B&B without paying. The Chief will start breathing fire if I ask for extra manpower to catch a petty crook. So unless you're volunteering for some door-knocking –'

DS Leyton shrugs stoically. His suggestion is a speculative retort to his superior's unreasonable expectation in the time available. However, it is common knowledge that Skelgill's rival DI Alec Smart has been commandeering staff in anticipation of a salvo of cash machine raids – the dubious product of a tip-off from among his netherworld network of informants. Undoubtedly he schemes to enlist the services of DS Leyton and DS Jones – and in this relatively arid period before the Lake District floods with visitors on Good Friday, Skelgill is struggling to justify otherwise.

'Seems like he's just disappeared into thin air, Guv.' DS Leyton rubs the top of his head absently. 'Then again, I suppose he came out of it in the first place.'

'What about Ukrainian contacts in the area?'

DS Leyton's sagging countenance foretells of limited news.

'There's a Carlisle branch of the Association of Ukrainians in Great Britain – mainly for those folks and their families who fled here after the last war – but there's only a scattering in Cumbria. The place is just a social club, Guv – like the Legion. They've got a *Facebook* page – but there's no indication of Leonid Pavlenko trying to get in touch. I spoke to the branch secretary and he didn't know of him – but he said they'd put out a request for information.'

Skelgill is leaning back with arms folded. With a stirrup kick he swivels the seat and gazes up at the map of the Lake District on the wall behind him. It seems likely he is revisiting his earlier remark about needles and haystacks, for his eyes dance about the shaded fells and green dales with their blue ribbon glacial lakes. Missing persons are a nagging thorn in the side of the police – every year some quarter of a million are reported, of which ninety-five per cent subsequently turn up safe and sound. The potential waste of police resources is therefore enormous – especially in times of austerity – and the 'thin blue line' does not easily translate into an effective blue drag net in a district as geographically challenging as the Lakes. And in this outdoor playground is the added dilemma presented daily by thoughtless enthusiasts who simply omit to mention they are spending a night or two wild camping in the hills. How is anyone to know whether they are safely tucked up in a sleeping bag, or bleeding to death beneath a precipice? Thus Skelgill's present predicament is far from unfamiliar. And more than nine times out of ten he would be justified in closing the file and letting nature take its course. Yet some inertia within seems to resist this easy option – perhaps some underlying sense of unease, some accumulation of subtle signals received to date, still to manifest themselves as a tangible or logical objection.

As he ponders – and while DS Leyton appears to be distracted by measuring his feet, one against the other, perplexed by a hitherto unnoticed size discrepancy – the office door opens and DS Jones slowly enters, listening to her mobile phone. Skelgill turns and stares, and DS Leyton inhales to greet her – but she puts a silencing finger to her lips – and then employs the same digit to terminate the call.

'Ah – that's interesting.'

'What is?' Skelgill's tone is harsh, as if he thinks it has been a social call.

DS Jones taps the display a couple of times, and then approaches Skelgill's desk and slides her mobile in front of him.

'Last night, Guv – about eleven-thirty – the duty desk took a call from this number. It was a female. She asked for the police and then rang off.'

Skelgill is still looking irked.

'How many people do that every day?'

'Well, there were a few hoax calls last night, Guv. But George is back on the desk this morning and he's been checking through them, just in case. He asked me to listen to the recording – and the girl sounded familiar. What's more, she asked for "Police who come today" – so I just rang the number.' Now she rests a manicured nail upon the screen of her phone. 'It's the Langdale Arms, Guv. The call must have been from the Polish girl, Eva.'

Skelgill is gnawing at a recalcitrant thumbnail, and now he leans over the handset and stares at the screen.

'You withheld your number?'

'Aha.'

'Who answered?'

'I'm pretty certain it was the landlord, Guv.'

Skelgill continues to gaze unblinking at the phone, but then – to DS Jones's dismay – he suddenly picks it up and tosses it to DS Leyton. Fortunately, despite a momentary juggle, he proves to be a safe pair of hands.

'Leyton, redial that number. Say you just got cut off. Then ask if they serve pub lunches – say you're about to climb Pike of Blisco from Great Langdale and you're thinking of stopping off that way.'

DS Leyton looks bemused, but he knows better than to question Skelgill when he is in a capricious mood.

'Hold your horses, Guv – I'd better write these down.'

He reaches for his notepad while Skelgill impatiently repeats the names. Then he presses the redial key and puts the handset to his ear. The call is answered promptly and he follows his superior's instructions. The conversation takes under half a minute.

'The geezer says twelve till two, Guv.'

DS Leyton looks pleased with himself. Skelgill is frowning.

'I know that, Leyton – we were there yesterday.'

Now DS Leyton glances from one of his colleagues to the other, as though he thinks there is some practical joke being perpetrated. He passes the mobile back to DS Jones and then turns to his superior.

'I don't get it, Guv.'

'What you get, Leyton, is lunch on expenses – you're going hillwalking.'

DS Leyton looks dismayed.

'What about outdoor kit, Guv? I've not got anything with me.'

'Never fear, Leyton – there's plenty of spare gear in my car.'

As this excuse is demolished, DS Leyton's expression of alarm intensifies.

'Have pity, Guv – I got blisters on top of blisters last time I wore your old boots.'

Skelgill glares impatiently.

'Leyton – you're not actually going to *climb* Pike of Blisco. I'm about to show you a photograph so you know what it's like, if asked. You just need to look the part. And for Pete's sake don't park too near the pub – at least arrive looking like you've done a bit of a hike.'

DS Leyton's demeanour now shifts to one of tempered dismay. He surveys his ample stomach as it spills over the belt of his trousers.

'That shouldn't take too much doing, Guv.'

Skelgill grins, perhaps a touch maliciously.

'You look out of breath just thinking about it, Leyton.'

DS Leyton gives a good-natured shrug of his broad shoulders. He glances appealingly at DS Jones.

'Thing is – I've been meaning to get the family out – but with all the rain this winter – you ought to try dragging a couple of whining kids past the cinema when it's blowing a gale and they can smell the pizza.'

DS Jones smiles sympathetically.

'I noticed the Langdale Arms were advertising home-made steak-and-ale pie on their specials board. There was a news clipping pinned up – about it winning some award.'

DS Leyton casts a surreptitious glance at Skelgill. His boss is tapping away at his computer – perhaps retrieving the threatened mountain image – but there is no disguising the fleeting scowl that crosses his features at the mention of the acclaimed fare. DS Leyton tries to make light of the matter.

'They ought to call it *Scafell Pie*.'

He forces a guffaw at his own joke – but Skelgill remains not amused.

'That aside, Guv – what exactly is it I'm doing?'

Skelgill abruptly flips his screen round so the others can see. There is in fact no mountain summit, but instead a map of what appears to be Eastern Europe.

'Finding out what the barmaid wanted – *and* why she hung up.'

DS Leyton's brow furrows.

'Couldn't we just phone, Guv – and ask to speak to her?'

Skelgill suddenly looks surprised. He raises a finger in apparent wonderment.

'Leyton – I never thought of that.'

'Really, Guv?'

Now Skelgill tosses his hands up to the heavens.

'Leyton, you dummkopf – of course I thought of it.'

'Oh, right, Guv.'

Skelgill looks despairingly at DS Jones – she appears unsure of how to interpret his mood – but he seems now to be seeking her corroboration.

'Yesterday, Leyton, when we called into the pub to ask about Pavlenko, this girl – I'm pretty sure – wanted to tell us something.' He glances again at DS Jones, and she nods reflectively. 'But the landlord was keeping a close eye on her. I let it pass – but I wouldn't if I'd known she was going to phone after closing time last night. Now if Jones or I go swanning back in there the guy's going to be suspicious – whereas you can pose as a dim-witted Cockney hillwalker.' (DS Leyton's features register some disapproval at this suggestion.) 'Get a table well away from the bar – when she brings your award-winning pie, identify yourself and find out what she wants to tell us.' Now he indicates loosely towards the map on his screen. 'The city she said she's from – *Lublin* – it's only an hour from the Ukrainian border.'

DS Leyton is nodding, now comprehending.

'Fair enough, Guv.'

Skelgill sits back and folds his arms.

'What else had you got on today?'

DS Leyton blinks several times and reaches for his pad. He flips over a couple of pages and inhales rather wheezily.

'Some mean assignments, Guv.' There is something faintly sarcastic in his tone, that hints at retaliation for Skelgill's disparaging remark about his provenance. 'Theft of a mobility scooter from outside the Post Office in Grasmere – suspected joyrider. An organised raid on the allotments at Pooley Bridge – bolt-croppers used and two sacks of seed potatoes taken.' He steals a glance at DS Jones, who is trying her best not to laugh. 'Oh, yeah, Guv – and a decapitated sheep over by Kirkstone Pass.'

Now he looks up somewhat artfully to see if Skelgill is buying into his humour – but he is confronted by an expression as black as thunder.

6. KIRKSTONE PASS

'The daffodils look unreal – they're like birds, Guv – like a great migration of yellow-headed geese that's descended on the shoreline in search of spring grazing.'

'You'll be reciting Wordsworth next, Jones.'

DS Jones chuckles.

'This was where he got the inspiration, wasn't it?'

'Aye – couple of miles further – Glencoyne Bay.'

They are silent for a moment, Skelgill concentrating upon the curves of the road, DS Jones watching the crowded banks, amidst the botanical multitude each individual bloom glowing golden in the late morning sunshine.

'You do have to pinch yourself sometimes, Guv – that we can be at work amongst this scenery.'

'Aye – it's double-edged though.'

'In what way?'

'Well – look at that.'

He lifts a hand from the steering wheel to gesture across the mill-pond-flat expanse of lake to their left.

'Ullswater, Guv.'

'Rising trout, Jones – and pike and perch – and even schelly.'

DS Jones grins. As he pronounces the latter name *skelly*, she can't be sure if he is serious.

'There's always the weekend, Guv.'

'Aye – and statistically it rains more on Saturdays and Sundays.'

'I thought that was an urban myth?'

'Weekdays, air pollution from commuters and trucks inhibits precipitation.'

'Don't we have more traffic at weekends?'

Skelgill grimaces at her unarguable logic.

'Anyway, Jones – since when did the weather need any excuse to rain in the Lakes?'

53

She nods.

'Maybe this dry spell will keep going, Guv?'

'Don't bet on it.'

They are heading south beside Ullswater, its nine miles of western shore hugged by the Penrith-to-Windermere trunk road. Considered by many as the most beautiful of the national park's nineteen major lakes (and innumerable tarns), it owes its existence to not one – not two – but three glaciers that once rumbled off the Cumbrian mountains, and which gave rise to the 'stretched-z' shape that creates a pleasing series of constantly changing aspects for the traveller. But their final destination lies a little to the south. Reaching the hamlet of Patterdale, and leaving the lake behind, the gradient steepens and in just a short distance climbs a thousand feet through Kirkstone Pass, the surroundings a sudden contrast of bleak foreboding fells and screes, themselves towering another thousand feet above the lonely road. Astride the head of the pass, in splendid isolation, crouches the Kirkstone inn, a welcome sight for weary wayfarers these past five hundred years, and it is here that Skelgill brings his car to a crunching halt. They disembark, blinking in the bright April light, the sky a cobalt blue that is unblemished by cloud, the air sharp and ringing with the staccato treble of meadow pipits.

'It's a couple of minutes down the Struggle – but it's safer to park here.'

'*The Struggle*, Guv?'

Skelgill is already striding away, weaving between weathered picnic tables that have been optimistically dragged onto the broad verge opposite the hostelry. Deserted now, certainly if the weather holds fair this elevated spot will be thronged in a few days' time, as curious holidaymakers venture forth from their lodgings. He stretches to point out a junction some fifty yards ahead, a narrow lane that dives down the fellside and winds away over the shoulder of Snarker Pike and draws the eye to a tantalising glimpse of Windermere, four miles hence.

'It's what they call the south side of the pass – the lane up from Ambleside – it's one-in-four in places – must have been a killer in the horsedrawn days when it was an unmetalled track.'

'For the poor horses, at least, Guv.'

'Aye – though the likes of us would have been hauling our bags barefoot.'

The Struggle is bordered on each side by dry stone walls and rocky verges, and admits passing vehicles only with difficulty. In what Wainwright rather ungenerously referred to as "the charabanc season" it can be a challenge to make the ascent from Ambleside to Kirkstone without sustaining damage to the undercarriage. But they encounter no such troubles; indeed they stride down the centre of the deserted lane. Skelgill is keeping a sharp eye out for a marker tied by the shepherd who yesterday evening reported the ovine casualty – a strand of blue baler twine wound unobtrusively around a post. After some four hundred or so yards, he spies his object.

'Here we go – it's beyond the opposite wall.'

A line of decaying stakes, formerly strung with wire, fronts the wall to their left – but the instruction is that the sheep's carcase lies hidden from sight over the right-hand wall. Skelgill's attention, however, seems to be focused on the verge itself.

'What is it, Guv?'

'Tyre tracks – see?'

The ground is well draining, and Skelgill's discovery is not immediately obvious. He indicates with a tip of his boot an area of grass, cropped short by rabbits and perhaps enterprising sheep (which could, of course, account for the fatality, as road kill). There is just a faint impression, a pattern of knobbly indentations. He digs in his pocket and produces a pound coin, which he places carefully at the centre of the patch.

'See if you can get a photo – you never know, it might be useful.'

'Sure, Guv.'

While DS Jones gets to work with her mobile phone, Skelgill approaches the wall and leans over. From his reaction – as he casts about – it is evident something is amiss.

'It's gone.'

He scrambles atop and leaps well away from the wall, landing to stoop and examine the area of vegetation immediately adjacent to the stonework. There is a distinct flattening of the clumps of soft rush, and several tufts of blood-smeared fleece. DS Jones's head and shoulders appear above him.

'Who would move it, Guv?'

'More to the point, Jones – who would know it was here?'

DS Jones taps her handset against her lips, pensive as she watches Skelgill.

'Would it be valuable as meat, Guv?'

Skelgill is still staring at the undergrowth. He shakes his head.

'You could be talking ten-year-old mutton – there's no butcher would thank you for that.'

'What would it weigh, Guv?'

Now Skelgill glances up.

'About the same as you lass.' He grins in a rather macabre fashion. 'Less with the head and innards missing.'

DS Jones winces by way of response.

'So one person could lift it?'

'Happen as not.'

'Do you think it was heaved over and driven off, Guv?'

Skelgill has now risen, and cursorily examines the surrounding pasture. There is no obvious sign of disturbance, though the harsh mix of rush and grass makes for an unyielding substrate. He surveys the fellside that rises above them, forming the western wall of Kirkstone Pass, a four-mile-long barrier known as Red Screes. North of where they stand is the outcrop of Raven Crag (one of many so-called sites in Lakeland), and as he turns towards the south he scans the summit of Snarker Pike, the last of four peaks along the ridge. Then he seems to freeze, and raises a shading hand to his brow in a salute to the sun's rays. He watches for perhaps two or three seconds, before he turns purposefully to DS Jones – who still awaits a reply to her question – and pulls out his car keys. To her surprise he tosses them in the air – but her reflexes are quick and though startled she makes the catch.

'Get the car – quick – another quarter of a mile down the lane there's a track on the right that comes from a quarry – block the entrance.'

And with this instruction Skelgill turns away and sets off at a run, making a beeline towards a scar of cliffs halfway up the hillside.

'Guv... what...?'

'Go!'

He does not look back; DS Jones heeds his exhortation and turns to jog up the lane towards the inn. The going across the enclosure is uneven and steadily steepening, and the rough pasture marred by rush and bracken gradually gives way to rocky scree. Skelgill, of course, is no stranger to such terrain – though he would not ordinarily choose heavy walking boots when speed is of the essence. The escalating gradient eventually defeats his will to run, and he is forced to clamber, picking his footholds as best he can – though he dislodges many a loose boulder – and heaving himself by hand in places.

It takes him a good three minutes to cover the five hundred feet of ascent – and a similar distance in yards – and when he gains his object, the flat rim of the quarry, he is panting heavily. Nonetheless he does not break stride, wiping his brow on his sleeve as he goes. Directly ahead is the manmade cliff where for the best part of a century green slate was hewn, and to his right a cluster of buildings in various states of dilapidation, their roofs orange with rust, windows bereft of glass, beams fallen across entrances. Of his personal 'quarry' there is no sign.

He checks about, taking care where he treads so as to move without incurring the crack of a stone. He circles the abandoned buildings, peering into their dark interiors – pausing while his eyes become accustomed to the stale gloom. It takes just two minutes to satisfy himself that he is alone here, and his coiled demeanour relaxes, if reluctantly so. He begins to search more minutely, paying interest to the ground, inspecting behind doorways and forsaken piles of unworked slate. He is just leaning over the parapet of what appears to be a well shaft when the sudden urgent crunch of tyres jerks him around. But it is only his own long brown estate – distinctive for its improvised aerial, bent from a coat hanger into the outline of a fish – DS Jones behind the wheel, her features visibly anxious even through the competing reflection of the windscreen. She slews the vehicle around – raising an eyebrow from Skelgill – and leans out of the passenger window.

'He went off-road, Guv!'

'What?'

Skelgill places his hands on his hips, gunslinger fashion.

'I did what you said, Guv – I blocked the gateway – but he spotted me from a good distance and just drove across the fell – it was an old green Defender, Guv – short wheelbase.'

'Did you get the plate number?'

She compresses her lips and shakes her head.

'Too far away, Guv – I couldn't even swear it was a male driver. I drove up to the point where he went off the track – from there you can see back down the pass – the wall disintegrates – he must have got through.'

'So he headed for Ambleside?'

Now DS Jones nods.

'I phoned for back-up, Guv – but the duty officer for the area has been called away on an emergency – I was hoping if he was around he'd be able at least to get the number – maybe intercept the vehicle.'

'You could have tailed him.'

DS Jones looks momentarily crestfallen.

'I don't like the sound of what's been happening to these sheep, Guv.'

She refrains from elaborating further – perhaps a more direct expression of concern for his welfare. Skelgill for his part folds his arms and exhales through clenched teeth. He pulls open the driver's door and reaches into the side pocket for his torch. Then he walks back over to the well. Just before he reaches the retaining wall he bends down and picks up an object from the stony ground. DS Jones has left her seat and now approaches him.

'What is it, Guv?'

He holds out a tuft of sheep's wool. DS Jones indicates towards the well.

'Think it's down there, Guv?'

Skelgill shrugs. He leans over and directs the flashlight into the depths of the shaft. Perhaps fifty feet down, a black circle of water reflects the beam.

'If it is, it's not going anywhere in a hurry.' He raises his palm to his lips and blows the wool into the opening of the shaft. 'But this could have come from any number of sheep – there's nothing to stop them scavenging round here.'

DS Jones is surveying the abandoned workings.

'What made you come up, Guv – how did you know he was here?'

Skelgill narrows his eyes.

'He was watching us – I saw the sun glint off a pair of binoculars.'

DS Jones nods.

'Whoever it was, Guv – he didn't want to meet us – that was fairly serious evasive action – even in a Defender.'

Skelgill runs his fingers through his hair, still damp with perspiration.

'Can you remember where he went off?'

'I think so, Guv.'

'As Leyton would say, let's have a butcher's hook.'

DS Jones guides Skelgill to a sharp left-hand bend in the trail. There are skid marks in the aggregate where the Land Rover evidently drew to an abrupt halt – no doubt upon spotting the estate barring the exit – before escaping diagonally across the open fellside. They climb out and approach the verge. Parallel wheel-tracks bruise the vegetation, and they follow these until a patch of bare earth seems to provide the confirmation they are looking for: the same off-road tread pattern – indeed clearer now – as that beside the wall from where the sheep's carcass has disappeared. DS Jones takes another photograph, and then falls in beside Skelgill as they make their way back to his car.

'Guv – it's odd enough behaviour – killing and mutilating sheep – but why try to cover it up a day or two later? You'd imagine the crank that's doing it would want the shock effect of his handiwork being found.'

Skelgill nods pensively. He is silent for a few moments, apparently preoccupied with picking a path through last year's crackling bracken.

'Arthur Hope's rung around half a dozen farms – he reckons there are more strays than usual being reported this spring – maybe they're not strays.'

'You mean there could be more of these mutilations – that the shepherds don't know about?'

'Why stop at three?'

'You'd think walkers would have come across them, though, Guv?'

Skelgill shrugs.

'Walkers stick to the paths – besides, most folk tend not to look too closely when they smell a dead sheep and hear the buzz of the flies.'

DS Jones nods.

'What do you make of the driver of the Defender, Guv?'

'I know that innocent birdwatchers don't normally take off like that.'

'Do you think it was someone that recognised us, Guv?'

Skelgill scowls dismissively.

'Jones – we're not exactly *Mulder and Skully.*' (She chuckles at his suggestion.) 'Like as not he thought we were the landowners.'

They reach Skelgill's car – as he pulls open the driver's door his mobile phone, still in its hands-free cradle, begins to ring. He answers it on speaker.

'Leyton.'

'Struth, Guv – got you – at long last.'

DS Leyton's phrases are punctuated by wheezy gasps.

'Steady on, Leyton – are you climbing?'

'It ain't that, Guv – what it is –'

'Leyton – what's the news of the girl?'

Skelgill's interjection seems to disorientate his sergeant.

'What? Er – well – she wasn't working when I got to the pub, Guv – so eventually I managed to get the landlord talking, about him managing on his Tod Sloan – and he said his barmaid had dropped him in it – just taken off and gone back to Poland – a family bereavement, but –'

'And did you believe him?'

DS Leyton finally circumvents the questions by leaping directly to his point.

'Guv – you'd better get over here – they've just fished a body out of the lake.'

7. LITTLE LANGDALE TARN

'This is a *tarn*, Leyton.'

DS Leyton stands alongside his taller superior officer, some twenty yards from the shoreline, as they watch a little knot of emergency services personnel go about their rather grisly business.

'I've never got my head round it, Guv – water, mere, tarn, lake – they all look the same to me.'

'There's only one lake in the Lake District, Leyton.' Skelgill turns inquiringly to his colleague. 'You know that?'

'I think you did mention it, Guv.'

Nevertheless, Skelgill looks like he is winding up for his pet lecture (that Bassenthwaite Lake – or *Bass Lake* to him – is the only such natural feature to contain the actual word *lake* in its name, and that to say, for example, "Lake Windermere" is the tautological equivalent of "Lake Winderlake"). But DS Jones detaches herself from the group dealing with the gruesome job of recovery and hurries towards them. Her alarmed expression is sufficient to postpone Skelgill's homily.

'Guv – the constable's originally from Great Langdale – he says he knows who it is.'

'Aye?'

'William Thymer – we read about him in the pub – he's the old man from the woods they called *Ticker*.'

DS Leyton looks inquiringly at Skelgill.

'You've heard of him, Guv?'

Skelgill shakes his head – although this action appears to be one of ruefulness rather than denial. He takes a step forward and silently surveys the scene. They stand at a point halfway between the shore and the nearest approach of the lane that leads on towards Wrynose and Hard Knott. In this respect, Little Langdale Tarn is relatively unusual, in that most tarns are found far from the highway, small pools suspended high in the fells, nestling in mountain combs. Moreover, it is perhaps large enough even to merit an upgrade in its nomenclature, being half the size of nearby Elter Water. That said, and despite its proximity to Little Langdale itself, the tarn lies in a conservation area and there is no public access. It is neither boated nor fished, neither swum nor paddled. A drowning in Little Langdale Tarn is therefore an extremely rare event indeed.

'Aye, Leyton, I have.'

DS Jones, still facing her colleagues, raises her right hand.

'This was wrapped round his wrist – clenched in his palm.'

Skelgill and DS Leyton lean closer. It appears to be an item of rudimentary jewellery, an ensemble of a leather thong about eighteen inches long, its loose ends untied or broken, and an opaque pale orange pebble, threaded through a drilled hole. DS Leyton reaches for it and weighs it in his own broad palm.

'It's light – what is it, plastic junk?'

Skelgill takes hold of the strap between forefinger and thumb and raises the necklace into the air, holding it against the bright sky. It seems to glow as it captures the rays of the sun.

'If it's light it could be amber – that's a natural plastic – makes for a good bass lure – floats in seawater.' He swings it like a pendulum. 'Pricey, though.'

DS Jones produces a small plastic evidence bag from her back pocket, and holds open the mouth while Skelgill drops the trinket into place.

'Anything suspicious?'

'There's a doctor on the way from Coniston, Guv – but the paramedics say there's nothing on the face of it – they think the body was in the water a good twelve hours.'

'Who found it?'

'A park ranger, Guv – he'd stopped to watch a pair of grebes displaying on the tarn when he spotted it floating face down. It was the paramedics that waded out and pulled it to the shore.'

'Any theories on what he was up to?'

DS Jones shakes her head.

'There's nothing to indicate anything other than he got into trouble – perhaps in the dark – if he'd been drinking, Guv?'

Skelgill nods.

'See what the tests tell us.'

DS Leyton waves an inexpert arm.

'Could he have been fishing, Guv?'

'There's no fishing allowed here.' Skelgill's expression is slightly wistful, and perhaps also rebellious, as if such a prohibition would not particularly have deterred him under similar circumstances. 'Water this size, not artificially stocked – it's not going to be your first choice if it's your tea you're after.'

DS Jones glances back towards the tarn; the paramedics are now preparing to move the body by means of a stretcher. Skelgill seems to reach a decision about their next course of action. He clears his throat.

'Jones – you go with Leyton – but call in at the pub first – ask for contact details for the Polish girl – they must have something. Leyton, you follow that up along with anything new on Pavlenko from the Ukrainian authorities. Jones – see what you can get on Land Rovers registered in the area – there can't be so many that fit the description – what we witnessed required local knowledge. Give Arthur Hope a call – explain I'm tied up over here – get a list of other farmers who might have had problems – see what you can piece together.'

DS Leyton shifts rather uneasily from one leg to the other and glances apprehensively at his feet. While his discomfort might stem from the prolonged wearing of Skelgill's oversized boots, his question suggests another concern.

'Think we've got enough to keep the wolf from the door, Guv?'

Skelgill grimaces. He understands that DS Leyton refers to DI Smart and his hunger for personnel – his team in particular. Now, with one of his sergeants investigating stray foreign nationals, and the other a spate of attacks upon sheep, Skelgill's position is hardly impregnable in the face of the Chief's likely assessment of priorities and risks. However, he appears unwilling to see it that way.

'Leyton – sheep farming's the backbone of the National Park – without these folks the Lakes would be an overgrown wilderness – it's our duty to take seriously any threat to their livelihood.' He scans the horizon to the south, dominated by the imposing bulk of Wetherlam, Swirl How and Great Carrs, outliers of the Old Man of Coniston. 'As for Pavlenko – when someone's gone missing, potentially at one of the most dangerous sites in the district – we need to clear that up for the sake of public confidence. What's a couple of cash machines ripped out of their housings by comparison?'

He glares at his colleagues, seeking their approval. They are perhaps not entirely convinced, but they nod obediently, accepting his logic as a metaphorical girding of the loins that will equip them in the event of an unexpected thrust from the enemy. DS Leyton rather resignedly digs his hands into his trouser pockets.

'What are you going to do, Guv?'

Skelgill holds out a hand to DS Jones, and flicks his fingers, indicating that she should pass him the bag containing the necklace. She complies, and he feeds it distractedly into a pocket of his jacket while the paramedics pass them bearing the stretcher, a blanket discreetly covering its human cargo.

'I'll just have a nose about here – while I'm in this neck of the woods, may as well get all the griff on this drowning – might save a trek back over later in the week.'

*

'Sorry I couldn't help you with the Land Rover, sir.'

Skelgill shrugs. He stands at the water's edge with the uniformed constable on whose extended rural beat both of the day's events have occurred.

'Don't worry about it, lad – you can't be in two places at once – despite what my boss keeps telling me.'

'I'll keep an ear to the ground, sir – it's a nasty business with these sheep being slaughtered.'

Skelgill nods grimly.

'Most flocks are in-bye now – let's hope that's enough to deter whoever's doing it.'

The fine weather has encouraged a hatch of insect life – indeed Skelgill is staring at what appears to be a little cloud of St Mark's flies – and the eyes of both men flick about as small wild trout sporadically sip unlucky emergers from just beneath the surface film of the tarn.

'Do you fish, sir?'

Skelgill turns his head to regard his young colleague. He is a short man, though stocky, with cropped ginger hair, lively blue eyes and a naturally eager countenance liberally scattered with freckles.

'Aye – never tried here though – looks too shallow for my kind of fishing.'

The constable nods.

'You could probably wade out thirty yards before it was above your waist, sir.'

Skelgill turns back to survey the water, his eyes narrowed.

'Not easy to drown.'

The constable shakes his head.

'I was thinking that, sir – unless you'd taken a lot of trouble to get out of your depth – you'd have a job to drown by accident.'

Skelgill nods pensively.

'No pile of beer cans by the shore?'

'No, sir – what I've heard of him, he was teetotal – you'd occasionally see him skulking round Coniston, but he wasn't the sort of tramp you'd find on a bench with a bottle of strong cider for company.'

Skelgill loosely casts a hand in a small arc before them.

'DS Jones tells me you're from round here.'

'Grew up in Great Langdale, sir – we had the Post Office – but we moved to Coniston when I was twelve.'

'So you knew of Ticker?'

'That's right, sir.' The constable blinks a little self-consciously. 'Me and a pal – we used to go up into Blackbeck Wood – birds' nesting and the like – secretly we were always hoping to find what we called *Ticker's Nest*.'

'And did you?'

The constable shakes his head, though the hint of a smile teases the corners of his mouth as he revisits the memory.

'I reckon we might have got close once or twice – he chased us out of there a few times – that was part of the fun – pretending he was a cannibal, living off his wits and stray nippers like us.'

Skelgill tips his head to one side in a gesture of approval; this is exactly the kind of adventure that formed part of his own childhood.

'I heard folk would leave food for him – in hiding places?'

The constable appears unsure about this possibility, though he frowns in a way that suggests it strikes some chord. He shakes his head uncertainly.

'I don't know about that – I can ask around – but there is a spot I've seen him more than once – when I've been driving through to Santon Bridge.'

'Aye?'

'Sir – you know the stone they call *Meg's Hat* – at the foot of Blackbeck Wood?'

Skelgill purses his lips – for once he appears stumped as regards his Lakeland heritage.

'I've heard of *Long Meg* by the stone circle over at Little Salkeld – named after the witch from Meldon.'

'That's her, sir – well this one's shaped like a pointed hat – it's easy to miss though – it's over the wall from the road, just where a little beck passes through a culvert – about halfway between the track to Blackbeck Castle and the Little Langdale village sign.' (Skelgill nods as though he can picture the location.) 'The story goes that Long Meg was travelling over to Boot and had stopped to drink – she'd knelt down and taken off her hat – but she was almost ambushed by a gang of witchfinders and had to flee into the forest. They say she cast a spell and turned her hat to stone so they couldn't carry it away as evidence.'

8. TICKER'S NEST

If Long Meg's petrified 'hat' is actual size, then indeed her stature would correspond to the eponymous megalith some twenty-five miles hence (as the broomstick flies) at Little Salkeld – the twelve-foot outlier of the circle reputed to be her coven of daughters, themselves turned to stone in the act of sorcery by Scottish wizard Michael Scott. Skelgill stalks cautiously around the object – perhaps inadvertently doing so widdershins (being left-handed?) – a rather sceptical expression creasing his features. Certainly it is roughly pointed, and dark in colour, with a greenish hue typical of the local slate, but in shape it lacks the tapered precision of the stereotypical enchantress's headgear. It is impossible to tell how much of its bulk lies below ground, but it protrudes to a height of about four feet – and thus is invisible to road users beyond the dry stone wall that borders the woodland. As the constable's anecdote had implied, it is set just a few feet from a small clear stream that plunges into an ancient-looking culvert beneath the base of the wall.

Skelgill's scrutiny, however, is not directed upon the jagged shard of rock itself, but on the ground that surrounds it. Try as they might (and not that they often *do* try), humans are far from expert at disguising their tracks. So, if tourists regularly visited this place, Skelgill would expect to see a patch of worn earth beneath the easiest part of the wall to scale, and around the monument itself. There is no such balding of the vegetation; indeed the only indication that any animal form comes this way is a six-inch-wide badger-path that leads away from the base of the 'hat' into the undergrowth. But even this assessment would be flawed. Badgers might be creatures of habit, over generations wearing distinctive tracks from sett to foraging grounds – but they are not prolific sightseers. In possession of this knowledge, Skelgill is unfoxed.

The bank of elder shrub into which the narrow path disappears is already in leaf, racing to put on growth before the budding woodland canopy steals the sun and casts a permanent shade. But elder is a friend to the adventurer, lacking the thorns and impenetrability of hawthorn, and Skelgill easily parts the spindly branches of adjacent bushes. Yet now he pauses, and pulls a handful of bruised foliage to his face – and inhales deeply. The constable was not the only boy to be a birds' nester – and the mephitic smell of elder evokes for Skelgill such heady days of discovery, spring evenings after school spent searching, probing into hedgerows, on tiptoes stretching precariously, twigs snapping, heart racing, small hands feeling for the hot shock of a fresh clutch of eggs, of song thrush, blackbird, dunnock or linnet. He detaches a cluster of leaves and rubs them vigorously between his palms, discarding them and then smearing the residue over his forehead, face and around his neck. In days gone by an ostler would wreathe his horses' harnesses with elder to repel flies – and Skelgill knows this same trick: the woodland midge is deterred by the plant's bitter aroma of cyanide.

Once he has slipped through the elder grove the forest floor becomes less crowded, as the gradient steepens and rocky outcrops forbid much undergrowth. The path, too, widens in places, and is more heavily worn where the terrain demands a high step. However, Ticker plainly knew what he was doing in attempting to conceal the whereabouts of his abode. Not only had he moved with great care near the standing stone, leaving only the impression of animal activity, but also he had another card up his sleeve. Now Skelgill finds the route traversing the hillside and returning to meet the little beck. And, here, it stops dead.

He casts about, but beyond the little rocky gully there is no trace of a regular footfall. The earth is thick with soft moss and tumbling lichen, a carpet that would certainly yield and soon betray the regular passing of human feet. Skelgill steps across the beck and regards the ground more carefully, checking that the path does not pick up again a couple of yards further on – but to no avail. At this juncture, a hound engaged to track the old man of the woods might be thwarted, but Skelgill is able to employ a detective's nose (and a good-sized one, at that). Though no reader of fiction, in effect he applies the maxim of Sherlock Holmes: when all other avenues are exhausted, that which remains must provide the solution, however implausible. The beck and the path are one and the same.

Accordingly he begins to follow the diminutive watercourse upstream. This is not a matter of wading, for the bed is rocky and the flow continually cuts between boulders and dives beneath fallen logs. There are level footholds aplenty, and indeed the route – taken without haste – is deceptively easy, a natural staircase that steadily takes its passenger up through the forest. Skelgill continues this way for several minutes, and though he frequently scans left and right in case the path returns to the woodland floor, he finds no cause to digress. However, when the ground suddenly steepens and the stream becomes a tinkling waterfall that pours glistening down a mossy cliff of some ten feet, Skelgill halts – this barrier would challenge a skilled climber, let alone a septuagenarian tramp.

At the base of the outcrop the brook tumbles into a clear pool, maybe a yard in diameter and a couple of feet deep. Skelgill inspects this and nods with some satisfaction. It is just the place to dip a pot (indeed it would accommodate his own *Kelly Kettle* – and he perhaps rues its absence). He notes that around the pool's edge large flat rocks have been arranged to create a level though natural-looking pavement. If he were to make a camp himself, it would be close to a reliable source such as this – for drinking, cooking and, on a discretionary basis, washing.

The main considerations for wild living and – perhaps more pertinently – *sleeping* are protection from rain, wind and cold. Overarching these requirements, the wish for concealment clearly figured high on William Thymer's list of attributes. On the face of it a cave would satisfy all of these criteria, and the preponderance of old mines in the vicinity might suggest an obvious solution for his hideaway. However, such tunnels are often damp, with an unforgiving bedrock that chills to the bone;

the air may be stale, and potentially poisonous and the darkness a depressing constant. Certainly, these would be Skelgill's perceptions, and consequently he follows his own instincts in an alternative direction.

Some fifteen yards from the pool, upwind in a westerly direction, the woodland appears to thicken. This shadowy impression is created by a clustering of mature Norway spruces, majestic evergreens that strike sixty feet skywards, to the exclusion of other less vigorous species. There is a silence now in the wood as daylight wanes, and only the faintest 'cork-on-glass' song of a tiny goldcrest emanates from high above. Skelgill tilts back his head and sniffs, rather like a stag that tests the breeze for danger. He appears perplexed, as if the resinous scent of pine is tainted, and sets off purposefully towards the conifers. They cast an apron that creeps beyond the tips of their boughs – a fine brown carpet of needles, scales of bark, finely toothed twigs and curling cones – that remains dry in all but the most prolonged of rains, and conveniently accepts no tracks. But Skelgill's course is driven by intuition. He ducks beneath a low sweep of branches and emerges into a hidden clearing, and – sure enough – there stands his object, a bender. Roughly the size and shape of a two-person tunnel tent, its frame of withies is cloaked with a colourful patchwork of split fertilizer sacks anchored to hand-carved wooden pegs by guys of orange baler twine.

And thus Skelgill's consternation of a minute earlier finds its explanation: however, it is not the sight of the construction itself that furrows his brow, but the leafy adornments recently added. Draped all over the shelter, and likewise dangling from the branches of the surrounding spruces, are perhaps as many as thirty bunches of partially wilted elder foliage. It seems that Skelgill is not alone in putting this rather nondescript shrub to good use.

A flap of clear though tarnished polythene covers the mouth of the shelter, and more elder hangs here; he carefully moves it aside before lifting what is the door. It is gloomy beneath the conifers, and even darker inside the bender – but as his eyes become accustomed to the lack of light it is a scene of some order that greets him. On the left is a bed – a cot made from strips of hazel interwoven between stakes hammered into the earth, this frame filled to overflowing with dry bracken – traditionally harvested for winter bedding for livestock – and overlaid with perhaps as many as a dozen threadbare blankets topped by a grubby sleeping bag. On the right is a wall of crates and boxes, plastic tubs, canisters and large tins. The open-top containers hold soot-blackened cooking utensils (pot, frying pan, kettle), plate, mug, cutlery and various implements; tools (spade with broken handle, wooden mallet, rusty hacksaw, a useful-looking axe); and a sizeable assortment of tinned food (though predominantly baked beans); while those vessels with lids – inspected by Skelgill – conceal such staples as oats, candles and matches, and desert island luxuries in the form of many new-looking bars of chocolate, and by contrast a yellowing collection of second-hand books, including titles such as *Food for Foragers*, *The Compendium of Magical Herbs* and *The Apothecary's Flora*.

Skelgill seems satisfied that this inventory is largely innocuous (although he ponders for a moment over the literature, and might reasonably question the provenance of the confectionery), yet he lingers upon his haunches, perhaps considering what life would be like inside this rudimentary dwelling, already beginning to feel at home. He tests the roof with the spread fingers of his left hand – though flimsy, it appears watertight, the slit fertilizer bags having been tiled from the ground up, and correctly overlapped along the sloping ridge. Eliminating rain and wind goes a long way towards defeating the cold – although when the mercury plummets the insulating bracken and pile of blankets would be a necessary refuge. He presses down on the bed with both palms – it yields with a reassuring crackling springiness, suggesting that the bracken has been recently replenished – *Ticker's Nest* is a fitting epithet.

He checks his watch – the hour has crept past six, and if he is to escape the wood before dusk he must soon depart. In a rather ungainly fashion he crawls out of the shelter, like an unpractised sprinter struggling to come to terms with his blocks. But he pauses overlong in the 'set' position – his eyes studying a pattern of hitherto unnoticed score marks in the ground. He hauls himself to his feet and steps away for a wider perspective. Enclosing the bender a ring is scraped into the pine needles and, at intervals, a succession of triangles each has its apex touching the inside of this circle. He extracts his mobile phone, and steps away to the rear and takes a photograph, the flash firing to emphasise the failing light.

Skelgill now hesitates – his job is done here at the campsite, and he must decide which route to take. His car is parked at the same spot he and DS Jones used yesterday, a good distance from the site of *Meg's Hat*, where the stretch of road is narrow and lacks a suitable verge or laybys. He rips open the flap of his trousers' map pocket and produces a compass. A quick check appears to confirm what he already suspects, and he sets off in the opposite direction from that in which he arrived, picking a path that continues to traverse the afforested hillside. After about ten minutes' steady walking the lie of the land presents him with a choice of a rising bluff or a slightly trickier boulder-strewn course. He opts for the latter, clambering between the rocks, greasy with algae and liverworts, as a cliff rises to his right. But the reason for his choice soon becomes clear – for in another minute or so he reaches the mouth of the ravine that he explored with DS Jones. Now, of course, there is a faintly trodden path, which brings him to the high boundary wall of Blackbeck Castle; from here it is a simple matter of retracing his steps of yesterday.

It is just after he has passed the impenetrable grey gate when something catches his eye. Bluebells – yet to flower – swathe good parts of the woodland floor with their prolific bottle-green foliage, and amongst one patch of these a metallic glint attracts his attention. In fact he continues for several paces before the visual incongruity registers with his consciousness and induces him to investigate. He steps cautiously through the foliage – as though to avoid damage to the tender shoots – and reaches tentatively to extract the foreign item. It is an old book, hardbound in black clothette, only three-and-a-half inches by five, though a good inch-and-a-quarter thick. The fine pages are gilt-edged – explaining its reflective gleam – and he rotates the spine to reveal the title: *The Holy Bible*. With reverent thumbs he separates the front cover from the first page. A small label announces, "Presented by the Blue Coat School, Everton" and inscribed in faded blue ink at the top left corner of the endpaper is the name, *W. Thymer.*

9. LITTLE LANGDALE

'Where are you, Guv – it sounds like you're in a pub?'
'You ought to have been a detective, Leyton.'
'Very good, Guv – I'll remember that one.'
Skelgill raises his eyebrows to nobody in particular.
'I'm still at Little Langdale, Leyton – bird in the hand.'
'I can recommend the pie, Guv – I was just saying to the missus I should have bought a couple and saved her cooking.'
'I'll bring you some back if you want, Leyton – you can have them tomorrow night.'
'Blimey, Guv – don't trouble yourself – know what I mean?'
Skelgill shrugs, this gesture also invisible to his colleague.
'Anyway – what's the story?'
DS Leyton hesitates for a moment – there are strident background noises that could be the sound of small children engaging in some form of aquatic sibling rivalry. Skelgill has evidently called his sergeant's mobile at bath time.
'Did you get my message, Guv – is that why you're ringing?'
Skelgill momentarily takes his handset away from his ear and taps at the screen. He scowls.
'I've had none come through – the signal's worse than useless over here – I've only got one bar now.'
'Oh, right, Guv.' The penny seems to drop with DS Leyton that his superior has called him not out of urgency but more likely boredom. 'Actually it was no news really, Guv – just that they'll have some preliminary test results on the drowning victim by about ten in the morning.'
Skelgill does not respond directly to this information. He glances across towards the bar and lowers his voice.

'I've not been able to raise Jones – did she get anything on the Polish barmaid?'

DS Leyton grunts painfully, as though an object has just hit him. There is the slam of a door and the commotion diminishes measurably.

'Sorry, Guv – I'll just leave them to drown each other – the Polish girl, you said?'

'Aye – Jones's mobile is going through to voicemail.'

'I think she said something about a fitness class, Guv.'

Skelgill scoffs dismissively.

'What's she up to that nonsense for?'

'Beats me, Guv – cost of these gym memberships.' (Skelgill inhales, as if he is about to pontificate further, but DS Leyton appears keen to return to work matters.) 'Apparently the landlord didn't have any details – reckoned she'd upped and left this morning – got the bus to Coniston and on to Manchester airport – story fitted in with what he'd told me.'

'Did you come in here – with Jones?'

'No, Guv – I thought, no point in blowing my cover as the dim-witted Cockney tourist.'

There is more than a hint of sarcasm in DS Leyton's tone.

'Very funny, Leyton.' Skelgill shakes his head mirthlessly. 'Still, it might come in handy, yet.'

'I reckoned so, Guv.' DS Leyton sounds a touch mollified. 'I thought employers are supposed to get ID details – for tax and national insurance and whatnot?'

'They probably are – but a pound to a penny she was paid cash in hand. Did we get a full name?'

'The geezer reckons she told him but he couldn't remember – claims it was unpronounceable.'

Skelgill again looks over to the bar, where the landlord is occupied in laboriously writing a customer's food order on a small triplicate notepad.

'So we've just got his word for her impromptu departure.'

'Want me to check out her journey in the morning, Guv? The bus driver will surely remember – can't be many folks get aboard in that one-horse place.'

'Aye, why not.'

Skelgill sounds pensive and lacking in enthusiasm. DS Leyton, meanwhile, is clearly under pressure to resume his peacekeeping duties – but out of politeness he evidently feels unable to terminate the conversation.'

'How did you get on, Guv?'

Skelgill's response is perhaps unfairly gruff.

'Found the old boy's hideaway – up in Blackbeck Wood.'

'Anything suspicious, Guv?'

'Leyton – I'm always suspicious – I'm suspicious when I find a dead vole on the doorstep – even though I live with a congenitally murderous cat.' He strums his nails impatiently on the wooden table. 'And when there's no dead vole I'm suspicious of the dog.'

'Right, Guv.'

Now it is DS Leyton who sounds distracted. The hullaballoo has intensified despite the barrier of the door between him and his unruly offspring.

'Guv – if you don't mind – I think I'm going to need to separate these two.'

Skelgill hisses an expletive.

'Leyton – that racket's only *two*?'

'You want to hear 'em when they're hungry as well as tired, Guv.'

*

'Your young lady not with you this evening, Inspector?'

Skelgill is roused from his thoughts. The publican, who has been kept busy manning the pumps, stands before his table with a clutch of empty pint glasses trapped between the plump fingers of each hand. Skelgill stares at the bitten nails before he raises his gaze; he glowers as though he suspects the man's inquiry to be disingenuous.

'You referring to Sergeant Jones?'

The man shuffles back an inch or two, sensing Skelgill's disapproval.

'That's it, Inspector – she called in this afternoon – nasty business in the lake.'

'Tarn.'

'Tarn – of course, Inspector.'

Skelgill does not offer any opinion on the incident. The silent hiatus obliges the loitering landlord to reveal the true purpose of his unsolicited approach.

'Was there some problem as regards Eva?'

'In what way?'

'When your... *Sergeant Jones...* was asking about her – I assumed there must be a connection with the drowning?'

Skelgill folds his arms and grimaces.

'Yesterday she was admiring the boots your barmaid was wearing – maybe she just wanted to know where to buy them.' If his disinterest is affected, he carries it off with authenticity. 'You know what women are like.'

The publican gives a nervous laugh, unconvincing in its bravado. He seems uncertain of where next to tread, and retreats to safer territory.

'Can I get you a refill, Inspector – the ordinary bitter's in good form – a decent driver's beer?'

Skelgill looks askance at his half empty pint.

'I was thinking of having supper.'

The man is resting the glasses against his substantial paunch; they rattle as he nods encouragingly.

'We've got faggots new on the menu tonight, Inspector.'

Skelgill frowns warily.

'I thought that was Black Country haggis?'

The publican grins accommodatingly.

'All ingredients sourced locally, Inspector – our butcher delivers daily from Kendal.'

Skelgill shakes his head somewhat ungratefully.

'I'll stick with the pie.'

'No problem, sir – would that be with chips and peas or with boiled potatoes and salad?' (Skelgill's scowl suffices as an answer.) 'Chips it is, Inspector – you're a man after my own heart. Be about ten minutes, sir – as we've got a few in tonight.'

Skelgill nods dismissively. His mobile rests on the table beside his beer, and he is distracted by the arrival of a text message. The man backs away, bowing rather subserviently, before turning to shamble off with his load of clinking glassware. Skelgill meanwhile opens the message – the number is unfamiliar, but its sender begins by introducing himself as the redheaded constable who attended the drowning earlier. Skelgill methodically scrolls through what is quite a lengthy communication and then slumps back in his seat, inhaling and holding the breath for several seconds while he ponders the message's import, his eyes glazed. Then his mind seems to focus – he rises and pulls his jacket off the back of the chair. He heads across to the bar, tugging his wallet from his hip pocket. The landlord is this moment emerging from the kitchen – having presumably placed Skelgill's order with the chef – and at the sight of his customer preparing to leave looks somewhat alarmed. But before he can speak Skelgill takes control of the situation.

'That pie – forget the trimmings and I'll take it in a doggy bag – in fact make it half a dozen and they'll see me through the week.'

*

'Clarice – you're certain it was William Thymer that you saw?'

The old woman – short and plump and wearing glasses that magnify her eyes so they appear to fill the lenses, and who has already informed Skelgill several times that she is ninety-two – adjusts her hearing aid with one hand and with the other presses down on the head of an uncomfortable-looking tortoiseshell cat that she has pinned upon her lap.

'What's that, young 'un?'

Skelgill leans closer and in the same movement helps himself to another chocolate digestive biscuit. He is seated upon a small sofa at right angles to the woman, whose own high-backed chair faces the television set – the picture still displayed, though the sound muted – in what is a cosy cottage-style sitting room, blackened oak beams lining its low ceiling. Opposite him on the sealed chimney breast a wall-mounted electric fire has all its bars glowing orange, and he has already removed his jacket in response to the stifling heat; the chocolate on the biscuits is melting, and he licks his fingers after transferring what will be his third to his plate. His eye falls upon a framed photograph of a group of small children clustered around the old lady herself – it is one of several such images hung about the walls – and the woman seems to notice it draws his attention.

'I'm a Great Nan, yer know? Eight so far and two in t'oven. That was me ninetieth birthday – they came from all ower.'

Skelgill smiles respectfully. He takes a sip of tea and a bite of his biscuit. He seems in no hurry to reprise his question – but perhaps a deliberate tactic underlies his silence, in order to avoid being subjected to an exposition of a dynastic nature. The constable's text message that has brought him here – hampered in its timeous delivery by the mountainous environs – has informed him that an eyewitness of sorts has come forward, Clarice Cartwright being that observer. Now, casually munching, he speaks again, more loudly this time.

'What made you look out of the bedroom window, Clarice – after midnight?'

The woman gives the cat several firm strokes, its features stretching as its fur is drawn tight from its head.

'I wo' lettin' in Lotty – she comes in when she knows I'm going to bed – sleeps ont' quilt, eh?'

Skelgill gathers that Lotty is the squished feline.

'And you saw William Thymer, Clarice – you saw Ticker?'

The woman nods several times.

'Looked like devil 'isself wo' after 'im.'

'He ran past – in the direction of the tarn?'

'Lowpin.' She pulls vigorously at the cat's skin. 'He wo' flaiten alright.'

In an exaggerated manner Skelgill raises his eyebrows to show he understands that her graphic dialect tells of the tramp jumping with fear. He glances across at the window; the curtains are still open and beyond the small mullioned frame there is complete darkness. Little Langdale, like many such hamlets set deep in Lakeland's fells, is not overburdened with street lighting. The woman seems to divine his misgivings. She fixes him with her bulbous fishlike gaze and lifts a finger towards the ceiling.

'Moon had risen ower yon pike – it wo' plenty bright enough.'

'And how long after you got into bed did you hear the other footsteps?'

'Minute or two.' She sucks in her lips momentarily. 'I'd 'ave deeked but I'd took out me teeth by then.'

Skelgill appears unfazed by this logic – he reaches for another biscuit and holds it up approvingly, which pleases the old lady.

'And it was more than one person?'

The woman gets to work again on the cat as a precursor to her reply.

'Sounded like when fell runners come through t'village – a group on 'em together.'

'But no voices?'

Now she shakes her head and, as Skelgill watches with some alarm, she dispenses a couple of solid thumps upon the tolerant feline's cranium – perhaps this action corresponds to a negative response. However, as he reaches for his cup of tea he can't fail to hear the creature's throaty purr.

'Is it unusual for folk to be up and about – at that time of night?'

Now the lady rubs the cat's head with a side-to-side motion – this could be an indication of uncertainty.

'Since these offcomers arrived there's bin goings on.'

'Clarice – do you mean at the Langdale Arms?'

'Aye – and ower at castle – yon foreign gadgee.' With the heel of a hand she gives the cat a solid dunt in one ear. 'He sacked local folk as wukt there – and they say he keeps wolves – roaming wild int' grounds.'

Skelgill narrows his eyes and leans forwards with his elbows on his thighs. It will not surprise him that Blackbeck Castle's proprietor's name – *Wolfstein* – and his conspicuous ownership of a brace of Alsatians have already become twisted by hearsay. (In fact he might marvel that the rumour mill has not made the leap directly to werewolf.) Though Clarice Cartwright is still mobile about her modest abode, she probably relies upon visitors for her news and gossip. Indeed it was from her twice-weekly charlady that she learned of William Thymer's unfortunate demise, and through the same woman's good offices that her report of his nocturnal flight was relayed to the local bobby and thence to Skelgill. Now, as he munches companionably, he must be speculating as to the reliability of her testimony. Witnesses are notoriously inaccurate at the best of times – and throw into the equation such variables as a hearing aid and thick-lensed spectacles (neither of which may have been worn at the time) and an unlit village street at well past midnight – and it is tempting to conclude that the account has been invented, imagined, embellished, or possibly even dreamt.

*

The charcoal-clad figure that drops noiselessly beside Blackbeck Castle's grey forest gate crouches for a second, poised like a panther in a patch of pale moonlight. He wears fine gloves and a close-fitting hat, and a *Buff* around his throat pulled up over his nose – exposing only glinting eyes that dart about, quick to alert him to danger. His top is a soft-shell that makes no sound, his climber's trousers likewise, and rubber soled trail shoes complement the burglar's silent ensemble.

What separates this intruder from the conventional sneak thief, however, is his next act. Still on his haunches he slips off a small backpack and extracts first a bulging hessian bass-bag, and then a leather sheath from which he draws a wicked-looking filleting knife. He spreads out the bag and sets to work upon its contents with the flickering blade. Some thirty or more cuts made, he regards his handiwork. Tugging down his muffler, he picks up a portion and stuffs it into his mouth: while the bag and knife owe their origins to angling, the comestible hails from the Langdale Arms – it is in fact a slice of pie.

The 'burglar' is DI Daniel Skelgill.

Munching pensively he considers the scene, for the time being seemingly at ease. Behind him the wall curves away north and south, disappearing behind trunks and dark gatherings of shrubs. If Dr Wolfstein's five-kilometre assessment of the perimeter is accurate – a circuit of just over three miles in Skelgill's money – then it encloses private grounds of some five hundred acres, and Blackbeck Castle itself stands about half a mile from his position.

Although his previous inspection – accompanied by DS Jones – revealed no footway outside the gate, this is not the case within. A distinct shadow ahead of him stripes the rough vegetation, wider than a badger-path, though as purposefully straight. It leads due west from the forest entrance, presumably towards the castle. He sets out along its course. His customary pace is brisk – a good five miles per hour – and a few minutes' walking should bring him close to the rear of the property.

And now he allows an insight into what might appear more madness than method as regards the pie (or in fact *pies* – for he has sacrificed four of his bulk buy of six). Thirty paces from the gate he delves into the bass-bag and takes out a second morsel. Rather than eat it, however, he drops it onto the path. For a man whose stomach rattles with a mere five chocolate digestives (and nothing else since a hurried bowl of dry cereal first thing), such self-restraint is remarkable – and would certainly confound his colleague DS Leyton, who at this instant ought to be dozing replete at his fireside before the ten o'clock news. And Skelgill's ascetic determination to eke out his supply solely for his mysterious purpose seems to hold, for at regular intervals he marks his progress with successive deposits.

A gentle north-easterly is cool across his shoulder, its murmur punctuated by the occasional *too-woo* of a Tawny Owl (and the unsynchronised *too-wit* of a mate in reply). Long-eared bats fresh from hibernation are on the wing, and more than once Skelgill's sharp ears pick up their shrill cries as they hawk skilfully about the canopy. Above all – above breeze and bird and bat – a waxing gibbous moon casts solid black shadows beneath towering ornamental conifers, ideal for emergency concealment.

But Skelgill continues to shun such reassuring cover; he travels unswervingly upon the path. The habitat is neither woodland nor parkland, but somewhere in between. The ground cover is short and mainly grassy, with new growth pushing through last autumn's crumbling leaf litter. Facing the moon, bare trunks and branches and their twin shadows beneath his feet are uniform in their blackness, sharper than their daytime counterparts – but, when he turns about, a different scene confronts him, dreamlike, a greenish monochrome, an indistinct water world of waving boughs and waiting claws, where distance and space cannot easily be judged, where pale boles of oak and beech take on a ghostly luminescence and glisten with the slick trails of slugs and snails; a world where the whispering sough of the wind might be the distant wash of waves, irregular and patchy in their breaking, sensed through the opaque depths that immerse him.

But now he halts, for the arboretum suddenly gives way to a croquet lawn, hoary with dew, perhaps twice the size of a typical village bowling green. To progress further will expose him floodlit to onlookers – the dazzling moon eclipses all but the brightest constellations, Ursa Major, Pleiades, Cassiopeia, Orion, and planet Jupiter of course.

Beyond the sward, the castle looms black and grey, like some great crouching spider, its many darkened windows watchful eyes, its central door an unforgiving mouth. Imposing towers bookend the main body, the crenelated silhouette stark and jagged against the milky midnight blue of the sky.

As Skelgill takes in the scene his gaze settles upon a vague outline – a construction – in the centre of the lawn. Around its base are clustered several small tussocks, dark shapes crested with silver – and then as if by magic one of these *hops* – for they are grazing rabbits – alert sentinels that tell him no one is yet afoot.

Drawn nearer, he scatters the creatures – and begins to perceive the form of the edifice. It is a simple ring of posts – twelve round stakes five feet tall – driven into the turf, creating a circle perhaps four paces in diameter. Ostensibly it could be something the gardener has rigged up to protect ground under repair. There are pale shapes draping each of the uprights. But as he closes to within a yard or so their nature becomes clear. His narrowed eyes signal his alarm – this is a crazy modern artwork, a circle of death – each post is adorned with a horned skull, bleached white, great eye sockets black as jet – jawbones gape in mute bleats, wired leg bones dangling and redundant.

The ghoulish arrangement sees Skelgill drop his bass-bag and free his mobile phone from the breast pocket of his outer shell. But now he must remove his left glove, and he plucks with his teeth through the fabric of the *Buff*. The glove slips off only with difficulty and he bites on it while he manipulates the settings on the screen. He cannot risk the flash, and to disable it delays him a moment, and – before he can attempt the shot – a light flickers high in the tower to his right. Instinctively he drops to one knee behind the ring of posts, though it makes only a partial screen. The window is narrow and arched – barely more than an arrow-slit – and the flame seems to be a candle or a lantern that is being moved as if to follow the flight of a moth. As he watches there is just the vague impression of a person within – a glimpse of head and shoulders – perhaps fair hair, or perhaps a pale hood – but it would be too easy at this moment to imagine the castle's white lady.

And now a sudden sharp sound splits the silence – the metallic clank of an iron latch – it emanates not from the direction of the arrow-slit, but the main door in the centre of the castle. And dogs begin to bark.

Skelgill is pricked into action. In a single movement he grabs the bottom of his bass-bag and shakes out the remaining contents, rises, turns and sprints away. Behind him the door throws a widening fan of neon upon the grass. The Alsatians spill out; their baying resonant about the stage-set created by the jutting towers. There comes the angry exclamation of a man – but Skelgill has breached the treeline – he careers onwards for another twenty yards, then strikes out at a tangent to the right of the path – and tumbles for the black shadow beneath a

Wellingtonia's low-slung boughs. He slithers against the great corked trunk and freezes.

But the cry was evidently not directed at him. A wiry figure stands halfway between the door and the wooden henge, facing back towards the tower. And, now – incredibly it seems – he raises a rifle at the window. Yet it is not a bullet but a powerful torch that strikes its target – it must be mounted above the sight of the weapon – and the man again yells – a bellowed warning "Oi!" drawn out for effect.

The beam illuminates the arched window, driving the shadows from its deep recess. Almost immediately the flame is extinguished and the man watches for a moment. Satisfied, he turns his attention outwardly. The dogs, their initial bravado short-lived, have fallen silent, and he tries to call them in by name – *Hansel* and *Gretel*, of course – and Skelgill might visualise the Grimms' cannibalistic witch, were it not for his recognition of the harsh tones as those of the equally disagreeable gamekeeper, Jed Tarr.

The man begins to play the flashlight methodically around the lawn, arcing slowly from right to left as Skelgill watches – and just in time he ducks low – the beam passes – but not by so many degrees – it steadies – there is the sharp crack of the gun – and the squeal of a wounded rabbit.

'Gretel – pick it up! Gretel – off yer go! Oi – Hansel! What the hell are yer doing?'

But the hounds have found Skelgill's lure.

When all is said and done, these indulged house pets might be moderately effective guard dogs, but they are not the trained retrievers Jed Tarr is accustomed to intimidating. Why fetch a bloody twitching louse-infested coney when award-winning fare is on a plate? Indeed, why obey a human at all?

The hounds neither dwell to savour the unexpected delicacy nor take any care to share – indeed, in the half-darkness it cannot be obvious to the man that they have fed. Ignoring Jed Tarr's expletives they simply follow their noses to the edge of the lawn where Skelgill's next titbit awaits. Thence, silver backed, black shadows hung beneath, they slink like wolves along the path, relentless in their pursuit of pie.

Skelgill does not move a muscle. He is apprised of canines' superior hearing and night vision, and their stratospheric sense of smell. As regards the latter, he is downwind (and upwind is the pub grub) – so an involuntary sneeze or twitch is his only enemy. Dog logic is anchored in the reptilian brain, where repetition rules, and as likely as not they have found discarded scraps upon this path before.

A third discovery drives them on, Jed Tarr outstripped, blowing and cursing, the beam of his torch jerking up and down as he hobbles along, rifle in hand. His language is colourful – and even has Skelgill raising an eyebrow – and his threats to the dogs murderous. Yet to Skelgill's ear there is suspicion in his voice – anxiety, too – for just *why* are the dogs behaving so?

Skelgill waits until the expletives become less intelligible – it is a reasonable measure of the distance between him and his would-be pursuers. He readies himself to head south for the wall – away from both castle and its distracted guardians. If the dogs do their job and consume the food ahead of their surrogate master – as they surely will – Jed Tarr need know nothing of his incursion. Invisible beneath the tree, he permits himself a grimace of satisfaction – that is, until he returns his mobile phone to his zip pocket... and realises his glove is gone.

10. CLUTCHING AT STRAWS

'Guv – who ate all the pies?'

'What?'

'These pies – it says on the box there's six.'

DS Leyton is inspecting the takeaway carton branded *'Langdale Arms'*, now resting upon the cabinet in Skelgill's office. Having arrived promptly, he has been waiting for the return of his superior for a scheduled ten a.m. meeting together with DS Jones, who is yet to appear.

'I used them – as ground bait.'

'You went fishing last night, Guv?'

'Why shouldn't I?'

DS Leyton retreats, though his features remain quizzical. Patently he suspects his boss of having eaten them.

'Bit expensive for ground bait ain't it, Guv?'

'Look, Leyton – I saved the last two for you, didn't I?'

'Sure, Guv – I appreciate that.' He digs into his back pocket. 'That's a tenner if I remember right.'

Skelgill glowers across his desk.

'Forget it, Leyton – I must owe you a tenner – call it quits.'

DS Leyton's expression of resignation tells a tale of *many* owed tenners – a story that may just have reached its unhappy ending as Skelgill blithely writes off the entire debt.

'Right, Guv.'

At this moment DS Jones materialises in the doorway bearing a canteen tray with two mugs and a glass of water. Tucked beneath one arm is a sheaf of papers, and as she attempts to push open the door with her elbow they slip from her grasp and scatter onto the tiled floor behind her. Immediately, from out of sight, the slick, suited personage of DI Alec Smart swoops to gather the spill. Apparently he has been shadowing her along the corridor. And also evident to those within the office is that his eyes are not on the job in hand. DS Jones sports a designer sweatshirt top and close-fitting stressed hipster jeans that showcase her athletic form. As she glances over her shoulder she notices the unwelcome attention – and, instead of crossing as she might to Skelgill's desk, and bending to deposit the tray, she turns to place it upon the tall cabinet beside the box of pies.

'Skel got you skivvying for him again, Emma?'

DI Smart rises and takes a step into the office, pulling at the lapels of his hand-stitched jacket with bony fingers.

'It was my turn, sir.'

DI Smart sneers and his gaze now appraises her figure – he has her at his mercy while he keeps her documents by his side. Then he casts a cursory eye over the top sheet, and holds out the bundle, hanging on a little longer than is necessary before releasing it back into her custody.

'I hear you're setting up a sheep protection unit, Skel.' He lifts a thigh and affects to brush away dust, his gaze tracking DS Jones as she takes her customary seat; she settles self-consciously, her knees pressed together and the papers covering her lap. 'Should keep your little flock busy.'

He cackles at his own joke. Skelgill is glaring at him, but has no retort to offer. DS Leyton is glumly watching his boss.

'Don't let me hold up your meeting.'

The collective silence at least seems to have the effect of advancing DI Smart's departure, though he is too self-important to take offence. He straightens his tie and casts a lingering look at DS Jones.

'Hasta la vista, baby.'

He nods to his male colleagues – DS Leyton reluctantly acknowledging in kind, Skelgill feeling no such obligation – and strides away.

DS Leyton reaches to close the door. Skelgill lets out an Anglo-Saxon adjective-and-noun combination popular with disgruntled motorists. He turns with a scowl to DS Jones.

'What was that all about?'

'I don't know, Guv.' She appears reluctant to elaborate, but Skelgill's glare is persistent. 'He passed me in the canteen and said he's got something that's ideal for me.'

'That's not for him to say.'

DS Leyton rises and ostentatiously distributes the drinks from the tray. The intermission gives DS Jones a chance to compose a response.

'He said he was going to set up a meeting with the Chief this afternoon, Guv.'

Sullenly, Skelgill leans back and folds his arms. Then he appears to come to some unspoken conclusion. He casts a hand at the documents DS Jones still grasps upon her lap.

'What's Herdwick got to say?'

DS Jones's shoulders relax, as she turns to matters less contentious. The pages have become disordered, and it takes her a minute to sift through them. She hands out a copy of a single sheet to each of her colleagues. Skelgill lays his on the desk without attempting to read it and looks at her inquiringly.

'On the face of it, Guv – nothing sinister.' She scans her sheet and then paraphrases its content. 'Cause of death: asphyxia due to aspiration of fluid into the air passages – i.e. drowning. No trace of alcohol or drugs in the bloodstream. No apparent injuries or illness – he was in good physical shape for his age.'

She takes Skelgill's silence as a signal to continue.

'There is this, though, Guv.' Now she turns her copy of the report towards her colleagues and indicates a sub-heading on the lower half of the page. 'Abnormal concentration of corticotrophin-releasing hormone.'

DS Leyton starts rather melodramatically.

'Steady on, Emma – some of us nearly got expelled for using language like that.'

DS Jones grins obligingly. Skelgill, however, is scowling – he looks unwilling to fall in with his sergeant's classification, and keeps his counsel.

'I've never heard of it before, either.' She taps the page. 'CRH for short – I'll read it out: "Normally present in the bloodstream in a natural twenty-four-hour rhythm in non-

91

stressful circumstances. Highest at eight a.m. – lowest overnight. Manages the body's response to stress. A sudden episode can lead to elevated levels. It triggers a cascade of related fight-or-flight hormones.'" She looks up to gauge the reactions of her colleagues. 'But here's the interesting thing – it says concentrations of up to ten times normal are associated with suicide victims who have been suffering from chronic depression.'

DS Leyton shifts his bulk in his seat and scratches his head and sighs.

'Sounds like he topped himself, Guv.'

Skelgill is gnawing tenaciously at a thumbnail. His thoughts appear to be elsewhere, although his expression darkens to suggest he disapproves of such a conclusion. Then he reaches for the report and transfers it to his in-tray.

'Aye, you're probably right, Leyton.'

*

'Where are we going, Guv?'
'Whitehaven.'
'Am I allowed to know why?'

Skelgill frowns. He wrenches the steering wheel two handed, right then left, cutting across the marked lanes to beat the amber lights of the Junction 40 roundabout.

'Happen I'll tell you when we get there.'

He floors the accelerator. DS Jones lets go of the strap above the door and allows inertia to pull her head onto the restraint. She knows her boss well enough to read between the lines, and must suspect his insistence that she accompanies him has its roots in DI Smart's attempt to hook her – possession being nine-tenths of the law (and Whitehaven being nine-tenths of the way to Ireland, as Skelgill puts it on occasion).

'Is it connected to what you found at Little Langdale, Guv?'

Now Skelgill flashes her a reprimanding glance – but her artful smile seems to disarm him – she will try her luck. He lifts his shoulders, both hands still gripping the wheel.

'Maybe – but I don't understand it myself – we'll see, lass.'

DS Jones watches him for a moment.

'The local constable was trying to raise you, Guv.'

'Aye – I spoke to Leyton.' Skelgill stares into his rear-view mirror. 'While you were at your aerobics.'

DS Jones grins.

'It's called *Body Tone*.'

Skelgill does not respond to this; he appears a little peeved.

'I do it with a couple of the civilian girls, Guv – you could come along, you know?'

Now he screws up his face – he seems to suspect she is humouring him.

'No thanks.'

His manner is ungrateful, and DS Jones seems a little offended. There is a pause of a few seconds before she speaks again.

'DS Leyton said you found the tramp's den in the woods?'

Skelgill nods, though he declines to elaborate directly.

'I had a chat with an old woman – claims she saw him belting down the street about half-past twelve.'

DS Jones is alert to the connection.

'Guv, that would correspond to the estimated time of death – between midnight and two a.m.'

'She reckons she heard footsteps a minute or two later – folk running the same way.'

DS Jones frowns.

'Someone chasing him, Guv?'

Skelgill grimaces.

'She also told me they're keeping wolves in the grounds at Blackbeck Castle.'

DS Jones nods slowly, comprehending his scepticism. She makes another link.

'These sheep mutilations, Guv – you don't think people with dogs could be involved?'

Skelgill ponders for a moment, pursing his lips doubtingly. He dismisses the hypothesis with a shake of his head.

'Ivver sin a worried yowe?'

DS Jones chuckles at his lapse into local dialect – though she knows he makes a serious point; at this time of year the local press is full of horror stories of heavily pregnant ewes falling prey to the dogs of ignorant offcomers.

'Thankfully not, Guv.'

'What did Arthur Hope have to say?'

'One dead – decapitated – in Eskdale. One injured near the Whinlatter. About fifteen per cent mortality – now that the shepherds have rung round and compared markings on the strays they've picked up.'

The muscles of Skelgill's jaw tighten.

'It's been a mild winter – ten per cent's more like normal for Herdwicks.'

DS Jones narrows her eyes with concern.

'If it continues, Guv – the killing – it's going to be down to pure luck that we catch someone – how can we police half a million acres?'

Skelgill stares ahead, his grey-green eyes unblinking. They are making swift progress westwards; much of the A66 between Penrith and Keswick is dual carriageway, with roller-coaster stretches that make for entertaining driving, especially at well over the speed limit.

'This is the old road, you know? Used to be two-way.' He tips his head to the right. 'The new section coming back east is over there.'

'I think I remember, Guv. We used to visit my cousins at a farm near High Lorton.'

Skelgill grins roguishly, exposing his canines.

'Sometimes – if I've got a passenger that's not paying attention – I pretend I'm overtaking blind – I tell them these roads are quiet and you can generally take a chance.'

DS Jones gives a little squeal of unease – though it corresponds to them cresting a rise and achieving lift-off; a 'butterflies' moment.

'That's cruel, Guv – twisting the knife.'

Skelgill frowns censoriously, as though he gathers she refers to their present velocity.

'You should try a trip with Leyton – he thinks he's Nigel Mansell.'

There is a pause before DS Jones replies.

'Nigel Mansell, Guv?'

Skelgill shakes his head with resignation. He glances briefly across, taking in her lithe form as she rides the undulations of the road with a relaxed ease. His features become rather brooding as he skims another blind summit.

'Before your time, obviously, Jones.'

DS Jones does not reply – but now her attention is drawn as they overtake a vehicle and she turns to inspect its occupants. It is a green Defender.

'Long wheelbase.' Skelgill points out the obvious discrepancy.

'I know, Guv.' She resumes her forward-facing position. 'There's at least thirty in the county like the one we're after, *Coniston Green* the paint's called – but I had a word with Traffic – they think there could be the same number again that have been de-registered and are just kept for use on private land.'

'That's how I learned to drive as a twelve-year-old.'

DS Jones raises her eyebrows; it could be an expression of wonderment – but also of enlightenment. Skelgill evidently suspects the latter, and reverts to his tactic of defence by comparison.

'Whereas I reckon Leyton was a teenage getaway driver for some East End gang.'

Skelgill's mobile is suspended in its hands-free cradle. He pokes at the screen.

'Speaking of the devil, I'd better have a word, since he doesn't know we're gone.'

It takes just a couple of rings for the sergeant to answer his mobile. His voice surrounds them, his breathing audible and wheezy.

'Guv – I was just looking for you – I'm in your office right now.'

'Aye – something came up.'

'Where are you, Guv?'

Skelgill surveys their environs, his gaze lingering upon the expanse of water flashing through the trees that line the highway to starboard.

'Just passing Bass Lake.'

'Right, Guv.'

DS Leyton's tone suggests he harbours some suspicion of Skelgill's motives.

'Don't worry – I've got Jones to witness I don't stop.'

'Course not, Guv.'

'Leyton – anything more on Pavlenko?'

DS Leyton lets out a grumbling growl.

'I missed a call from my contact in Kyiv, Guv – while we were having our meeting. He's not been answering his phone since. I've tried their main switchboard but they don't understand English.'

'Probably they don't understand Cockney, Leyton.'

'Could be that, Guv.'

'Aye, well – keep trying. In the meantime see what you can find out about the owner of Blackbeck Castle – Wolfstein.'

'Doctor.'

This is DS Jones who pipes up.

'Aye, that's right, Leyton – he called himself "Doctor" when we crossed paths.'

'Righto, Guv – any particular angle you have in mind?'

Skelgill tuts impatiently – perhaps it is the proximity to Bassenthwaite Lake that irks him; so near yet so far, on such a fine day with little prospect of fishing.

'I don't know, Leyton – use your initiative – start with any previous as a werewolf.'

DS Leyton emits a nervous chuckle; uncertain of whether this is a joke or an insult. An outright laugh carries the risk of riling his superior.

'Leave it with me, Guv.' Now he hesitates for a moment, though he inhales to make it clear he has something to add. 'Er, when will you be back, Guv – in case anyone's looking for you?'

They all know he refers to the Chief – or, at least, to DI Smart, should he be successful in his quest to conscript DS Jones.

'No idea, Leyton – this could take all day. You know what it's like.'

Though the explanation makes no sense whatsoever, DS Leyton is obliged to yield.

'Right, Guv...'

Still he hesitates to offer a farewell.

'What is it, Leyton?'

'Er, nothing really, Guv – just that I was going to take the pies home later – for me and the missus, like.'

'Be my guest.'

'Thing is, Guv – there's only one left in the box.'

'Can't help you there, Leyton.'

Skelgill reaches forward and terminates the call. DS Jones glances sideways at her boss, but quickly averts her eyes when he senses her gaze. She must be wondering if, despite his denial, they are in for an unscheduled halt at Peel Wyke, "just to check the boat". However, as the turn for the old coaching inn approaches, Skelgill leans over the helm and hammers on towards Cockermouth.

'Wolfstein translates to *wolf stone*, you know, Guv?'

Skelgill raises an eyebrow.

'You do German, too?'

'Only a little, Guv – I studied it for a year.'

Skelgill scoffs.

'A year? I did French for five and I can't remember what day of the week it is.'

DS Jones laughs at his cryptic logic.

'I looked up the origin – apparently when a corpse had to be buried in a shallow grave – such as stony ground – they'd lay a large flat rock over it – to stop wolves from digging up the remains.'

Skelgill seems intrigued by this notion.

'Cairns – they'd do the same job – you know, out on the fells, I've often wondered if it's more than a pile of rocks I'm passing.'

He takes in a sharp breath, almost a reflex. 'They built one over Mallory.'

'It's a scary thought, Guv.'

Skelgill shakes his head. Then he digs into the right-hand pocket of his jacket and produces an object in a foil tray.

'Bite of pie?'

11. THE HAVEN

'A*witch*, Guv?'

They have turned into a narrow truncated street that appears sheared off to the sky. It can only be an optical illusion, caused by the upward slope, and a cliff top. Indeed this is Whitehaven, northern England's most westerly outpost, perched on the edge of the Irish Sea, two centuries ago a major commercial port for coal and iron ore. Today it is the haunt of tourists admiring the fortified harbour that withstood American raiders during the War of Independence, and its intact Georgian town plan, reputedly the inspiration for the design of New York City.

Parallax aside, George Place on the outskirts of the small town is no Fifth Avenue. A mere three parked vehicles ranged against a dozen satellite dishes tell their own tale; the properties bleak and harled and huddled, and fronting directly onto the patchy asphalt of the inadequate sidewalk. Skelgill conducts the car with care as they count the numbers; it turns out the house they seek is the last on the left, its nameplate *'The Haven'*.

Skelgill yanks up the handbrake and kills the engine. Then he regards the view that has now unfolded. Ahead of them across a t-junction rusting railings enclose ramshackle allotments that tumble into unruly scrub. Somewhere below is the shore, and, seventy miles beyond the watery horizon, County Down.

*

'Mrs Roberts, it's very good of you to see us.'

'Inspector, Sergeant – you are most welcome.'

The woman bows graciously towards each of her guests. They are seated around tea things in a tiny sunroom enclosed in a walled yard at the rear of the property. There have been passing peeks at a sitting room with television and sofa, framed graduation photographs of offspring; and a kitchen-diner where a pot bubbles quietly on a hob, filling the small property with the resinous pungency of rosemary. Rhian Roberts could be in her late sixties; she is unostentatiously attired in a white blouse with lacy sleeves, and a matching calf-length white skirt of soft material and a fine floral pattern in violet; her jewellery is conventional, a modest gold chain around her throat, a wristwatch and bracelet, and pendant earrings with small white opals that correspond to the stone set in a ring on her right index finger. More distinctive is a thick head of wavy raven hair, though cut short in a kind of bonnet; this, along with skin that is smooth and unseasonably tanned, and a pronounced physiognomy, contrives a Mediterranean look enhanced by eyes so deep a brown as to approach black.

Skelgill begins uncharacteristically with an *'ahem'*, as if he has neither rehearsed his opening line nor finds the right words materialising in the moment. Since their admission at the front door there has been no mention of their purpose, and little conversation beyond them having had a safe journey from Penrith (and the agreeable weather, naturally). DS Jones sits demurely, while Skelgill wrestles with what is – to the two detectives, at least – the proverbial elephant in the room. But the woman waits serenely for him to find his tongue, like a veteran doctor schooled in forbearance by a lifetime of apprehensive patients.

'Mrs Roberts –' (she nods encouragingly) 'I've heard of you through my family – I believe you – helped – an aunt of mine some years back – by the name of Graham – from Buttermere.'

'And how is she – Mary Ann?'

There is an involuntary straightening of Skelgill's posture.

'She's doing good – thanks – fit as a fiddle.'

'I am glad to hear it – perhaps it was the spell.'

From such mundane pleasantries this little word – *spell* – leaps clanking and hooting into their midst like a one-man-band that has been conjured from some Victorian street scene. Rhian Roberts, of course, is entirely unperturbed, and regards her guests with an inquiring look. Skelgill is clearly disoriented, though he eventually manages to force a response.

'Perhaps?'

'Inspector – I could not honestly claim to be one hundred per cent sure of my magic – because it may be that in some cases it is the power of suggestion that achieves the desired effect, and in others it might be sheer coincidence. Of course, there are hundreds of people who consider I have assisted them – and I could refer you to many of these.'

Skelgill nods willingly. The woman looks at him with a glint of amusement in her eye.

'But demonstration is not easy – I cannot turn you into a frog because that is contrary to the laws of nature. But I can for instance help you with a matter of the heart – for it is quite possible that someone may fall in love with you – these are forces that already exist and thus I can bend them to my wishes. Were I able to turn you into a frog and back there could be no denying I can work magic. That I can make a beautiful girl fall in love with you could happen anyway, and so it could be attributed to coincidence or suggestion.'

She watches Skelgill for a moment and then turns her gaze with gentle admiration upon DS Jones. Both officers look scared to death. Skelgill has his hands clasped firmly on his lap.

'So you do... do actual... spells?'

She smiles patiently.

'When I was learning my craft, I found it important to adhere to spells – to the letter; it facilitates concentration. I have an ancient grimoire that was bestowed upon me at my initiation, four decades ago. But as my confidence grew I discovered that I could often work without such a crutch. The most powerful weapons a witch can possess are her own mind and her will. With correct training and experience she should be able to perform magic simply of her own volition.'

On Skelgill's brow is enacted a little battle between bewilderment and the business at hand.

'If you don't mind my asking – what exactly happens?'

'I channel natural energy – my own, that of my subjects, that which envelops us.'

'And it causes real changes?'

'I believe so. Although there are some things I cannot accomplish alone. I take them to the coven to which I belong. The combined strength of thirteen minds is very powerful.'

Having somewhat awkwardly surmounted the hurdle of spells, by comparison Skelgill now seems to take the idea of a witches' coven in his stride.

'What sort of things do you try to achieve?'

'As I have intimated – people seek help concerning romance – then there is health and wellbeing – and of course financial hardship.'

Skelgill glances about the room, an involuntary a clue to his thoughts.

'You are wondering why I live so modestly, Inspector. If I could work magic to make money?'

He holds apart his palms, realising there is no point denying such.

'It is not for a witch to act for her own ends.' She speaks with a calm assuredness, and no hint of regret or avarice. 'I would not even wish to enrich a subject – our power is primitive and dangerous, it seems to take the shortest possible route to fulfil itself. Imagine if the outcome were compensation for the loss of a limb, or insurance for the tragic death of a loved one.'

She stares hard at Skelgill as this rather macabre idea sinks in. He nods grimly to reflect his comprehension.

'To focus upon the person's career would be more prudent. But I can only help those who help themselves.'

'In what way, Mrs Roberts?' Skelgill's eyes narrow as though he envisages some participation in a mysterious ritual.

'If you want a new job, Inspector – or promotion, Sergeant – I can only assist if you fill out some applications!'

She chuckles and they follow suit, relieved to learn of such a mundane necessity.

Skelgill grins wryly.

'Keeping mine's normally more to the point.'

'But you are not here for your own advancement.'

It is a statement rather than a question, again reflecting the acuity of her perception.

'I suppose the first thing I wanted to be sure about – to understand – is that there *is* witchcraft taking place.'

'Of all shades – from white to black, with fifty of grey in between – from genuine to sham.'

'What makes the difference – for it to be genuine?'

'Inspector, the word *witch* – it means *wisdom* – an ancient descriptor derived from the Anglo-Saxon *wicce* – just look online.' (Skelgill nods – it would appear he has done some rudimentary research.) 'The inner circle of witchcraft is effectively closed – you have to be born a witch to enter.'

'So – Mrs Roberts – how do you go about becoming involved?' Skelgill appears perplexed. 'I mean – it's not like you can walk into a church or something.'

Her dark eyes shine like polished chestnuts; she looks calmly from one detective to the other.

'In my case I began to experience a degree of clairvoyance from a young age. My powers gradually developed and I was introduced to wise people who were able to guide and instruct me. Witches recognise one another sooner or later. I was initiated into a coven of which today I am the *Magistra*.' She glances briefly at DS Jones. 'The leader is always female, Inspector.'

'And – black magic – are you saying it's all a sham?'

A shadow seems cross her features.

'There are witches who prefer the left-hand path, Inspector – one I know has been a lifelong friend – but the dark side attracts the psychologically disturbed who see it as a short cut to their heart's desire. So there exist occult groups that make useful receptacles for such would-be witches, the self-deluded, the highly suggestible. They may however be led by those with genuine ability.'

Skelgill has been captivated (and DS Jones likewise; she sits unmoving, out of deference refraining from her customary brisk taking of notes), but now he seems to notice his tea. He lifts the cup; it has cooled and he drains it in one go. His hostess responds by reaching for the pot to provide a refill.

'Ah, thanks – very much – Mrs Roberts.'

While she pours Skelgill ferrets in the inside pocket of his jacket. He produces the clear polythene bag that holds the necklace prised from the dead fingers of William Thymer. He pulls it out by the broken leather cord and holds the bead dangling. Carefully, but without hesitation, she takes it from him. A wry grin creases the corners of her full lips, though she awaits Skelgill's explanation.

'A man has been found drowned in suspicious circumstances. He had this in his possession.'

The woman's demeanour stiffens respectfully.

'Inspector – I thought for a moment you might be intending to test me – like a vampire with a cross or bunch of garlic.'

'I'm sorry?'

'This is a charm to ward off witches.'

'Ah.'

'But a white witch would have no fear of such an amulet – though I don't doubt it is an authentic talisman – and there is a hex sign lightly marked.'

'What's that?'

Skelgill leans forward as she proffers the item for his closer inspection. Indeed there is engraved – scratched so faintly as to be almost invisible – a rough circle containing a star.

'Amber was revered by the ancients – for possessing the power to repel witches – and the hex sign is of pre-Christian Teutonic origin – if you know your German...?'

Intuitively she looks to DS Jones, who responds to the unspoken command.

'*Hexe* – it means witch.'

Skelgill casts a somewhat piqued glance at his colleague. Perhaps not to be outdone, he fishes out his mobile and locates the photograph of William Thymer's forest bender. He presents the handset to Rhian Roberts.

'This is the place in the woods where we believe the old man lived. His camp was draped with bunches of recently harvested elder twigs – you can see the leaves are only partly wilted.'

'A more local tradition.' She nods slowly and weighs the phone thoughtfully in the palm of her hand. 'Like the rowan it protects against evil – planted at the door, and hung over the chimney breast and from a rafter in the barn.'

'There were markings on the forest floor.' Skelgill leans across and indicates with a finger. 'See around the shelter, scored into the earth – a circle with points – another of these hex signs?'

Surprisingly she shakes her head with some determination.

'No – it is a pentagram – perhaps an amateur attempt to deter hag-tracking – when a black witch will circle her victim in their sleep, making an incantation.' The woman's eyes narrow. 'But in vain I fear – for there is a more sinister thing.'

She proves to be adept with a smartphone – with a swipe and a flick she enlarges a portion of the background of the image. Then she presents the handset at arm's length for both detectives to view. DS Jones lets out an involuntary cry of revulsion. Illuminated by the flash – and fixed to a tree beyond the entrance of the bender – is the horned head of a sheep, its dead eyes staring purple and opaque.

'It's a tup – Herdwick ewes don't have horns.'

Such taxonomy seems somewhat superfluous, and Skelgill's interjection is perhaps borne out of self-reproach for overlooking the gruesome object in the evening gloom of the forest. Hence it is DS Jones who pursues the underlying issue.

'Mrs Roberts – what can it mean?'

The woman does not answer – indeed she sits back, her wicker armchair creaking, and presses Skelgill's phone between her palms; simultaneously she closes her eyes. When she opens them, she is staring directly at Skelgill, and her expression seems to flush with wonderment – contrary to the disquiet that might be expected, given her macabre discovery. For a few moments she is silent, until she blinks decisively and turns her attention back to DS Jones.

'The ram is a recognised symbol of the occult – records of its worship reach into the mists of time – the oldest depictions of *Amon* the ram-headed god can be traced to Berber mythology dating back over ten millennia – cults have worshipped something similar ever since – right up to the *Wicca* of today.'

Skelgill must make some inadvertent movement, for she fixes him with a penetrating stare.

'Inspector?'

He shifts uneasily in his seat and then, with the heels of his hands pressed together and his fingers spread and pointing upwards, he forms a kind of crown.

'What about a ring of posts with sheep's skulls and bones attached to them?'

'How many posts?'

'A dozen – but the circle was small – it would fit into this conservatory.'

The woman considers the area around them, a shrewd smile pulling at the corners of her mouth. Meanwhile DS Jones has fixed Skelgill with a frown of consternation. From where does this information spring?

'I can tell you that when my coven meets, the *Magistra*' (she touches her breastbone with the fingers of one hand and then extends the arm with a sweeping motion) 'marks out a consecrated circle with a ritual knife called an *Athamé* – one's reach is rarely more than five or six feet from the centre. Yet there is ample space for twelve members – and the leader.'

'I've always imagined something more on the scale of Castlerigg – or Long Meg and Her Daughters.'

Rhian Roberts shakes her head.

'A pre-match huddle of the *Marras* would be closer to the mark, Inspector.'

Skelgill grins; she refers to the local rugby league team.

'Thirteen players, as well – they could do with a bit of your magic.'

Now she smiles modestly – but she turns inquiringly to DS Jones, divining her wish to speak.

'Mrs Roberts – what would someone be trying to do – by displaying the sheep's head near his camp?'

'It is hard to know – what can you tell me about him?'

'His name was William Thymer – the locals called him *Ticker* – he'd lived as a tramp for over twenty-five years in the forest above Little Langdale. We understand he gave character readings at shepherds' meets and village fairs.'

'It is plain he knew some folklore – in trying to protect himself – he must have believed someone wished to harm him – or perhaps to drive him away.' She still has Skelgill's phone, and she hands it back to him with a flourish. 'The symbolism seems rather territorial, don't you think?'

DS Jones reaches to place a hand on Skelgill's sleeve.

'Guv – there was that skull hanging in the mine entrance – that felt like a warning not to enter. And the mutilated sheep – it's as if they're saying they can act with impunity – wherever they choose.'

Skelgill stares at her broodingly; then he turns to Rhian Roberts.

'Sheep have been found – with the head cut off and the thorax split open.'

She receives this information dispassionately.

'I have heard that in some traditions a sheep's heart is studded with nails – in lieu of a human sacrifice. From what you have told me, Inspector – it sounds that a black coven may be at work – or at least a group that is masquerading as such.'

Skelgill grimaces at the prospect.

'The shepherds don't believe local folk could be responsible.'

'People will travel a long way for their beliefs, Inspector – it may be part of their secrecy.'

Skelgill nods.

'How would we know them?'

'I could tell you if someone is a *true* witch.' She smiles coyly. 'A kind of identity parade – though I do not imagine my opinion would carry much weight in law. But mere minions are unlikely to be riding broomsticks – it is not as if there are signs so obvious as those that indicate you are left-handed, Inspector.'

Skelgill starts; she chuckles mischievously.

'I say that not because of telepathy, Inspector – but by the way you drink your tea and wear your watch – it is easier to fasten the buckle with one's good hand, is it not?'

She raises her own right arm to make the point. Skelgill grins ruefully.

'What about coven meetings – are they always held at the same place?'

'There is no such requirement, though certain prehistoric sites are more auspicious – by their very nature they are likely to facilitate meditation and concentration. I suspect those misguidedly drawn to the occult would be more impressed by stereotypically eerie surroundings.'

Skelgill nods. However, before he can respond she adds a rider.

'Meticulous precautions are normally taken to avoid discovery, Inspector – although timing would be in your favour. The moon is a reliable calendar.'

'The full moon?'

She pauses to consider her answer.

'For a white coven the power is greatest when the moon is waxing – especially just before it is full. The waning moon and dark period are when black magic is practised. As a rule covens meet once per month – and in addition celebrate four main festivals – Candlemas, Beltane, Llamas and Halloween. These ancient dates have a power of suggestion in their own right – it strikes me that a black circle would endeavour to channel such energy.'

Skelgill inhales to speak but DS Jones pre-empts his response.

'Mrs Roberts – what could be their underlying intention?'

But now she shakes her head.

'It is not within my direct experience. For someone such as myself the craft is a vocation – a calling. I have been bestowed with certain limited powers and believe I am to use them for the purposes of good. I spent my working life as a nurse, and in many ways the sense of duty is indistinguishable. My coven executes work of a benign and beneficial nature – we go to great lengths to ensure nobody is harmed as a result of our magical influences.' She looks from one detective to the other, her eyes deep coal-black pools. 'For those that take the left-hand path – for their personal ends, whatever they may be – one can only conjecture that it concerns the attainment power of over others, perhaps for financial enrichment, perhaps for self-gratification.'

DS Jones is leaning forward, clenching her hands, fingers interlocked.

'Can black magic really do this – if it's just ordinary people who've decided to become involved – without actually having any special ability?'

Rhian Roberts holds out her creased palms in a reluctant gesture of powerlessness.

'The answer to your question may be academic, Sergeant – it is what people believe that matters – just look at the influence of the world's major religions upon the actions of their adherents throughout history to this day – and those religions cannot *all* be right.'

Skelgill nods vehemently; her point evidently strikes a chord. He makes to rise – as though this is an appropriate juncture and he is concerned about overstaying their welcome. But now it is Rhian Roberts who springs to her feet with an alacrity that belies her years and places a gently restraining hand upon his shoulder.

'Inspector, and Sergeant – you cannot have failed to detect the smell of food – and I could not possibly allow you to leave on empty stomachs having tantalised you with the aroma.'

Skelgill begins a half-hearted protest, but she is already past them and on her way to the kitchen.

'Make yourself comfortable, Inspector, please – it will delay you only a few minutes.'

Skelgill grins rather sheepishly.

'Don't mind if I do, madam.'

He glances at DS Jones, who is smiling at him knowingly.

Rhian Roberts disappears from sight, but then her head pops back around the door.

'Inspector, I ought to mention – given our conversation there is one unfortunate aspect – it is lamb hotpot.'

*

'Guv – you look like you've seen a ghost.'

Skelgill is staring at the screen of his mobile phone. He stands, stock still, one arm loose at his side. The street is silent, and empty but for the two detectives, the front door of 'The Haven' now closed at Skelgill's back. DS Jones is a couple of yards away beside the car, waiting for him to finish and find his keys.

He looks up – directly at DS Jones – but there is apprehension in his eyes and he seems to see straight through her. Then he turns to his left and walks away, continuing across the little t-junction until he comes up against the iron railings that separate the local residents' allotments from the road. He appears to halt only because of the barrier, like an automaton that otherwise would keep going. Now, facing the glassy blue curve of the Irish Sea, he stands again, unmoving.

DS Jones is unsure of what to do – but, watching him from behind, an expression of alarm seizes her features – for he seems to wipe a cuff across his eyes. Gingerly, she crosses the twenty yards of tarmac that separate them, treading softly in her rubber-soled sneakers.

'Guv – are you okay?'

Skelgill does not respond, though neither does he object as she nears, tentative in her approach and wary of eye contact. She stops half a pace short, a yard to his side. Beyond the fence, immediately in front of them, this particular household uses its plot for leisure purposes: there is a meagre area of patchy grass, some half-trodden daffodils around the edges, an obliquely leaning swing, and discarded child's playthings.

'I've got three brothers.'

Skelgill stares seawards, his eyes glistening, his jaw jutting. His words are a statement but DS Jones replies.

'Aha.'

The breath hisses between his teeth, and then he inhales deeply through his nostrils.

'Older than me by ten years and above.

'I was the baby of the family.
'They thought I was the last mistake.
'Until little Carol came along.
'I was six when she was born.
'Reckon I was jealous – nose out of joint.
'She was a live wire.
'Like a kitten on a skate.
'This night she was ill.
'Two years old, she was then.
'Ma didn't get a wink of sleep.
'But the fever was worse in the morning.
'My brothers were away at the crack of dawn.
'They all worked on farms.
'I'd wanted my breakfast before school.
'But they needed to take Carol to the hospital.
'My dad had this old battered van.
'It was frosty and it wouldn't start at first.
'Then he got it going and he came in for them.
'But I'd pestered Ma to cook me egg and bacon.
'Carol was in a chair by the fire.
'Wrapped in the pink blanket she'd had as a baby.
'They carried her out, I remember she looked at me.
'I went to school, I just used to walk it.
'Came home for my dinner.
'There was no one in.
'I made a jam butty or something.
'Then I went back to school.
'Got back after school finished – still no one.
'I wanted my tea.
'I was starving by then.
'And angry – I couldn't get the telly working.
'I remember waiting.
'For ages, looking out the window.'

He pauses, almost panting, as if the entire monologue thus far has come on the back of a single lungful of air. His irises seem enlarged and greener than their regular greyish hue; it must be a constricting of his pupils and the reflected blue scatter from sky and sea. His lips barely move as he continues.

'Then finally the van pulls up.
'Dad walks round dead slow and opens the passenger door.
'I dash out, shouting I want my tea.
'Then I see Ma's face.
'She's got Carol's blanket folded over her arm.
'Only the blanket's come home.
'I keep running down the path and straight past them.
'I'm in the fells all night.
'It takes the Rescue to bring me back.
'I'm convinced it's my fault.
'Those ten greedy minutes this morning.
'Else they might have got her there in time.
'She had meningitis.
'A light's gone out today.'

Now he falls silent, unmoving, though his eyes track a Herring Gull, its melancholy cry fading as it passes out to sea and fades from sight.

'That's why I joined the Rescue when I was still a kid.
'Lied about my age.
'Probably why I joined the police, too.
'I never had the brains to be a doctor.
'But I figured if one day I could save just one life...'

He turns to look at DS Jones; tears are streaming down her cheeks. He steps close and hugs her. While his outward manner might be parental, his childhood brogue clings on.

'Hey up, lass – Ah should be bubblin' – not thee.'

12. ESKDALE TO LANGDALE

'I've never breathed a word about Carol, not to a living soul.'

Skelgill is driving again. They have departed Whitehaven, heading south on the coast road. This is not the way back to Penrith, but if DS Jones has noticed she has perhaps concluded that to interrogate her superior along such lines would be an intrusion during these first few miles. Now, his statement breaks the reflective silence.

'What made you, Guv?'

Skelgill stares at his companion – for overly long – and she looks alarmed that he takes his eyes off the road.

'Don't worry, lass – we're protected by magic.'

DS Jones gives a nervous giggle. To her relief he tightens his grip on the wheel and gazes ahead.

'You won't believe this – but when I checked my phone – you know how you get a preview of the texts and calls you've missed while it's been on silent?'

'Aha?'

'I saw the words, "Carol" and "Peace" – I swear it – but then I unlocked the screen,' (he shakes his head) 'and there was nothing there – just junk from Leyton and HQ and whatnot.'

DS Jones's eyes widen, though she seems to want to offer a plausible explanation.

'Guv – perhaps it was just a combination of words – or even letters – that your brain selected from all the phrases that were displayed? It sometimes happens to me when I'm reading.'

Skelgill's demeanour is dark and brooding.

'But she had my phone, didn't she?'

'Mrs Roberts?'

'Aye.'

They round a curve in the road and the towers and chimneys of Sellafield nuclear power station swing into view on the horizon. It is possible to live in the Lakes and imagine that Mother Nature's beauty abounds on all sides, soaring fells and tumbling becks, gambolling lambs, walled pastures rolling on endlessly. Not so. If their conversation had not anyway reached an abrupt hiatus, this disquieting vision provides one. It is another minute before Skelgill speaks again.

'Look – don't mention any of this to Leyton – that we've seen the Roberts woman.' (DS Jones nods obediently.) 'He thinks I'm barmy enough as it is.'

'What about me, Guv?'

'You know I am.'

DS Jones chuckles, but her mirth is short-lived. Skelgill has slowed the car to a crawl: they are following a lycra-clad cyclist up an incline towards a blind summit, and it is not safe to overtake. Except, as Skelgill puts it (with expletives deleted) the impatient "idiot that's been up their backside for the last five minutes" does overtake. A gleaming black Porsche Cayenne, driven by a balding male in late middle age, roars past towing a shiny aluminium trailer loaded with purchases from a builder's merchant. As he does so a car crests the brow of the hill. The Porsche cuts in, its trailer missing the cyclist by a whisker, and forcing the approaching vehicle to take evasive action, rattling up onto the footpath (where thankfully there are no pedestrians). The cyclist throws a middle digit in irate protest, while the oncoming driver blasts his horn. Skelgill and DS Jones can only watch helplessly as the near miss unfolds, DS Jones making a sharp intake of breath while Skelgill trots out his full repertoire of curses.

But in a flash the incident is over. The Porsche disappears from sight; the oncoming car resumes its position in the carriageway and continues north; only the shaken cyclist remains ahead of them, pedalling rather more unsteadily than before. Skelgill waits all the way over the rise – until he can see the road is clear – before taking a wide berth. The rider raises a thumb of approval, and they exchange glances to the effect that the Porsche driver should be committed.

'That's when you wish you were on traffic patrol, Guv.'

'Aye.' Skelgill nods grimly. 'I'm tempted to catch him as it is. I've seen a guy get six years for causing a death doing an identical overtake.'

'I got his number, Guv.'

Skelgill casts a sideways glance at his efficient subordinate.

'You've memorised it?'

'Aha.'

Skelgill raises an eyebrow.

'Maybe pass it on to the Whitehaven boys – he's no tourist, not with that trailer. At least they can keep an eye out for him.'

DS Jones nods reluctantly. The incident has grounded them, an uncomfortable touchdown on planet police work, a land where misdemeanours minor and major abound – a reminder of the continual need to assess where and when to intervene. The interview with Rhian Roberts must begin to seem distant, metaphysical, and somewhat unreal.

Skelgill slows the car – a junction approaches, and a sign for Santon Bridge.

'Where are we going, by the way, Guv?'

'Home – by the scenic route.' He scowls innocently. 'I've got a thing or two in mind.'

DS Jones grins. She must suspect that afternoon tea is next on his agenda. However, her geography of Lakeland is sufficient to tell her that not only will this circuitous route take them over the oft-treacherous Hard Knott and Wrynose passes, but also that it leads into Little Langdale. So maybe there is more to Skelgill's navigation than fruit scones and the eating up of time that may otherwise see her ensnared by the scheming DI Smart.

But first they find themselves cast upon the horns of a dilemma.

Rounding a sharp right-hand bend beyond the hamlet of Santon Bridge, beneath the wooded hill known as Irton Pike, the southern outlier of the Wast Water Screes, they come upon a road accident. It involves only one vehicle – a black Porsche Cayenne.

In trying to negotiate the corner too fast it has met side-on with a dry stone wall; the sturdy ancient boundary unyielding, unlike the buckled coachwork. The aluminium trailer is detached, a wheel missing and badly misshapen, its load of rough-sawn timber and paving scattered along the verge. The driver – the balding middle-aged man – surveys the wreckage. He is short in stature, his distended stomach bulging from a Tattersall shirt to spill over the belt that supports his corduroys.

Hearing the approach of the detectives' car he looks up to reveal a face flushed red and distorted with anger. Quickly he takes a step out into the road, raising a palm that demands they stop and provide assistance. Skelgill swerves past him, watching with some curiosity in his wing mirror as the man fumes and yells and hops and stamps and disappears from sight as they slip round the next bend.

'Guv – shouldn't we...?'

Skelgill cuts her short with a severe glance.

'Jones – this is a murder investigation – I've not got time for folk with manners like that.' He gives a flap of his arms and concentrates on the road ahead with renewed vigour. 'Besides, there's a café at the station at Dalegarth – they might still be serving if the last train's not left.'

He looks pleased with himself, as if a little wager has just come to fruition; with exaggerated craning of the neck he affects to admire the scenery that rises into relief as they penetrate deeper into fell country. Resignedly, DS Jones sinks back into her seat – although after a few moments' silence she suddenly strikes up.

'Guv – you just said *murder* investigation.'

'Aye.'

'Did you mean it?'

Skelgill hesitates for a moment.

'I was thinking of the sheep.'

He produces a wry grin, and says no more – yet there is something about his manner that suggests this is more than a joke. DS Jones switches tack.

'I thought she was convincing, Guv – Mrs Roberts.'

'There's some in my family reckon so.'

'You mean you don't?'

Skelgill forces out a breath, his compressed lips vibrating.

'I'd say after today's experience I'm a shade north of agnostic.'

'She was so matter of fact, Guv – and people come to her – it's not like she's publically advertising miracles or trying to get rich or famous.'

Skelgill nods; he seems largely in accord with his sergeant.

'Few generations ago in these parts, if you were sick the nearest doctor was two days away in the back of an uncovered cart – if you could afford a doctor – or a cart. Small wonder folk knocked up the old crone at the top of the village, with her cauldron and her cat.'

'But it *would* be old women, wouldn't it, Guv – they lived the longest and their skills were in the kitchen – they'd know about herbs and natural cures – they'd be the keepers of the family wisdom – the *wicce*.'

Again Skelgill can only agree.

'Aye – my Granny could make a mean poultice – would draw a splinter overnight. Ma was always sending us round to her. She'd mumble some old gobbledygook while she was bandaging it up.'

'A spell, Guv!'

Skelgill frowns.

'Aye – but where our Mrs Roberts crosses the line is this idea of energy – willing it, directing it.' Skelgill narrows his eyes and performs a series of grimaces, as though he is running through a scenario in his mind. 'I can't see the Chief buying into this line of investigation – much as she has her own broomstick.'

DS Jones smiles, and then nods reluctantly. They both fall silent, whether contemplating the supernatural aspect itself, or its questionable value as a bargaining chip to help Skelgill keep his team together. As they round a bend a white shape drifts out of the trees on their left, followed by another, and then another. DS Jones starts, but does not speak, as though she might be wondering if her imagination is playing tricks upon her. Then Skelgill laughs.

'It's the train, you wally.'

Indeed, the ghostly shapes are puffs of steam; the road and the Ravenglass-to-Eskdale railway track have converged and they are rapidly gaining upon one of the little engines with its payload of early-season tourists. DS Jones relaxes, though she watches with interest as they overtake. The rolling stock and loco have a Lilliputian quality, hijacked by their oversized boiler-suited driver and his giant passengers, cramped and bowed in their coloured cagoules in the open-sided carriages.

'They look frozen, Guv.'

'Aye – they'll be wanting their cocoa – we need to beat them to it.'

Of course, the train is no express; it takes forty minutes to cover the seven miles from Ravenglass on the coast to Dalegarth station near Boot in Eskdale – but who would wish to rush England's most scenic rail journey, whatever the weather? Thus Skelgill's phobia of queuing whilst hungry (a phenomenon that must apply each and every time he lines up) is quickly left behind with the clouds of steam that mark the engine's gentle progress.

*

'Look at that, Guv.'

'Aye, it's Birker Force – worth a visit on a rainy day.'

Refreshments taken on board – mineral water in DS Jones's case and tea and a brace of scones in Skelgill's – they are back on the road, the fells beginning to close in on either side as they press deeper into Eskdale. Skelgill seems in good spirits, perhaps fortified by carbohydrates and excited by the prospect of the driving challenge that lies ahead. He cocks a head in the direction of the waterfall.

'Here's one for you and your languages – know why it's called a *force*?'

DS Jones ponders for a moment.

'I've always assumed it's descriptive, Guv – of the force of the water coming down over the edge.'

Skelgill smirks rather superciliously; as he must have hoped, she has opted for the obvious explanation, and now he can demonstrate his superior knowledge.

'How about if I said to you that Dettifoss in Iceland is the most powerful waterfall in Europe?'

'Ah – I see, Guv – is it Nordic?'

Skelgill looks a little deflated, that she has so speedily made the connection. Cumbria's era as a Viking fiefdom is reflected in many local names. Reluctantly he is obliged to confirm her hypothesis.

'Aye – it's not force – not as we know it – it's never been force – it's *foss*.'

DS Jones has a follow-up question.

'So what does foss mean?'

'Waterfall.'

'No, Guv – I mean in Norwegian – or Old Nordic, more like – the original etymology. In French it means *pit*.'

Skelgill scowls; he looks like he regrets bringing up the subject. DS Jones raises her hips and slips her phone from her back pocket – she intends to ask the oracle. But then she makes a disappointed sound.

'No signal.'

Skelgill tuts disingenuously.

'That's the trouble with coming this way.'

DS Jones grins – she knows Skelgill's renegade alter ego is never happier than when he escapes the shackles of the electronic tag that is the mobile communications device. Meanwhile he is ducking his head to get a view through the passenger window.

'Never mind the Vikings – here's the Roman fort.'

Skelgill does not jest. The incline has steepened, and the character of the surrounding landscape has made a swift transition from wooded dale to barren fell. Here the route snakes between Harter Fell and Hard Knott, where the col reached in due course takes its name from the latter. About a quarter of the way up this ascent is what must have been one of the Roman Empire's least celebrated commissions, Hardknott Castle, a well-preserved garrison that once guarded the 'Tenth Highway', the route from the Roman naval base of Glannoventa (today's Ravenglass) to the fort of Galava at Ambleside and on to Kendal. It is difficult to imagine what its detachment of five hundred Croatians would have made of such an assignment, the rainstorms of summer, the snowstorms of winter, and Skelgill's unruly Brittonic ancestors snapping at their heels.

'It's turning into quite a history tour, Guv – you could almost say magical.'

'Very witty, Jones. Want to stop?'

She appears surprised by his suggestion.

'Actually, Guv – I kind of figured we'd be calling at a less ancient castle.'

Skelgill gives an involuntary tip of his head.

'Aye, well – you're right there.'

DS Jones waves a hand at the roadside Roman ruins.

'I've been here on school trips – it would seem strange to wander around without a clipboard and questionnaire, and teenage boys making rude noises in the bath house.'

Skelgill forces a wry grin.

'I can probably help you on the latter.'

DS Jones suppresses a snigger.

'Maybe we should just continue, Guv.'

Skelgill pushes back into his seat and accelerates sharply.

'Hang on to your hat – here comes Hard Knott.'

This is not such an inappropriate statement – for in no time the track becomes improbably sheer and winding – a gradient of one-in-three makes it the steepest road in England, with hairpin bends treacherous beneath the thinnest skim of ice. But conditions are good today, and the route almost deserted, and Skelgill has no need to rely upon oncoming motorists to anticipate and yield to their climb. As they reach the col and begin the descent into the wilderness that stretches beyond, Skelgill's phone signal cuts in and almost immediately a call comes through. Skelgill answers on speaker.

'Hey up, Leyton.'

'Guv – where are you?'

'Just heading for Wrynose Bottom.'

DS Leyton hesitates – of course to his Londoner's ear this description sounds like a wind-up – but he is quick to fashion what he thinks is an apposite response.

'Yeah, well – you can keep your rhino, I'm in the flamin' lion's den, Guv – Smart's been prowling everywhere looking for you both.'

'Let him prowl – what's the griff?'

'Nothing more yet on Pavlenko or your Doctor Wolfstein – other than we've got a line on him as formerly being a university professor in Prague – but it's something else that I've remembered.'

'Aye?' Skelgill sounds underwhelmed.

'What it is, Guv – when I was in the pub yesterday, incognito – and I'd ordered a pie –'

'Leyton – you're not still going on about the missing pie.'

'No, Guv – it's not that,' (though he hesitates, evidently reminded of the said item) 'but just then the phone rang on the bar and the Brummie geezer answered it – and he came over a bit strange – said he couldn't talk now – so he hung up and went through the back with my order –'

'Leyton does this have a punch line?'

'Give us a break, Guv – I'm getting there – so I'm waiting on me Sweeney Todd, and then me old copper's nose starts twitching – I don't know why – and I pick up the phone and dial that code that gives you the last number – and I write it down – then the next thing all hell breaks lose – the National Park ranger bursts in shouting there's a body in the lake – I mean *tarn* – and the phone business slipped my mind until –'

'Leyton – we could lose the signal any minute.'

'Sorry, Guv – anyway – this morning I rang that guest house in Keswick where Pavlenko stayed – in case he'd pitched up –

and then just a while ago I was going through my notebook and I came across the phone number from the pub –'

Skelgill inhales as though he is reaching the end of his tether, but DS Leyton detects this and blurts out what is indeed a kind of punch line.

'It was the *same* flippin' number, Guv – it was the B&B that phoned the pub at Little Langdale.'

Skelgill glances searchingly at DS Jones.

'We never mentioned that Pavlenko had stayed in Keswick.'

DS Jones shakes her head vehemently.

'Not even when I went to get details of the Polish girl, Guv.'

DS Leyton's wheezy voice comes back on line.

'I didn't think you would have, Guv.'

'Remind me Leyton – the phone was in the hall, wasn't it – under the stairs?'

'That's right, Guv – with a gnome money-box – so guests cough up when they use it.'

Skelgill looks thoughtful – but DS Leyton breaks back in before he can pontificate.

'Oh-oh, Guv – here's the Chief just marched into the open plan.'

'Tell me about the pie.'

'Come again, Guv?'

'You're speaking to your wife, Leyton – about your dinner.'

'She's heading for my desk, Guv – she'll be able to see your number on the display.'

'Can't hear you, Leyton – the signal's going.'

'Guv – I can hear you fine – what shall I –'

Skelgill reaches forward and deftly terminates the call. Then he rips the handset from its mount and tosses it to DS Jones. Without needing to be told, she switches it off. Then she checks her own phone.

'I've still got no signal, Guv – your network must be better than mine.'

'Aye, well – you never know when you're out in the fells and you might need to order a curry.'

13. CASTLE & INN

'Guv – the gates are opening.'

Skelgill engages first gear and edges the idling estate towards the receding barriers that guard the main entrance of Blackbeck Castle. It is only a minute since he suggested they need a minor miracle to avoid being refused access, or simply ignored, and now his wish has been granted. A chestnut courier van is champing at the bit, waiting for the gap to enlarge sufficiently to squeeze through, but the gates hinge inwards and Skelgill goes with them. There is a short-lived mimed stand off, the driver gesticulating with frustration, until Skelgill presses his warrant card against the windscreen and the van backs up. The castle walls are breached.

'This is a trick I learned from my dog – when you're going in and she's coming out there's no getting past her.'

DS Jones chuckles apprehensively.

'Let's hope the Alsatians are not on the loose, Guv.'

Skelgill shrugs indifferently, though he drives right up to the front door, and slews the car around so that the passenger side is nearest to the building. There is no obvious bell – the main entry phone system being located beside the perimeter gate, so Skelgill gives three raps of a large brass knocker in the shape of a woven Celtic triqueta. Immediately the dogs strike up from somewhere within, although their barking remains distant as the sound of light footsteps approaches and the door swings cautiously ajar.

'We're here to see Doctor Wolfstein.'

Skelgill is again brandishing his credentials.

'I sorry?'

The female is in her mid-twenties, of medium height with short black hair and contrasting milky skin, and very pale blue eyes beneath fine arched brows. She is quite strikingly attractive, but equally distinctive is the two-piece orderly's uniform she wears, which owes more to martial arts than domestic science. Charcoal in colour, it is of a soft material and well tailored, such that the belt tied around her midriff emphasises an hourglass figure. The trousers fall just below calf length, and on her feet are matching black ballet pumps. She glances nervously over her shoulder.

'Doctor Wolfstein.' Skelgill takes a step forward. 'It is important. We are the *police*.'

He speaks with exaggerated enunciation and stresses the final word. It seems he has detected both her deficiency in English and her surprise and confusion at their unannounced arrival within the normally impregnable confines of the wall. It is likely she assumed the courier had returned for some reason. As she backs away from his advance he sidles past, surreptitiously pulling DS Jones by the sleeve. Now they are inside, and turn to face her as she clings uncertainly to the door. Skelgill continues to display his warrant card.

'Doctor Wolfstein.'

It could be that he banks on the authorities – from wherever she may hail – having a rather more sinister reputation than the British police. If so, his hunch perhaps proves correct, for she closes the front door and with a tentative wave of one hand indicates they should follow her across what is a large shadowy hallway that extends along the front of the building. The décor is heavily oak-panelled, and huge oil paintings occupy much of the walls, Dantean scenes the minutiae of which are difficult to discern in the dimly lit surrounds. Skelgill is more taken by a stack of large boxes and oddly shaped parcels that bear customs stickers – presumably the delivery just received. She guides them into what might be the anteroom to a larger chamber, though it is sizable in its own right, with two long sash windows that overlook the croquet lawn at the rear. The walls are papered in flock of a fine heraldic pattern, and the pictures traditional hunting scenes. A pair of austere chesterfields face one another across a low coffee table on which are arrayed various county set and field sport periodicals; there is the air of a waiting room in a country medical practice.

Without speaking the girl slips out, her pale eyes anxious. As she closes the door Skelgill scoops up a glossy fishing magazine – but rather than settle down to peruse it he strides to a window and gazes out. DS Jones remains near the entrance – indeed a noise must reach her sharp ears for, very carefully, she turns the handle and re-opens the door by just a crack. After listening for a few moments she crosses to Skelgill. She speaks in hushed tones.

'Sounds like the girl's getting told off, Guv – but he's talking in a language I don't recognise.'

Skelgill is about to reply, but there is the crescendo of approaching footsteps and he gestures towards the nearest sofa. When Doctor Wolfstein enters, Skelgill is staring at a spring salmon and DS Jones admiring a country house interior. It behoves the tall man to speak first, though it is with grudging civility that he makes an oblique greeting.

'To what do I owe the pleasure – the second time in three days, Inspector?'

Though he addresses Skelgill his icy blue eyes appraise DS Jones as the two detectives rise, and under his scrutiny she self-consciously brushes back hair from her cheek. He does not suggest they sit again, nor make an offer of refreshments. Beneath his outward composure there is an underlying tremor – in his voice, and the muscles of his jaw. No doubt he disapproves of their guileful entry – however, he does not deign to acknowledge the feat.

'It's a different matter, sir – you are aware of the drowning in Little Langdale Tarn?'

He nods slowly.

'I believe I heard mention of it on your local news – some worthless vagrant.'

Skelgill narrows his eyes – the man's condescending manner is plainly not endearing.

'Then you may have heard mention of our laws on squatter's rights.'

There is a stiffening in the man's demeanour.

'I don't see what that has to do with me, Inspector.'

'I believe your estate includes Blackbeck Wood, sir.'

'That is correct.'

'Then there may be some legal relationship – there's such a thing as adverse possession.'

A hint of a furrow appears above the bridge of his aquiline nose.

'Inspector, I have almost six thousand acres – to most of which there is unrestricted access – I can hardly be held responsible for people who camp without permission.'

'It's not quite that simple, I'm afraid sir – you'll have read what the English courts can be like – *Bleak House* and all that.'

The man is beginning to be rattled, and his tone becomes increasingly terse.

'I don't doubt that my lawyers can provide all the information you require, Inspector.'

Skelgill puts his hands in his trouser pockets and gives an exaggerated and magnanimous shrug of the shoulders.

'That may not be necessary, sir. It appears to us the drowning was accidental.' He glances pointedly at DS Jones who nods in confirmation. 'Meanwhile we have a tip-off that an organised crime syndicate is poised to commit a string of cashpoint robberies across the county – we're keen to wrap this case up – but we are obliged to investigate to the satisfaction of the Coroner – another of our laws.'

'I see.'

It is apparent that Doctor Wolfstein doesn't quite 'see' – but that he senses there is some deal about to be made. He raises a hand to his chin and rubs his neatly trimmed beard with a forefinger.

'So if we could just get brief informal statements from you and your domestic staff to confirm what contact you have had with the deceased – we ought not need to trouble you again, sir.'

The man folds his arms and tilts back his head, like an aristocrat unwillingly held at bay by a couple of impertinent peasants.

'In my case the answer is that I have not set eyes upon the man – and I can assure you that my staff have certainly had no contact with him.'

Skelgill nods generously.

'How can you be sure of that, sir?'

'They do not leave the property – they have no such desire or requirement.'

'With respect, sir – you'll appreciate that for the sake of the record we would need to ask them directly.'

Now the man smirks, rather superciliously.

'How is your Russian, Inspector?'

Skelgill turns hopefully to DS Jones, though the alarm in her eyes rebuffs his inquiry.

'Perhaps you would do the honours, sir?'

The man hesitates, but the remnants of the grin continue to play at the corners of his mouth. After a moment he produces a tiny black and silver two-way radio from his belt at the small of his back. He presses a button and almost immediately a woman's voice answers. He barks a curt order, the only intelligible word being the last, the name *Martina*. Within a minute the familiar young woman appears, along with another girl sporting the same uniform and who could almost be her twin – and might certainly be a sister. He introduces them as Natasha and Martina, the former being the woman who admitted them. They walk to within a couple of paces of the detectives, and stand facing them obediently. Still Doctor Wolfstein makes no suggestion that anyone be seated – it is clearly his intention to render the meeting as brief as possible.

DS Jones pulls her notebook from the pocket of her denim jacket, but Skelgill gives a slight shake of the head to indicate it is not necessary. Via the landowner he provides a brief explanation of William Thymer's background and demise, and asks whether either of the girls have seen him within the past week, and of their whereabouts in particular on Monday night. Not unexpectedly, answers are relayed back to the effect that neither of them is aware of Ticker's existence (or lack of), nor have they left the castle grounds within the last month. While, of course, it is possible that Doctor Wolfstein puts words into their mouths, their economical responses are nothing if not rapid, which implies a certain legitimacy.

They are dismissed, Doctor Wolfstein staring after them until they have left the room. He turns to Skelgill.

'So you see, Inspector, it is as I anticipated.'

Skelgill nods, perhaps a little humbly.

'And just the two members of staff, sir – for a place this size?'

The man does not appear disconcerted by the question.

'My needs are simple, Inspector.' He flicks a cool glance at DS Jones. 'Cooking and housekeeping.'

There is a silence. Skelgill is nodding, his face puckered into an expression of practical agreement. He tugs at the lapels of his jacket in a gesture of finality – but then he casually takes a couple of paces towards a window.

'How about the grounds, sir – they must be a bit of a handful?'

Doctor Wolfstein moves into line so as to achieve the same view as Skelgill.

'I allow them to grow in a largely natural state, Inspector – my gamekeeper can assist if necessary.'

'It's a fair-sized lawn – I shouldn't like to have to do that with my *Flymo*.'

'I have a ride-on machine, Inspector.'

Skelgill seems interested in this concept, and takes a couple more steps closer to the window. He peers through the glass.

'Looks like your dogs have been getting to work with their bones, sir.'

Doctor Wolfstein does not join him, and indeed now walks across in the opposite direction, to the door.

'We have a mole infestation, Inspector. As I say, my gamekeeper is on hand for that sort of thing.' He opens the door and keeps a grip of the handle, standing to one side in a manner that indicates he is waiting for them to leave.

Skelgill shrugs amenably and obliges, indicating with a tip of the head to DS Jones that she should fall in. Doctor Wolfstein strides before them across the lobby. The hallway extends some sixty feet to either side, where it terminates in stone walls similar to the exterior of the building.

'Must be a good view over the dale from the towers, sir.'

The man seems to hesitate in the act of unfastening the latch.

'They are follies, Inspector – mere decoration – there is no access. They would have to be scaled from the roof.'

Skelgill makes an enlightened face to demonstrate his edification, but any further discussion is pre-empted by a boisterous reception from the German Shepherds, which have found their way to the front of the castle. Following an initial roll call, they seem drawn to Skelgill, nosing in a friendly but pushy way at his jacket.

'Treats all gone – someone beat you to it.'

Skelgill pats his pockets to demonstrate his point, and then squats on his haunches to fuss the animals.

Doctor Wolfstein watches inscrutably, his eyes closely following the movements of Skelgill's hands.

*

'What was all that about squatter's rights and adverse possession, Guv?'

Skelgill is driving slowly down the track from the castle, peering from side to side into the woodland.

'I made it up.'

DS Jones raises her eyebrows.

'It sounded convincing – well, maybe until you mentioned *Bleak House*.'

Skelgill forces a grin.

'It did the job.'

DS Jones looks like she is not entirely sure to which 'job' he refers.

'And the back garden, Guv – the moles?'

Skelgill glances sharply across at his sergeant. It is evident from her tone that she suspects some ulterior motive is at play.

'There were mounds of soil in the middle of the lawn.' His voice sounds rather distracted and he pauses reflectively before he continues. 'Unless I was imagining things.'

'He seemed a bit touchy about it, Guv.'

Skelgill grimaces.

'He wanted us out.'

'I got the distinct feeling he didn't want us *in*. I notice he didn't ask if we'd found Leonid Pavlenko.'

Skelgill nods grimly.

'What did you make of the KGB bodyguards?'

DS Jones chuckles.

'Actually, Guv – I didn't think they were Russian – not from their accents.'

'No?'

'I've heard a fair amount of Russian used in my family – my great aunts and uncles from Ukraine – it's still the lingua franca of the former Soviet Bloc – these girls could speak Russian and be from any one of twenty countries.'

Skelgill remains pensive.

'Guv – the information we got from them – you couldn't really describe it as statement material?'

Now Skelgill grins sardonically.

'Aye, well – happen they wouldn't notice that.'

He is no more forthcoming on this point – but clearly things do not quite stack up – to go to the lengths of visiting and breaching the security of the castle simply to obtain information of a quality that could equally have been achieved with a telephone call – unless it comes down to wiling away the afternoon.

'What about the gamekeeper, Guv – are we going to see him?'

Skelgill scowls.

'I think we know what his answer's going to be, Jones.'

She nods.

'I can't say I'm sorry, Guv.'

Skelgill shoots her a searching glance.

'What did you think of Wolfstein's performance?'

DS Jones folds her arms; perhaps she detects an underlying nuance in Skelgill's question.

'He's creepy, Guv.'

Again Skelgill nods.

'Funny looking cleaner and cook.'

DS Jones squirms in her seat; there is something that disconcerts her about Skelgill's blunt yet oblique observation. It takes a few moments before her thoughts regroup along practical lines.

'It will be interesting to hear what the team unearths, Guv – how come a professor from Prague ends up owning an English country estate?'

'Aye – maybe there'll be something there.'

'Do you think there's a connection, Guv – between Wolfstein and Pavlenko?'

Skelgill hesitates for a moment.

'Best not to look too hard for connections, Jones – you can usually find the wrong one.'

His reply is characteristically cryptic, though DS Jones knows him well enough by now to understand this is not necessarily a case of being cantankerous. He simply dislikes to be pressed when he doesn't yet know himself. Though she must wonder what cards he holds close to his chest, she does not pursue the point. As they reach the road he settles broodingly over the wheel. The time on the dashboard clock now reads almost six p.m. – if wiling away the afternoon was an objective he has succeeded. However, call it belt-and-braces, but as they weave through the tiny hamlet of Little Langdale he draws up outside the village inn.

The landlord is nowhere to be seen, and it is to their evident surprise that a new barmaid comes forward to take their order. There is a cluster of early evening patrons loitering around the servery, and Skelgill despatches his colleague to bag what is becoming a regular table over by the window. Meanwhile he watches the girl as she inexpertly wrestles with a hand-pump. She is shorter than her predecessor, with shoulder-length dark brown hair and hazel eyes. Her nose is long and a touch bulbous, and combines with relaxed smile lines to give her a somewhat melancholy appearance. She works purposefully, and does not attempt to engage him in conversation. Her attire is just a plain white close-fitting t-shirt and jeans; her figure modest, small breasts, a narrowing at the waist, and the plump curve of a belly suggestive of the very earliest showing of pregnancy. She must sense Skelgill's attention, for she glances up at him, but then quickly lowers her eyes; however his stare is inquisitive rather than ogling.

'Where are you from, love?'

'Poland.'

'Good for pike.'

He grins mechanically and turns away with the glasses. There is a log fire crackling in the hearth close to their table and he sets down the drinks and shrugs off his jacket; DS Jones has already done likewise. Skelgill fishes a silvery object from a pocket and flicks it deftly into a brass coal scuttle.

'What was that, Guv?'

'Pie tray – I've been meaning to bin it all afternoon.'

DS Jones chuckles.

'So that was why the Alsatians were so friendly?'

'Shortest way to a dog's heart – ask Cleopatra.'

'Aw, Guv – I'm sure she's more loyal than that.'

'Jones – she'd have your dinner off your plate the second you're out of the room – she ate three quarters of a keema naan the other night – and the lime pickle.'

DS Jones looks pained, though she must be secretly amused by the irony of Skelgill getting a taste of his own medicine. She cranes around to read the specials board beside the bar.

'The steak-and-ale pie's not on tonight, Guv.'

'Tough on Leyton – I owe him one.'

The new barmaid notices their interest – perhaps she thinks they seek her attendance – she picks up a pad and begins to round the end of the bar. Skelgill mutters under his breath.

'He's not hung around getting a Polish replacement.'

DS Jones raises her eyebrows, but the girl is upon them.

'Yes please?'

She addresses DS Jones, but Skelgill does not stand on ceremony – here is a gift horse as far as speed of service is concerned.

'Cod and chips, love – and mushy peas.'

The barmaid casts a suspicious glance at him – but she writes down some version of his order, and then nods to DS Jones.

'Could I have the grilled sea bass with a salad instead of rice, please?'

The girl makes more diligent notes.

'I ask chef – I am sure no problem.'

DS Jones smiles engagingly.

'Spasybi.'

'Bud' laska.'

The girl's reply comes automatically as she turns away. Skelgill inhales to speak, but DS Jones's eyes widen and she puts a finger hurriedly to her lips. When the barmaid has disappeared from sight she leans forward over the table. Skelgill frowns.

'What?'

'Guv – that was Ukrainian.'

'Come again?'

'I just said *thank you* and she replied *you're welcome*. In Ukrainian.'

'Maybe she's got a granny like yours.'

DS Jones ponders for a moment.

'It's an ingrained thing, isn't it – in every language there's a *gracias* and a *de nada*, a *merci* and a *de rien* – someone thanks you and you say you're welcome. In your native tongue it's a reflex – you do it without thinking.'

Skelgill looks perplexed – it is impossible to tell if he is more preoccupied by the idea that the girl might not be all that she claims, or the novelty of DS Jones's premise.

14. LIFT OFF

'Now we're sitting comfortably, shall I begin with Wolfstein or Pavlenko?'

DS Leyton glances apprehensively from one to the other of his colleagues. They are ensconced in Skelgill's office, suitably provisioned with hot drinks and – predictably in Skelgill's case – a bacon roll from the canteen. The energetic spring song of a blackbird drifts in through the open window, carried on the cool, fresh morning air. In contrast, Skelgill and DS Jones both appear less than lively – Skelgill is yawning periodically, and the normally immaculate DS Jones has perhaps overslept, and arrived in a hurry in yesterday's clothes and make-up unevenly applied at traffic lights. She has her slender fingers wrapped around an Americano.

Skelgill sighs and shakes his head.

'Can't believe we're sitting here talking about folk with names from a *Bond* film. Where are good old Burke and Hare these days?'

DS Leyton seems surprised by his superior's nostalgia.

'That's the EU for you, Guv – what is it now, half a billion people?'

DS Jones nods in accord with her fellow sergeant, her expression thoughtful.

'Potentially another forty-five million if Ukraine eventually joins – then there's Turkey.'

DS Leyton grins and taps his chest with the fingers of one hand.

'Won't be long before you have to consider me as a local, Guv.'

Over the rim of his mug of tea Skelgill raises his eyebrows, as if that is no more than a distant possibility.

'Start with Wolfstein.'

DS Leyton opens his case file and begins to thumb through its contents. Skelgill looks at DS Jones – she senses his attention and returns his gaze, but he only stares absently and she averts her eyes.

'Here we go, Guv – it's not a lot so far – but it might explain what he's doing here.' DS Leyton extracts a single sheet of paper. 'Article in February last year from the *Westmorland Gazette* – property section – shall I read it out?'

Skelgill, now chewing, nods.

DS Leyton moves the page back and forth like a trombone player, until he finds his focal length.

'The title says, "Blackbeck Castle sells to overseas buyer." Then there's the rest. "The six-thousand acre Blackbeck estate in the Langdale area has been bought in its entirety for an undisclosed sum by a buyer from the Czech Republic. On the market for almost three years, the spectacular Victorian property is believed to require considerable renovation. Originally the domain of a Whitehaven shipping heiress, the castle has a chequered past, with previous occupants including a reclusive American industrialist during the early part of the twentieth century, the War Office between 1939 and 1964, and a New Age religious sect in the 1970s. Most recently it has been operated as a country house hotel, offering rough shooting and quad biking, together with rock climbing and cave exploration in the abandoned Blackbeck mines, which are situated on the estate. It is believed that the isolated location, and stiff competition from Lakeland's burgeoning outdoor activity businesses and gourmet hotels, were the main factors contributing to the closure and sale. Land agents *Pope & Parish* were not available for comment, but a source close to the *Gazette* reports that the new owner is a former professor of medieval history from the University of Prague, who intends to use the castle as a study centre for his private research. Due to the change of use, it is not known at this stage if existing staff will be retained."'

DS Leyton inhales wheezily and looks expectantly to Skelgill. But his superior is preoccupied with the remnants of his bacon roll – he jams the last of it into his mouth and casts about for a napkin – and in the absence of such he settles for a less-than-clandestine wipe of the fingers on his trousers. It is DS Jones who speaks next.

'Going by what we saw, Wolfstein has certainly invested. The décor was fully restored – and that art collection in the hall must be worth a small fortune.'

Skelgill is nodding.

'Aye – the boundary wall's been made good – and the gates and electronic entry system wouldn't come cheap.'

'He surely must have money behind him, Guv – my lecturers were always pleading poverty.'

Skelgill grimaces.

'Unless he's famous on the continent – why would we know that?'

Now DS Leyton chips in.

'Not much comes up online, Guv – we're waiting for the university in Prague to get back to us – the boys found some academic papers that have been archived as pdfs – but we'd need to get them translated from Czech or whatever it is.'

Skelgill appears uninterested in this prospect. His subordinates wait in silence as he ponders – he seems reluctant to move on, and yet it must appear to them that the connection of Blackbeck estate and its idiosyncratic proprietor to the matters they are investigating is largely circumstantial, and any 'foreign' commonality – hardly rare these days, as DS Leyton has pointed out – no more than a coincidence.

'What about the local plod?'

DS Leyton nods, his fleshy jowls absorbing the downward movements of his square jaw.

'He's asked around, Guv – not that there's many folk lives over there – but he's a Langdale lad.'

Skelgill, knowing this, waves an impatient hand.

'What he's gleaned bears out the press report, Guv – apparently this Doctor Wolfstein hosts academic conferences – some of the delegates lodge at the Langdale Arms – kind of overflow accommodation.' DS Leyton glances at his notes. 'Also he's pally with one of the regular UPS drivers – he reckons they get shipments of historical artefacts up to the castle from time to time.'

DS Jones is nodding.

'That could be what we saw being delivered.'

DS Leyton looks pleased with this corroboration.

'There's some word the locals have got the hump, Guv – like it says in the paper, there must have been a few hotel jobs lost – but what can you expect – it had gone bust, after all. Just 'cause he's employing foreigners – who doesn't these days?'

'The keeper's got a Whitehaven accent.'

Skelgill makes this observation but does not elaborate. After a few moments DS Jones offers a suggestion.

'I don't suppose it's a skill you could so easily, import – wouldn't you need local knowledge and experience, Guv?'

That she phrases her remark as a question appeals to Skelgill's vanity.

'Aye – to do it well, you would.' He leans forward, elbows on his desk. 'But why does he need a gamekeeper at all if he's a boffin?'

His subordinates assume they are to play devil's advocate. DS Jones is first to make a suggestion.

'It might just be his hobby – it appears he could afford it – and he dresses like a country gent.'

DS Leyton proposes another angle.

'Maybe they still do some shooting, Guv – as part of the conferences – you know how these team-building jaunts are all the rage.'

Skelgill puckers his lips. He does not appear convinced. He stares challengingly at DS Jones.

'How many pheasants did we see?'

'Pheasants?'

'When we walked up through the woods and down from the mines?'

DS Jones looks a little uneasy.

'I didn't notice, Guv – there were those deer, and the tracks.'

Skelgill transfers his gaze to the rolling farmland beyond the office window.

'This time of year you'd expect cock pheasants to be crowing all over the place – I didn't hear one.'

DS Leyton chuckles.

'Maybe Wolfstein's potted 'em all, Guv?'

Skelgill scowls.

'Either way, his keeper's not done much of a job.'

DS Jones is frowning.

'When we met him, Guv – he could have had no idea we were about to turn up – but he looked the part – and he was repairing those bird traps you warned him about.'

Now Skelgill shrugs, as though this argument proves nothing to him. DS Leyton – perhaps unintentionally – tests his superior's attitude.

'Want me to run a check on him, Guv?'

Skelgill ponders for a moment.

'So long as you don't rattle his cage.'

'Righto, Guv.' DS Leyton nods, understanding the caveat, though he sounds a little disappointed. He scans his notes and turns a couple of pages. 'That's about it for Doctor Wolfstein – got a bit more juice on Pavlenko, though – I've had an email from a new contact in Kyiv – seems like he's on the ball.'

'Aye?'

'Captain Shevchenko, Guv.'

DS Leyton grins expectantly, but Skelgill – far less of a soccer aficionado than his sergeant – appears not to grasp the allusion and returns a rather accusatory stare. DS Leyton affects a cough to cover his awkwardness. He blinks several times before he continues.

'It appears Pavlenko is no angel, Guv – he's got a string of petty convictions for handling stolen goods – and as of now is officially wanted for jumping bail – on suspicion of smuggling.'

Skelgill is rubbing a knuckle pensively against his unshaven chin.

'Any bright ideas what he might be doing here?'

DS Leyton leafs through his papers until he comes to a page printed in colour, an enlarged photograph of rather grainy quality. He reaches with a grunt and slides it across the surface of Skelgill's desk.

'The officer forwarded this, Guv – from social media, taken about a month ago – that's Pavlenko on the right.'

Skelgill glowers as he considers the image. Certainly Leonid Pavlenko is recognisable, albeit more animated than in his passport photograph – a laugh that reveals a missing upper left premolar, his prominent eyebrows curved upwards, his hair longer and more unkempt. He raises a celebratory beer bottle, and three-quarters in shot is another male who reciprocates – though with some reluctance it seems, for he is mirthless, his bulging eyes empty of emotion, and he leans away from his companion as if he might wish to escape the frame of the camera.

'The other geezer, Guv – he's got underworld connections – Captain Shevchenko's tracked him down – reckons he's meeting him tomorrow.'

Skelgill's taciturn features reveal little of his thoughts. After a few more moments he releases the page into the air and it planes towards DS Jones, making a last-second loop that defies her attempt to catch it. He watches as she reaches to retrieve it from the floor; her hair falls to cover her face, and she has to brush away stray strands before she can examine the picture in comfort.

'We've got a mobile number, Guv.' DS Leyton raps his file with his knuckles. 'Believed to be Pavlenko's – we're expecting a report later today – should be able to tell if it was used in the area.'

Skelgill nods, though again his expression reverts toward the sceptical.

'How difficult is it to pick up a pay-as-you-go phone?'

DS Leyton shrugs rather helplessly.

'It's all we can do, Guv – it's worth a try.'

'Guv.'

The cautioning inflexion in DS Jones's softly spoken entreaty has both of her male colleagues turning abruptly from their exchange. Her eyes are wide with disbelief. Now her voice rises.

'Guv – he's wearing the necklace – the amber charm!'

She stands and holds the photograph for Skelgill to see. But he rises too and pulls it from her and crosses to the window. He tilts the image to catch the daylight, his eyes narrowed to slits.

'It could be.'

DS Jones looks a little crestfallen – for his tone lacks enthusiasm – though it may be he chastises himself for missing the obvious.

'Some factory in Shanghai probably turns these out by the thousand, Jones.'

He hands the page absently to DS Leyton, who is hungry for a look.

'Cor blimey, Guv – it's one heck of a coincidence if it is one – if you get my drift.' He grins sheepishly at his tautology. 'It's even got the same leather strap like a square bootlace.'

Skelgill resumes his seat and pitches back to scrutinise the ceiling, gnawing at a thumbnail. But DS Leyton is eager to advance the debate.

'So how did old Ticker get hold of that, then, Guv?'

Skelgill folds his arms; he looks rather like an unwilling patient in a dentist's chair.

'If it's the same one.'

'It must prove Pavlenko was knocking around Little Langdale, Guv – Ticker couldn't have roamed all that far – not as his age.'

Skelgill twitches his shoulders in a gesture of ambivalence.

'The local bobby said he'd seen him in Coniston – that's five miles.'

DS Leyton squints hopefully at the map on the wall above his boss.

'It's near as dammit, Guv – same neck of the woods.'

DS Jones clears her throat – since Skelgill's underwhelming response to her 'discovery' she has remained silent, but now she appears to have gathered her thoughts.

'Given what we know about William Thymer's –' (she hesitates, realising she is restricted in what she can say in front of

DS Leyton) ' – *superstitions*... it would suggest he understood the purpose of the charm.'

She regards Skelgill keenly, and then glances at DS Leyton; he has the look of one who realises he is in the dark. Skelgill decides to enlighten him – on a limited basis, at least.

'When I found the tramp's shelter – it was decked with branches of elder – and there was a circle marked around it, called a pentagram – these are supposed to ward off... spirits.' He fishes behind him into a jacket pocket and extracts the necklace, still in its polythene bag. 'So is an amber charm, apparently.'

DS Leyton's pained expression suggests he would like to understand how his superior has arrived at such wisdom – but that he knows it is not for him to ask. After a moment he grins amiably, and shifts his bulk with a groan.

'You sure he wasn't batty, Guv? I mean, twenty-five years in the forest – if you'd asked him he'd probably have told you Mrs Thatcher was still prime minister.'

Skelgill looks perplexed.

'Is she not?'

DS Leyton seems relieved, and laughs at Skelgill's jest – but now DS Jones seems determined to keep the discussion on a more serious track.

'Logically, Guv – he could only have been given it, found it, or stolen it.'

Skelgill is unmoved.

'Charity shop?'

Though just plausible, this suggestion seems more designed to avoid jumping to one of the other conclusions offered by DS Jones. It is typical of Skelgill – and frustrating for his subordinates – that he will resist linear thinking at all costs – sometimes apparently flying in the face of perfectly good reasoning. At this moment he looks content to accept what is a quite startling piece of new evidence – that there may have been some interaction between Leonid Pavlenko and William Thymer – and then to park it, so to speak.

However, when the smug countenance of DI Smart insinuates itself between the jamb and the door of his office, evidently preparing to deliver some bad news, Skelgill casually rises from his seat, dispenses a curt, "Don't go away" to his bemused sergeants, and barges past his adversary without a greeting, apology or farewell.

He reappears about ten minutes later to find his subordinates have done his bidding, and DI Smart gone. Their glum and guilty expressions, however, portend of an outcome they are each reluctant to impart. Skelgill, on the other hand, is strangely exuberant. He dons his jacket and loads its pockets with his essential accessories.

'Right Jones – let's go.'

'Go, Guv – but DI Smart said –'

'Smart's overruled. I've just seen the Chief. Come on.'

'But... where, Guv?'

'You're going home – toothbrush, passport, overnight bag.'

DS Jones rises; she holds out her arms in an appeal for more information.

Skelgill, already at the door, turns back.

'Manchester airport – noon flight for Kyiv – via Schiphol.'

Now DS Leyton apes his female colleague's pose.

'What about me, Guv?'

'Leyton – you're giving me déjà vu – is it you that speaks Ukrainian, or Jones?'

'But, Guv –'

'Leyton – I need you here – we'll be back tomorrow night – in the meantime email your Captain Shevchenko and tell him we're coming to his meeting.'

15. KYIV

'There's a McDonald's!'

'Shouldn't we get checked in, Guv – in case there's any problem with the reservation – you know what Admin can be like?'

'I'm starving, Jones – those in-flight meals wouldn't feed a hamster.'

'There'll be plenty of cafés for a snack – our hotel's near the city centre.'

Skelgill sinks back reluctantly in his seat. The taxi driver, surly and swarthy in equal measure, shows no indication that he comprehends his hungry passenger's wishes. The interior of the cab smells of stale cigarette smoke; the creamy tan upholstery is creaky and cracked with age; and there are no rear seatbelts. Externally, the speed limit appears to be optional. With a hawk-like anxiety Skelgill has been watching passing sights en route from Boryspil – unkempt farmland stretching flat to the horizon, the sudden high-rise shock of Darnytsia Raion with its quarter-of-a-million inhabitants, and the colossus Rodina-Mat, an Iron Lady of sorts, a severe stainless steel amazon rising with sword and shield from the silvery Dneiper's wooded banks on the outskirts of the city proper. As they strike through the suburbs his expression of alienation grows with the proliferation of signs, Cyrillic script shrouding the mundane in secrecy; thus good old McDonald's has double cheeseburger appeal. He voices his concern.

'Aye – but what are you getting? – this is all gobbledegook.'

'I can read some of it, Guv – look – over there, for instance.'

A rank of cloud is invading from the east, hastening the arrival of dusk; in anticipation, Kyiv is lighting up. DS Jones indicates a huge yellow neon ahead and to their left that runs along the roof of what resembles a grand Parisian hotel: it reads both *ARENA CITY* and *APEHA CITI*. Skelgill ducks to get a better view, screwing up his face.

'So what are you saying – P is R and H is N?'

'That's right.'

'Why?'

'*Y* is *U*, Guv.'

Skelgill is about to berate her, but he notices the grin that she is unable to suppress.

'I think I'll leave this up to you.'

He folds his arms and resumes his twitchy surveillance. The traffic is dense; ubiquitous moulded saloons jostle with luxury limousines and SUVs, and battered boxy Soviet-style vehicles, an amalgam that is foreign to his eye and in the wrong carriageway. There are plenty of pedestrians abroad – the weather, at least, seems not dissimilar to that they have left behind, now cooling to single digit Celsius; most figures wear dark coats, though younger females he notices splash colour, a gold bag, a silver jacket motif, extravagant spangled boots with bouncing trimmings. The architecture thus far has been irregular and unremarkable, largely twentieth century; sporadic high rise, chimneys, aerials; more often austere-looking apartment blocks, generally five or six stories in poor repair, an assortment of precarious balcony extensions stealing ramshackle air space; occasional shabby shops at the ground floor; cranes and bill-stickered hoardings mark work in progress; indeed he is reminded of Manchester – and their hotel, a concrete 1990s tribute to Soviet-style architecture, built on an island of high ground in correspondingly inauspicious surroundings, reinforces this impression. They halt beneath utilitarian cement arches that must surely conjure fast food. The driver abandons them to clamber out unassisted, though when DS Jones tips him a Euro note in exchange for their bags his countenance illuminates and he wishes them a successful visit, in impeccable English.

Skelgill's appetite thus further subliminally whetted, he insists they register, drop their bags in their rooms, and meet in "two minutes" to head straight out. However, while DS Jones more or less complies with their compact, he keeps her waiting a short while. When he arrives in the lobby she is resting in a casual seating area that overlooks the vehicular approach and car park; he notices she has attracted the attention of a couple of brown-suited porters who loiter untidily inside the sliding glass doors. They observe his movements as he picks her up and together the detectives cross the broad floor; however, when approached they straighten respectfully and give a coordinated bow of their heads.

'Get the feeling we're being watched?'

'Not especially, Guv.'

Skelgill perhaps unfairly stares down the bellhops; his features remain stern as he and DS Jones begin to move away from the doors.

'You know how they give you free toiletries – like in a kit, in your bathroom?'

'Aha.'

She sounds apprehensive, anticipating what is coming.

'Mine had condoms in it.'

Skelgill's gaze picks up the trajectory of a pigeon, as though the bird is an unexpected sight. There is a pause before DS Jones replies.

'So did mine, Guv.'

Skelgill lifts his head in silent acknowledgement. The pigeon passes beyond view and he looks briefly sideways at his colleague.

'What's that all about?'

'Maybe it's a marketing campaign.'

They are descending flights of steps towards a busy road – four lanes of fairly heavy traffic flow in either direction. This conversation seems to peter out, but their emergence from the hotel's semi-private environs brings new distractions. Though they move purposefully, it is not clear which of them leads – until Skelgill reveals he has delegated (if not communicated) the task.

'I take it you've sussed out the rendezvous?'

As is frequently the case, DS Jones is one step ahead.

'We're meeting Captain Shevchenko just off Khreschatyk – that's the main street. It's the way up to the *Maidan* –

Independence Square – I thought we should at least see that in case there's no time tomorrow – we've got about half an hour.'

Skelgill shrugs. It is probable he would prefer any such casual sightseeing to take in the river – especially since the airline magazine has informed him that the Dneiper, Europe's fourth longest, is noted for the legendary *beluga*, the European sturgeon, and once produced a specimen of fifteen feet and the weight of five men. Absently he takes a series of pronounced breaths, and then exhales, as though the act has brought a revelation.

'You can tell we're a long way from the sea – the air's not fresh, like back home.'

DS Jones glances skywards, as if she expects Skelgill's notion to be somehow manifested as a visible phenomenon.

'You know, Guv, it reminds me of London – apart from...'

'Aye?'

'Well – the people.'

Skelgill's eyes become busy with passing citizens. A stream of elderly women all seem attached to plastic carrier bags. A youngish man has a laptop satchel, its strap a diagonal black sash across his pale mackintosh. A plump older man in a bulky blue ski jacket and a grey tartan cap is reading a pink notice plastered to a lamppost; the foot of the page is perforated and he reaches up and tears off one of the strips. An officer in smart greenish-blue military uniform, matching collar and tie, gold buttons and braid and insignia, and a ridiculous field visor hat, stops – and stoops – to present a coin to a female beggar, soot-blackened though well-fed and semi-larval, half emerged from a grimy sleeping bag.

'I don't think they look so different from us.'

'That's my point, Guv – do you see anyone who's not Caucasian?'

He nods pensively, but any further comparison to London is dispelled as they round into the southern end of Khreschatyk. This grand boulevard is unequivocally Iron Curtain, lined as it is by continuous ranks of neoclassical Stalinist architecture. Such an impression is not lost upon Skelgill.

'I can just picture the Red Army tanks rolling along here.'

DS Jones glances anxiously about.

'Not too loud, Guv – I think it's a sensitive subject.'

Skelgill chastises himself with a gurning expression.

Ranged around the north-east end of the Maidan self-important buildings converge like infantry battalions that have advanced so far and now realise they are not all going to fit. In somewhat garish contrast to their stark socialist modernism, their vertical masculine lines standing to attention, that capitalism has seduced this city is revealed by their incongruous crowning tiaras: giant neon logos, effeminate and elaborate, supported by extensive scaffolding. Skelgill is surveying these sponsors for a not-so-hidden meaning.

'Jones – look – there must be another McDonald's round here.'

His colleague grins, though she checks the time in her palm.

'I think we ought to head to the meeting point, Guv – it'll probably take us five minutes to walk back – we'll be able to eat there.'

Skelgill casts about forlornly. It will soon be dark – almost eight p.m. – and perhaps the two-hour time warp is contributing to his premature hunger (though his subordinates might testify that it is a permanent condition). The sky is blanketed by an evenly padded quilt of stratus, the gentle bulge of each pocket tinted pink by the setting sun; indeed its rays pick out the lavish golden domes of the city's holy places as if they radiate of their own volition.

But with no fast-food joint actually in view, Skelgill makes up his mind.

'Right, let's go.'

He has his bearings, and strides away, and DS Jones scampers to catch him. He remains a yard ahead as they retrace their steps southwards along Khreschatyk, until – prompted by her maps app – DS Jones reaches to pinch his sleeve and veer across the broad pavement towards a high stone arch. Beyond is a narrower thoroughfare, immediately distinctive for its chic. Raised terraces wrapped in smart awnings mark several restaurants; there are boutiques and a high proportion of luxury

147

cars, mostly prestigious German marques – though a gleaming white Range Rover catches Skelgill's eye.

'Now it reminds me of Bond Street, Guv.'

'Aye, well – you'd know better than me.'

'It's this one, Guv – *Pechera Vid'my.*'

'Sounds like a fish restaurant.'

DS Jones shakes her mobile phone.

'I could see what translate says.'

Skelgill's response is to take a striding leap at the wooden steps, but once over the threshold he halts and widens his eyes in an effort to adjust to the relative gloom. Beneath the canopy the terrace is more like the interior of a bar. There is scant lighting other than ambient street neon, and candles in jars upon the tables. A western pop video plays out from screens suspended at either end of the space. The seating recalls the VIP area of a nightclub, low-backed rectangular sofas in pale leather arranged around broad glass-topped coffee tables into a series of cubicles, in two rows. Despite a healthy sprinkling of patrons, the terrace is unmanned as far as staff are concerned. No one seems to be dining as such, though he discerns that some customers have plates of finger food.

He leads the way down the aisle to a vacant booth on the balcony side, achieving a view both along the street and back towards the entrance. DS Jones settles on the sofa perpendicular to his, facing the curtained doors of what must be the restaurant proper. While she appears relaxed, Skelgill is agitated and looks unwilling to drop his guard. In the next cubicle, seated together in the same position as DS Jones, are twin girls, perhaps aged twenty. They are strikingly attractive and immaculately presented. Their dresses, one a shimmering silver, the other pearl, look expensive, silky, clinging to contours and exposing bare shoulders; Skelgill's darting gaze, ostensibly seeking a waiter, continually returns to the groomed blonde heads and smooth bronzed cleavages. Occasionally sipping French mineral water, they lean in together, conspiratorial, swaying over mobile gossip, tapping with crimson talons at what amuses them.

DS Jones must notice Skelgill's continual distraction, for she turns to glance pointedly to her right.

'No sign, Guv?'

Skelgill affects to notice something in the street and leans out behind his sergeant to stare beyond her.

'Not that I know what to look for.'

'DS Leyton's email said he'd be wearing a three-stripes jacket – but I wondered if something got lost in translation – you know, to do with his rank?'

But Skelgill is only half listening – his gaze has become fixed upon the darkened doorway of a designer store – and there it is again: the firefly glow of a cigarette. As he narrows his eyes, the tiny orange ember reappears – apparently one last long draw, for it is sent tumbling through the air and a slim figure of medium height detaches itself from the sentry box of shadow and swiftly, easily, unobtrusively moves beneath the glow of the streetlamps and crosses towards the restaurant steps.

'This could be him.'

Now Skelgill reclines, as though he has been calm all along. DS Jones turns expectantly to watch the entrance.

'That's the right jacket, Guv.'

The young man – for he can be no more than mid-twenties, and possibly inferior in years to DS Jones's twenty-six – walks with the casual purpose of one who is returning to his seat, knowing where he is going, and already familiar with those around him. Indeed, he slides in at right angles to DS Jones, on her other side from Skelgill.

'Imagine I visit the restroom – there is no need to attract attention.'

His Slavic English has a mid-Atlantic drawl, as if American television has been his formative fare. His clothes fit him well, a sporty ensemble of shell jacket, t-shirt, slim jeans and trainers – though cuffs and hems show signs of wear that suggest, if he owns a new wardrobe, he has not dressed to impress them. Equally, if they were expecting the stereotypically wooden undercover policeman in oversized square shoes and ill-fitting brown suit with 1970s lapels, then he does not remotely conform. Indeed, as if to allay any such concerns about his rank or identity, he slides a palm across the table and lifts it briefly to reveal his credentials; he seems to require nothing in return.

'Inspector, welcome – I am Shevchenko.'

Skelgill nods; there is no suggestion that they shake hands.

The newcomer has longish, neatly styled black hair, light olive skin, and deep brown eyes fringed by extensive lashes; a handsome Mediterranean rather than typically Slavic appearance. His features are well defined, though lean and perhaps slightly harried. Still hunched forwards, he turns to look at DS Jones and takes in her apparel – a cropped black leather jacket over a snug white vest top, stretch hipster jeans, black ankle boots.

'Ukrayins'kyy?'

DS Jones seems momentarily startled, though she responds in kind to his inquiry about her nationality.

'Ni, Brytans'ka.'

He shrugs phlegmatically, as though this can't be helped. He holds her gaze for a moment.

'Krasyvyy.'

DS Jones giggles involuntarily, and immediately blushes, clearly taken by surprise by some compliment. But Shevchenko looks with a concerned expression to Skelgill and gestures to the bare table.

'We have a saying in Ukraine – no drink, no fun.'

And with this he rises and disappears through the curtains as though he is acquainted with whatever lies beyond.

Skelgill – perhaps unwittingly – is scowling.

'What was that about?'

For a moment DS Jones is tongue tied.

'He thought I was maybe Ukrainian, Guv.' Her cheeks still tinged with pink, she adds, unconvincingly, a rider. 'That I was your translator.'

'Aye, well – let's stick to English, eh?'

He folds his arms and glares across his right shoulder into the street. An elderly female flower-seller has drifted into his line of sight on the opposite pavement. Holding a basket of lilac carnations in the crook of an arm, she halts more or less facing him. She wears a green tailored coat with a marbled pattern, a high blue polo neck sweater and a tightly drawn brown floral headscarf. Her flesh has a deathly pallor, and her pale eyes are sunken into a long, lined countenance that exudes austerity. Her bearing is one of brave endurance, of mourning, her expression humble; she nods meekly to passers-by, offering gentle, hopeful glances from within an all-consuming aura of pathos.

But as he watches, this practised graveside manner suddenly transforms; like the screen vampire rudely woken by a hovering stake her eyes widen and her teeth become bared, and she lets loose a string of (unintelligible) invective: for an interloper has trespassed upon what is evidently her beat! It is another woman, younger, unkempt, large and rotund, partially wrapped in a threadbare serge greatcoat with rope for a belt, and clutching only a single tired posy in each unwashed fist. The intruder at first begins to protest, but when she sees that the old woman means business and is bearing down upon her she turns and begins to hobble away, receiving a solid – and surprisingly athletic – boot in her ample hindquarters for her trouble.

'Is doggy-dog world, no?'

While the modest drama has been unfolding, Shevchenko has slipped back into their cubicle. Skelgill turns to face him, looking a little startled. DS Jones laughs – perhaps she prefers to believe the malapropism to be intentional. But the officer does not wait for further approbation; he breaks open a new packet of cigarettes, and offers first to her, then to Skelgill. When they each decline he makes no comment but takes one himself and strikes up.

'How is your hotel?'

Skelgill is surprised by the mundane question.

'Seems pretty quiet.'

'It gets interesting later.'

Keeping his eyes on Skelgill, Shevchenko leans back into the sofa, blows a stream of smoke from his nostrils, and makes a short and sharp though deliberate jerk of his head, indicating the two girls at his back. DS Jones, detecting the signal, glances to see Skelgill's reaction – but he has already turned away: a pair of waiters approaches their table. The first grasps by its neck a bottle of clear liquid, and in his other hand three shot glasses, which he proceeds to fill and slide like a croupier, one before each player. He places the bottle in the centre of the table; then he unloads from the tray borne by his colleague a large steaming dish of what, beneath Skelgill's critical scrutiny, looks vaguely like dim sum. Finally he roughly distributes side plates, cutlery and napkins and bows to Shevchenko – who ignores him – and backs away. It is left to DS Jones to intercede with a modicum of protocol.

'Spasybi.'

'Bud' laska.'

Shevchenko has already lifted his glass. He holds it out, obliging the others to reciprocate. However, he toasts DS Jones.

'To your accent – it is very convincing.'

Skelgill looks mildly irritated.

'She's got a Ukrainian granny.'

Shevchenko squints as smoke drifts into his eyes.

'Then you have tried *horilka*.'

DS Jones sniffs the liquid experimentally.

'I'm not sure.'

Shevchenko grins knowingly.

'*Bud'mo!*'

He swallows the drink in one. Skelgill and DS Jones exchange glances; Skelgill makes a 'when in Rome' kind of face. They follow suit.

During the hiatus in which the two English detectives are unable to speak, Shevchenko first refills their glasses and then presents the bottle so they can see the label more clearly.

'You might know this as Russian vodka – but horilka was invented by Ukrainian Cossacks in the fifteenth century. We have many varieties – but basically it is grain spirit – think of it as white whisky without the headache.'

'It certainly hits the spot.' Skelgill's expression may not convey this precise sentiment, but nonetheless he now drinks about half of his second measure, this time merely grimacing as it goes down. 'The trick's just to swallow.'

He turns to DS Jones for approval, but she is not looking at him and instead gestures with an outstretched hand to the food.

'Varenyky, Guv.'

Skelgill empties his glass and slides it closer to Shevchenko for a refill. He leans to get a closer look at the little crescent-shaped doughy parcels, garnished with diced fat and fried onions and accompanied by a dish of sour cream. Shevchenko addresses DS Jones.

'Your grandmother make?'

DS Jones nods.

'When I was young.'

'You are young.'

Her eyebrows flicker but she avoids eye contact with Shevchenko. Instead she gets to work with a ladle; Skelgill is watching and seems content when she serves his helping first. Unsure of precisely what to do he slices a parcel in half and eats it from his fork; it is almost too hot and he has to employ his cheeks like bellows. Shevchenko simply uses his fingers, and dunks a parcel into the cooling sour cream before taking a bite.

'As I recall there's usually a selection of fillings, Guv.'

Shevchenko waggles his remaining portion.

'Mine is offal.'

'This one's alright.'

DS Jones grins apprehensively at Skelgill's remark – it is never easy to tell when he is joking, and the retort is quick-fire, which might suggest otherwise. However, perhaps the horilka is getting to work, for he has a punchline.

'Chicken Kyiv, I reckon.'

'Is not chicken in varenyky, Inspector – maybe you have cheese.'

Shevchenko's straight response suggests the British irony has evaded him. Meanwhile Skelgill is starting on his second parcel. He cuts it open and examines the contents, which could be minced cabbage.

'Make a decent fry-up, these would.'

Shevchenko speaks as he chews.

'We fry the leftovers – the next day.'

Skelgill frowns, leftovers being something of a scarce commodity in his kitchen. He glances to see how DS Jones is getting on – but, as he does so, behind her in the street a car slowly draws up. It is a large Mercedes, its stealth both enhanced and simultaneously undermined by distinctive matt black paintwork that singles it out as some kind of statement. Behind tinted glass the occupants are invisible – until the driver, a stocky dark-suited character of Slavic appearance sporting a severe expression and matching haircut gets out and rounds to the passenger door. He checks about and then opens it for a small pale man in his early forties, who slips on a pair of aviator shades to accessorise his smart-casual ensemble of stressed jeans, crocodile shoes, black crew-neck cashmere sweater, Italian jacket and prominent designer wristwatch. He is speaking into a mobile phone, and continues to do so as he enters the restaurant and – monitored surreptitiously by Skelgill – self-assuredly joins the two blonde girls. In the absence of an acknowledgement, the females fall silent and retreat dutifully from their handsets. The nearest of them delves into an extravagantly branded leather purse that rests upon the cushion beside her and pulls out a compact – but what now fascinates Skelgill is not the rather sensual manner in which she adjusts her make-up, but that peering at him from over the rim of the bag is a tiny white bat-eared dog.

'We should discuss business, Inspector.' There is a note of warning in Shevchenko's voice, as if he seeks to divert Skelgill's attention.

Skelgill shrugs and pops another slice of varenyky into his mouth. He turns to DS Jones with a pronounced nod of the head. She seems to understand and reaches for her shoulder bag. From a small folder she produces Leonid Pavlenko's passport and the photograph of the blonde girl that had originally fluttered from it. As she positions these on the table for Shevchenko, Skelgill seems to be drawing a comparison between the image and the two females beyond him. Shevchenko is bent over the picture, but does not touch it. His reaction suggests he thinks along similar lines.

'I could show you a thousand girls like this in Kyiv tonight.'

He sits upright and drains his glass. Then he stretches for the bottle to dispense top-ups. Skelgill looks pensive.

'What are you saying?'

'Is only one reason why a woman has this type of photo shoot.'

Skelgill's gaze again falls upon the girls in the next cubicle. Almost imperceptibly, Shevchenko seems to be nodding in confirmation.

'Maybe two – second to attract western husband.' Now he smiles boyishly, showing even white teeth. 'I expect you already have English wife, Inspector?'

Skelgill simpers; he glances at DS Jones, who is concentrating hard upon a page of notes. But before he can fashion a reply there is a distraction, for the two blonde girls rise in unison and sweep elegantly towards the exit, turning a succession of heads. The man is still engaged with his telephone conversation, but as he too stands he swivels to look at the trio of detectives, catching them in the act of observation. From behind the sunglasses the precise direction of his gaze is indeterminate, though to Skelgill's eye it appears he exchanges the merest of nods with Shevchenko. The females are already being fed into the rear compartment of the charcoal limousine by the driver, and in another thirty seconds the man has joined them and the vehicle pulls away.

'Know him?'

Skelgill's inquiry is casually spoken over a sip of horilka.

'Let's say I know who he is.'

It appears Shevchenko will be no more forthcoming. Skelgill turns his attention back to matters lying before them.

'About the photograph.'

Shevchenko nods.

'You think this girl go to England – she hide from the authorities and now Pavlenko, he join her?'

Skelgill seems unwilling to confirm this version of events. He picks up the horilka and replenishes their glasses – though only he and Shevchenko have finished their latest measures. The bottle emptied, he raises it and examines it critically.

'How easy is it to get into Britain?'

'Not so difficult. We have a five hundred kilometre border with Poland that leaks like a sieve.'

He clicks his fingers, as though it is as simple as that. But DS Jones has a caveat.

'Captain – we're not in the Schengen Area – they'd still have to get past British Immigration.'

Shevchenko is starting on another cigarette. He glances up from the act of lighting it with an amused glint in his eye. Of course, he has not offered a Christian name, and DS Jones is perhaps unsure of how she ranks alongside him.

'It is Juri.'

'I'm sorry?'

'My name – it is Juri.'

He raises his drink to her – then he looks back to Skelgill, who drains his glass with a grimace. Shevchenko shrugs languorously.

'Inspector – these questions – they will be better answered by Pavlenko's associate – *tomorrow*.' He seems to vacillate over the word tomorrow. 'Tonight you are guests in my country and you must relax – and eat.'

'Eat?' Skelgill gestures loosely to the remnants of the varenyky.

'This is appetiser – and aperitif.' He flicks the rim of his glass with a nail. 'This bar easy find for rendezvous – but I take you to place where is more interesting – more... cultural.'

Shevchenko does not elaborate upon the definition of cultural – nor does Skelgill request such an explanation. Instead he sinks back into the sofa and for a second his eyes seem to roll in his head. Perhaps the half-pint of horilka is kicking in. It falls to DS Jones to raise one of the points they had wished to discuss.

'We believe we found the necklace that Pavlenko is wearing in the photograph you sent us – it's an amber charm – it could be to ward off evil.'

Shevchenko grins mischievously.

'We are big on amber – our Baltic neighbours pick it up on their beaches by the bucket – and we are big on superstition – in fact we are big on *everything* – peasants, poverty, billionaires, beautiful girls – horilka.' He grins and swallows the last of his own drink. 'This is the Wild East – if you want a crazy time, you have come to the right place.'

With a smirk he slides DS Jones's glass towards her, and watches as – under subtle duress – she finishes the drink. Then he rises and beckons them to follow with a quick flick of his head that sends a ripple through his hair. Skelgill stands up, but too quickly perhaps, for he remains still for a second, as though his balance has momentarily deserted him. DS Jones, though a good glass-and-a-half behind her companions, is nonetheless more circumspect. Carefully she gathers her things into her bag, and then raises it symbolically.

'Juri – can we pay the bill?'

He dismisses her offer with a casual wave of the hand – though he smiles with some satisfaction at her use of his name.

'Is taken care of – come, I have driver nearby – my colleague, Lieutenant Stransky.'

16. FIXER

'Is heaven, yes?'
'Uh?'

When Skelgill wakes it is in a darkened room and he lies naked upon a stone slab. A muscular young man wearing only a leather thong is lathering his body.

'You turn.'
'What?'
'Turn.'
'No way, pal.'
'I – sorry?'

'Wait till I see Shevchenko – I'll swing for him.' Skelgill adds a further phrase, an unbecoming descriptor drawn from his Anglo-Saxon lexicon of stressful situations.

'No understand – no speak English.' This is just as well.

Skelgill brings his arms from his sides and rests his chin upon his overlapped hands. His field of vision is limited to the marbled wall a yard away. It streams with drips condensed from the steamy atmosphere. Relaxing music is piped from somewhere, and the irregular splash of running water may be real or otherwise. Every so often there is the slap of one of the masseur's sandals as he adjusts his position. Skelgill's expression hovers between rage and dismay.

That he gives the impression of having been somehow spirited into this peculiar predicament without his knowledge would not be entirely accurate, although he might have a case for feeling somewhat manipulated, press-ganged even, and that an accidental excess of horilka had significantly impaired his free will. As it was, upon leaving the chic bar off Khreschatyk, he had probably consumed more alcohol units in half an hour than he would in an entire Saturday night's drinking session, and – as Shevchenko had intimated – that was just the aperitif.

Lieutenant Stransky had been idling in a shadowy mews at the wheel of a newish ZAZ that had already seen its share of action – if its scraped doors and dented fenders were anything to go by. Skelgill had paused to finger what appeared to be a bullet hole in the hood when Shevchenko invited him to ride up front – an unexpected courtesy that became all the more confusing when he clambered in. A tight black leather catsuit and long slick raven hair proved a quantum leap in the surprise stakes. Lieutenant Stransky had acknowledged the bewildered English inspector with a superior smirk of her glossy scarlet lips, and his startled colleague with a cursory nod via the rear-view mirror. She had then wasted no time in pinning them to their seats with a display of driving that went much of the way to explaining the state of the coachwork.

Their harum-scarum journey lasted no more than five minutes, and took them to a poorly lit, Bohemian district of unevenly cobbled streets and shabby grandeur, elaborate but crumbling Art Nouveau, a loosely defined ghetto to which the former Soviet authorities must have turned a blind eye, allowing the true spirit of Ukrainian hedonism to survive, tolerated just below the totalitarian radar. As if symbolically, a pair of burly doormen, stern Khrushchev lookalikes, had nodded them through a low arch to descend a steep flight of stone steps into a dark basement of vaulted chambers that throbbed to the underground beat of the day; a humid dungeon complex thronged with the bodies of hundreds of revellers, shouting, drinking, swaying, in places dancing. Shevchenko had led them to a section most distant from the music source, where bench-style trestle tables lit by candles wedged into empty vodka bottles were crammed with informal diners, arguing and toasting and generally in party mood. Somehow he had negotiated a co-operative concertinaing of patrons, and Skelgill had found himself compressed between Lieutenant Stransky and a large Hell's Angel type who had greeted him with unintelligible grunts and a thump between the shoulder blades whilst simultaneously eating and drinking and grinning. DS Jones had slipped in directly opposite, tight alongside Shevchenko.

No sooner had they settled than a waitress in what might have been traditional dress – most notably a tight sleeveless velvet bodice fastened over a white cotton blouse embroidered with detailed coloured stitching – had heaved a litre of horilka into their midst and Shevchenko had quickly done the honours. Lieutenant Stransky – who could not have failed to appreciate she was a few drinks behind her companions, and with scant regard for her status as designated driver – had raised her glass to Skelgill and downed its contents in one, obliging him, in the name of chivalry, to reciprocate. Shevchenko and DS Jones – he had noted – were closely engrossed, though such was the ambient cacophony that it forced a certain intimacy.

DS Jones appeared amused by Shevchenko's patter – her dark eyes were glittering in the flickering candlelight. But Lieutenant Stransky had her own ideas about where Skelgill's focus ought to lie. Her English was at least as good as her colleague's, and her guile more subtle – for she was of an age with Skelgill (he would have guessed mid-thirties, though he had the good grace to avoid the subject). She had mischievously asked him why the British called her country "*the* Ukraine" – to which his on-the-hoof logic, in defence of his misguided compatriots, had resorted for erroneous corroboration to "*the* USA" and "*the* UK" – although he had been forced to admit that "*the* Germany" and "*the* France" were not common parlance. She had encouraged him to regale her with his adventures at work and beyond, though he had skirted around matters of the heart, craftily evasive beneath the cover of inebriation. When he had turned the tables and asked if she were married, she had thrown back her head with abandon and cried, "Of course!" – then proceeded to press a hot palm upon his thigh and hiss something into his ear in Ukrainian that amused her greatly.

Some drinks later – with no sign of food appearing – she had straddled the bench to face him. She tilted back her torso and supported her weight with her hands behind, so that her close-fitting outfit strained against her figure, feminine curves united by a slender waist beneath his captive gaze. Then she had grabbed his arm and stood, and – stepping out of the seat –

pulled him to his feet. "We dance," had been her command. Skelgill had anxiously looked to DS Jones – but she was preoccupied, Shevchenko's fingertips on her wrist as he made some point – and when she did glance up it was with a contented smile that did not falter as Skelgill was led away, and she returned her attention to her earnest petitioner.

The club was nearing capacity, and dance floor at a premium – it was just a matter of shouldering through the swell until a small pocket opened up – when (to Skelgill's relief) there was insufficient space to do much other than shimmy upon the spot. Lieutenant Stransky had taken him close to a bank of speakers – conversation was out of the question – but perhaps this was her strategy, for a more base form of communication seemed to be her goal. Cocooned in heat and dark and noise and anonymity, alcohol-loosened inhibitions were easily shed, and Skelgill offered scant resistance to the advances of firm hips, soft lips – and found himself becoming acquainted with the lithe brunette, who left him in little doubt about how she would like the night to end.

When eventually thirst had driven them back to their table, they discovered Shevchenko and DS Jones to be absent. Not even DS Jones's leather jacket – nor Shevchenko's sports shell – were folded on the bench. Skelgill had experienced some dismay, but pressed with horilka and the continued close attention of his catsuited companion, his cares had waned and he was subverted to her will, the passage of time becoming indeterminate. Incredibly, it had seemed, at around four a.m. dishes of steaming stew had arrived – can he dredge from his memory the word *guliash*? – and he had fallen upon his like a half-starved dog. By now Skelgill was operating on autopilot, holding a tenuous thread that connected his physical self to the joystick of his consciousness. There had been a ringtone, audible above the more subdued beat – Lieutenant Stransky had prised a mobile from some hidden nook – the conversation had seemed strained, a reluctant acceptance in her tone as she abruptly ended the call.

And his next recollection, if it is to be trusted, was in the back of a car (*her* car?) – with DS Jones beside him, limp and compliant, her hair damp with exertion – a rumbling roller coaster ride through streets empty but for the blur of taxi taillights and kiosk neon. And then the hotel lobby – and a cajoling conversation – Shevchenko's voice, persuasive, perverse in its insistence – something about Russia? – here it is most famous in all of Kyiv – no need to sleep – it is so much better – an essential experience – look, it is open, after five a.m. – there, it is organised – go now – sleep later – adieu!

And thus in some state of vague awareness – he could not vouch for DS Jones – they had been conducted to the subterranean sauna complex for which the hotel was renowned – its Russian *banya* – a sequence of treatments alternating temperature, pleasure and pain that would prove – in Skelgill's case, and aided by his unplanned 'power-nap' – a remarkable antidote to the intoxicating effects of horilka (if not the associated hangover).

Alert, trapped prostrate in a small darkened chamber with a scantily clad young man, if Skelgill revisits in his disturbed mind the sequence of events that has brought him here he may recall it began with a reception by a stout female, uniformed and impassive, who spoke no English but had supplied them with towels and peculiar felt hats, and abandoned them with some obscure gesticulation in a waiting area beside a plunge pool and a bank of communal lockers. DS Jones had remarked that she thought they had been told to get completely undressed, a suggestion that Skelgill had consigned to an unprintable fate lacking sunshine. Shortly, two watchful males had silently materialised – evidently employees, surly cavemen in standard issue pelt miniskirts – they had conferred slyly in a corner before the elder had directed them with grunts into a fantastically hot sauna, and indicated that they should don the hats, and – yes – remove their undergarments (which they had retained as proxy swimwear). He had then disappeared, leaving them to sweat, in due course complying on the hat front, but not as regards their modesty.

After a short time the younger man had returned (minus the miniskirt, now stripped down for action to the thong beneath) and signalled to Skelgill that he should follow him. Unenthusiastically parting from his colleague, Skelgill had stumbled to a steam room, where he had been soundly thrashed with switches of birch soaked in a mentholated concoction, before being led out to a marble bench on which he was ordered to lie so as to be doused with ice – at this juncture screaming out with shock something about the secret police. Next he was sternly commanded to take off his boxer shorts, before being hauled into a freezing cold shower – and then led into the contrasting steamy warmth of the chamber in which he currently reposes. The treatment here is a prolonged full-body lathering with rich soapy bubbles at the hands of the masseur – a situation from which Skelgill would ordinarily have bolted like a colt with a firecracker tied to its tail. However, at the time not knowing what to expect, and subdued by the lingering effects of the horilka and the softening-up KGB-style, he had complied and lain face down on the slab. In his efforts to distract his thoughts from what was occurring – but perhaps lulled by this very process – he had swiftly succumbed to slumber.

He draws the line, however, at turning over. And his masseur's request has come as more than just a literal wake-up call. As Skelgill stares helplessly at the damp marbling that tricks his eyes in and out of focus, he must now be pondering the fate of DS Jones, one stage behind him in the sequence, presumably at the mercy of the rapacious senior masseur – who, on reflection, had determined the staff-client pairings. Meanwhile, evidently marking the conclusion of this soapy step – its unhappy premature ending brought about by Skelgill's obstinacy – his own attendant begins to rinse him with warm water from a hand-held shower hose. The man clears his throat, preparatory to delivering a rehearsed line in stilted English.

'Next for full body honey-wrap cling-film.'

*

As DS Jones approaches the waiting Skelgill, crossing the foyer from the elevators to the casual seating area beside the windows, there is a fascinating exchange of glances, one that an onlooker would not find easy to characterise. On either side there could be flashes of reproach, jealousy, embarrassment and guilt.

Skelgill, seated, glances habitually at his wristwatch.

'No sign of Shevchenko – it's twenty past eight – we don't want to miss this meet.'

DS Jones hovers uncertainly a couple of yards short; she wears a fresh white vest top with narrow shoulder straps, and there is a flush upon her chest and throat and cheeks that might be a residual effect from the banya.

'I need to explain something, Guv.'

'Aye?'

'When I went out – with Juri – for such a long time – why he won't be meeting us this morning –'

She seems unsure of how to broach the subject that drives her desire for confession; Skelgill looks away and stares at the unsightly apartment block that rises up beyond the hotel parking lot like a cliff of dull grey limestone, cracked and crumbling and streaked by the stains of half a hundred faulty cisterns.

'He took me to meet someone, Guv – the *fixer*, he called him – Leonid Pavlenko's contact.'

'What?'

Skelgill turns back, dumfounded.

'The meeting wasn't meant to be this morning, Guv – or rather it *was* this morning – in the early hours – but Juri had this brilliant idea –'

Her voice tails off. Skelgill is glaring furiously – although it is impossible for her to discern what exactly might underlie his ire – it could be anything along a broad spectrum of issues: his hangover, which must surely be stellar – or that she has unilaterally met the gangster he has travelled almost two thousand miles to interview – or that she disappeared with Shevchenko and now is on intimate 'Juri' terms with him – or even that, when he had rebelliously unpeeled himself from the sticky honey-cling-film treatment and escaped the cell in which it was applied, in tiptoeing past the 'lather room' he had heard her throaty chuckle, and a minute later, upon retrieving his damp boxer shorts from the back of a lounger in the central pool area, he had discovered her silky white underwear neatly folded, bra *and* briefs.

'What brilliant idea?'

DS Jones casts about – as if for a waiter. There is a bar at the far end of the extensive reception zone; a dark head bobs busily but makes no attempt to court custom. She takes a step towards Skelgill, her arms extended in an appeal.

'We can penetrate this business, Guv – I can go undercover.'

Leaving him to digest this startling suggestion, she turns and with her elegant figure skater's poise bisects the reflective millpond of the lobby, leaving him staring, becalmed in her wake. She waits at the counter while the order is prepared, returning with two tall milky coffees upon a small round tray.

'What do you mean, *undercover*?'

DS Jones, given a choice of seats opposite and perpendicular to Skelgill, opts to settle beside him on the same settee. Whether this is a gesture of reconciliation or a tactic to avoid direct eye contact is a matter for conjecture. She arranges their drinks as she seeks to compose a reply.

'It's trafficking, Guv – Ukrainian girls – Juri knows a lot more than he admitted in writing to DS Leyton.'

Skelgill scowls.

'Let's stick to calling him Shevchenko, eh?'

'Sure, Guv.'

'So what was his bright idea?'

'He introduced me – they were speaking Russian – the fixer's a Russian Pole called Yashin and he couldn't tell I wasn't Ukrainian – Jur –' (she corrects herself) '*Shevchenko* – told him I was a mutual friend, of his and the girl in the photo – that I wanted to go to the same place in England and team up with her.'

'What's Shevchenko on – doing deals with a crook?'

Studiously, DS Jones stirs the froth into her latte.

'*That* was his idea, Guv – on the spur of the moment – he'd been asking me what we knew about the case – he said we could meet this guy officially – as British police – but he doubted if he'd tell us anything useful – or truthful.'

Skelgill's expression has moderated to mildly peeved.

'Where was this?'

'A flat nearby, Guv – I don't know if it belongs to Shevchenko or if it's just one the police use. We waited about forty minutes and Yashin appeared.'

Again a frown clouds Skelgill's features. He fiddles with a spoon – he has not yet tried his coffee.

'Why would he trust a cop?'

DS Jones glances up, as if surprised by his question.

'Like Shevchenko says, Guv – this is Ukraine – the land of blurred lines.'

Skelgill appears uncomfortable with this reference. He takes a deep breath, as if it is the precursor to a sigh.

'So, what's the story?'

DS Jones gathers herself; it is plain she is eager to get to the heart of the matter.

'He was dead cocky – Yashin – but I could see he was scared of Shevchenko.' She brushes away an unruly strand of hair from her eyes. 'He said we were in luck – his contact in the Lake District – he actually spoke it in English – is looking for someone else – to work as a chambermaid.'

She turns to face Skelgill, and holds his gaze as he searches for underlying meaning.

'I don't suppose he named the contact?'

There is a cynical note in his voice that anticipates the negative.

DS Jones shakes her head.

'Jur – Shevchenko – said there's no way he'd reveal his network – he reckons he's got people all over Europe – most probably Poles, too – he said the guy considers himself as a kind of international recruitment consultant.'

Skelgill is looking pensive; but now his thoughts are jumping ahead.

'So what's supposed to happen?'

'Shevchenko told him that he'd take care of getting me across the borders – he said he didn't want me suffocating in the boot of a car – it's the job and accommodation at the British end he wants arranged.'

'What's the catch – the price?'

DS Jones shrugs.

'I don't think there's either, Guv – I guess the fixer considers there's a quid pro quo – Shevchenko's got tabs on him, so if he does him a favour it gives him some leverage.'

'Why would Shevchenko take the risk – are you sure we can trust him?'

Now it is DS Jones's turn to frown.

'He wants to nail him, Guv – this might be a way of doing it – if we can get witnesses who are prepared to testify. Shevchenko believes he's responsible for hundreds of Ukrainian girls going missing.'

Skelgill is silent for a moment as he considers this proposition.

'And what about Pavlenko?'

'Shevchenko thinks Yashin doesn't know Leonid Pavlenko went after the girl – neither of them mentioned him – as far as I could gather.'

'So where does Pavlenko fit in?'

'Shevchenko believes he and the girl must have been an item – of sorts – but that she fell for Yashin's story of easy money – she suspected Pavlenko would object, since he knew the Pole's game – and left without telling him.'

'And then found our grass not so green.'

'That's it, Guv – but instead of handing herself in to the authorities, she must have called Pavlenko to get her out, undetected.'

Skelgill, despite his reservations, is evidently making some analysis.

'I doubt Pavlenko would have told this fixer – pal or not – in case he'd warned his British contact he was coming.' He at last takes a long draught of his drink. 'But if he'd disappeared from

Kyiv it wouldn't take a genius to guess where he might have gone.'

DS Jones is nodding.

'I know, Guv. He might have been intercepted.'

Skelgill puts down his latte glass and punches a fist into the opposing palm.

'If only we could get the British contact.'

'But I can lead us to him, Guv.' She raises the spread fingers of both hands to her chest. 'All I have to do is turn up at a meeting point in England – Shevchenko is going to let us know.'

'But they'll blow your cover in an instant.'

'No, Guv – I can easily pretend I only speak Ukrainian – and the chances of a Pole speaking Ukrainian are low.'

'But what about ID? That's the first thing I'd ask for.'

'Shevchenko says he can sort it – a Ukrainian identity card. We just need to email a photo of me and wire him four hundred dollars.'

'Four hundred dollars!'

'If we want it done express, Guv – otherwise it takes a month through the official channels.'

Skelgill is shaking his head.

'How do I explain that one to the Chief?'

DS Jones grins.

'She would expect nothing less, Guv.'

*

'Aw, Guv – look at that – how cute.'

Skelgill is already staring with eyes narrowed – though it might be the acute morning sunshine that rakes between stuccoed buildings, as much as the curious sight to which his colleague draws his attention. They have ambled from their hotel shirt-sleeved, amidst crowds in bright spring garb, through unexpected heat, covering the kilometre of Khreschatyk to the Maidan, and thence uphill to marvel at the shimmering golden domes and twirling white brides of St Sophia's cathedral. Now arriving at the foot of Andriyivskyy Descent, having run the gauntlet of eager artisans touting multi-coloured crafts, they happen upon an altogether different appeal for their money – and one that, as he digs into a back pocket, breaks Skelgill's hitherto stern resistance.

For here is a Mother Theresa of sorts – a bag woman who has struck camp in the shade of a peeling, bill-stickered wall, where she squats surrounded by some fifteen slumbering dogs, splayed listlessly over the cobbles, half black, a quarter toffee, and a quarter unclassified, though hairy. Her collection of bulging carrier bags is mostly stacked at the foot of the wall, though a couple hang straining from a truncated zinc downpipe at head height – perhaps foodstuffs judiciously placed beyond reach of hungry hounds on hind legs.

Despite the growing warmth the woman – diminutive, perhaps late fifties – wears the greatcoat characteristic of so many of her compatriots; this one is camel, and seems nearly new, but it is oversized and she has the cuffs turned back. Beneath is a navy blue ankle-length dress with paler hoops; she has a matching woollen muffler around her neck, and a black headscarf emblazoned with a bright red and green rose print. Her brown face is wrinkled like a prune, but she looks clean and her attire freshly laundered. The same cannot be said of the snoring pack, whose coats are tinged with grime and oil, and whose fitful itching suggests the presence of an unseen class of micro-fauna. That DS Jones has cooed over this scene of dubious charm relates to the ostentatious raising by the woman of a sleepy pup by the scruff of its neck, and its repositioning in a more suitable spot – although the cynic might submit this is a well-practised move calculated to win the hearts of passers-by. If so, it has worked. Skelgill extracts from his wallet two five-hundred hryvnia notes.

'That's thirty pounds, Guv.'

'Better she has it – I'll only spend it on ale.'

DS Jones suddenly chuckles, for the woman has stooped to swig from a brown bottle – a brand of Ukrainian beer. Skelgill shrugs and steps forward. Propped up by a wooden crate and held fast by two uneven cobbles, a large rectangle of torn cardboard advertises a proposition in neat marker-pen lettering. In front of it sits a cut-off plastic water bottle for donations. This arrangement is guarded on either side by a massive recumbent mongrel, their broad muscular heads and malevolent slits for eyes leaving little to the imagination as far as biting an uncharitable hand is concerned. Allowing the sleeping dogs to lie, Skelgill gingerly releases the notes and retreats.

'There you go, love.'

The woman raises the bottle in a gesture of thanks and bows her head. Then she settles on a folding stool and picks up a hardback book. Judging by its monochrome cover – a bare-breasted woman striking a stiff Edwardian pose – it is not the kind of reading one might have anticipated. Skelgill however is staring at the hand-printed sign.

'What does it say?'

'Something about gullible foreign tourists, Guv.'

'Ha-ha, Jones – wait till *you* start shopping.'

DS Jones grins.

'I look like a local, remember, Guv.'

'Don't remind me.'

Skelgill saunters away – he is following his nose and senses the river is not too far from their present location. They cross a tram stop, an open siding where pitted iron rails buckle from irregular rows of piano key paving. A massive-billed piebald bird is picking at something between the tracks, standing astride a bloody splatter of crimson entrails and grey feathers.

'Look at that – a hoodie – we only get them in Scotland.'

'What's it eating, Guv?'

'A slow pigeon.'

'Aw, gross.'

In recoiling she places an involuntary hand on Skelgill's upper arm – and perhaps her lingering contact acknowledges that, in revealing his chagrin a moment ago, he has opened a little door on his unspoken feelings. She keeps in step, close alongside him. Then as a preface to speaking, she makes a nervous giggle.

'It was probably down to me that we ended up in the sauna, Guv – I insisted we went back to the hotel – I think they might have had other plans for us.'

Skelgill jerks his head in a gesture of accord, though he continues to gaze ahead, unblinking.

'I figured you're a big girl.'

DS Jones shrugs coyly.

'Not always, Guv.'

He looks sharply at her; as though her tone bears a nuance he cannot read. If he is reviewing events post-midnight through the fractured kaleidoscope of his recall – then perhaps the revelation that it was she who was responsible for their homeward transition, albeit from frying pan to fire, casts a modicum of clarity upon a confusing maelstrom of emotions. Indeed, when he responds, his concerns appear to have shifted from the immediate past to the near future.

'Having second thoughts?'

'You mean about...?' But DS Jones has not made the same leap, and it takes a moment for her to realise what he is talking about. 'Oh – look – I know you – you guys – will be watching over me.'

Her frank admission draws from Skelgill a paternal frown.

'Beats me how you think you'll get past first base – what if the contact is someone we've met already? They'll take one look at you and leg it.'

'But – whoever it is almost certainly Polish, Guv – in which case we surely haven't met him – plus he'll be expecting a Ukrainian.'

Skelgill clearly harbours doubts about the scheme – and perhaps new concerns surface with each passing minute's cogent analysis.

'We're going to have to think this through, lass.'

DS Jones nods obediently – but all of a sudden they are distracted, as jay walking becomes a necessity. They have reached the busy Naberezhne Highway that borders the west bank of the Dneiper and Skelgill – in contrast to his apprehension for her safety a moment ago – is striding out with scant regard for the vehicles that flash past them. In a series of jerky darts they reach the sanctuary of the promenade, marked off from the hurtling traffic by motorway-style *Armco*. Skelgill makes directly for the waterside balustrade, and gazes across the river.

He appears mesmerised by the vast body of water; like a great lava flow from some distant eruption it slides past, silent and ominous, solid and mercurial, with the opacity of molten glass. There is a conflict unfolding before them, a battle of nature's force and human industry, an inland port of girders and pontoons, rusting wharves and cranes, stone breakwaters and steel buoys – yet amidst these manmade obstructions graceful terns flit and twist and dive for fry, and beyond, a third of a mile away, conscientious objectors basking in the sun speckle yellow beaches backed by the thick green mangrove shrub of Trukhaniv island.

'Thinking of Bassenthwaite Lake, Guv?'

Skelgill yawns imperiously.

'When aren't I?'

17. UNDER COVER

'I'm sorry, Miss – you can't just turn up to see a senior officer – Inspector Skelgill's a very busy man.'

To say that George, the desk sergeant at Penrith Police HQ, is a little hot under the collar would perhaps be something of an understatement. Monday morning generally witnesses a gasket or two blown – when members of the public jostle to demand the whereabouts of their carelessly lost pets or to brandish "outrageous" parking fines (issued by an altogether different authority). Today has been no exception, compounded by an influx of Easter tourists asking for sightseeing recommendations. And now his thermostat is additionally challenged by the undoubtedly alluring though insistent young foreigner of striking appearance – spiked peroxide hair and heavy mascara, skin-tight white hipsters, jaunty silver ankle boots, matching metallic-and-black leather jacket slung casually over one bare shoulder, a figure-hugging vest-top in shocking pink with a *Rolling Stones* motif – who taps slender pink talons casually upon the counter. Her look of insouciance seems to grow as his complexion reddens and a film of perspiration forms a glossy sheen upon his bald crown.

Skelgill might be a busy man – but at this moment he happens to be crossing the foyer amidst a band of darkly muttering colleagues, having attended the Chief's Monday sermon – and the exasperated mention of his name has his antennae twitching. And others'.

'You've got a biker chick on your case, Skel – grease-up the old machine at the weekend, eh?'

DI Smart is quick to quip, the snide insinuation in his voice all too apparent – but as Skelgill rounds upon him disparagingly he cannot fail to notice his fellow inspector's eyes are elsewhere engaged, and upon proverbial stalks.

'I'll see to her – if you're too busy with your sheep, Skel.'

'No thanks.'

Skelgill, his jaw set firm, pushes past DI Smart and steps swiftly towards the girl. But whatever baser instincts drive him – competition with DI Smart being among them – his eagerness is suddenly dampened. Rather ineptly, he assumes a casual stance, and digs his hands into his trouser pockets, and makes a face that suggests he has known (whatever it is) all along.

'It's alright George, she's got an appointment.'

He levels a hostile stare at the loitering DI Smart. After a moment's standoff the latter shrugs indifferently and backs off, employing a series of gunslinger finger gestures, with a flourish blowing imaginary smoke from the barrels. It is not entirely apparent what this means, and all the time his gaze is fixed on the girl, who watches him with bafflement. He tips an invisible hat, spins on his heel and disappears through the interconnecting doors.

DS Jones bursts into laughter. For it is *she* – the mystery caller – and Skelgill, if she deceived him with radically altered hair and striking make-up, has perhaps recognised the ensemble. This was purchased for the purposes of authenticity – along with other such new and second-hand personal possessions – while he kicked his heels outside various Kyiv emporia on Friday morning. She turns back to the counter and raises her palms in apology.

'Sorry, George – I couldn't resist it.' Her regular Cumbrian accent has returned, with additional emphasis.

'*Emma* – is that you lass?'

She beams endearingly.

'You've been a big help – I figured who better to test my disguise on.' She shoots a tentative glance at Skelgill, who is now scrutinising her as if he disapproves of most aspects of her appearance. 'I have to get the photo done, Guv – so I thought I may as well try the whole look.'

Skelgill nods grimly; he cannot really object to this logic.

'Aye – you'd better shoot downstairs and get it sent.' Now he grins reluctantly. 'I'll see you in my office – you can play the same trick on Leyton.'

'I'll bring canteen teas, Guv.'

She nods at George and glides from reception, her departure observed in thoughtful silence by the two males.

'You've got your hands nicely full there, Skelly lad.'

*

'Morning, Emma.'

For the second time in fifteen minutes DS Jones breaks out into laughter. DS Leyton has greeted her with his usual phlegmatic cheeriness.

'You're supposed to ask who I am.'

He taps the side of his nose with an index finger.

'Shall I tell you the giveaway, girl?'

She nods, still smiling.

'Four mugs of tea, three people. Only you would know that.' (She holds out the said offering.) 'Much obliged – plus I was in the car park – listening to the end of the sports report – saw you hop out of your motor.'

DS Jones places the tray on Skelgill's desk and slides it with his double ration to within his reach (he makes a vague grunt of acknowledgement, though it is clear his thoughts are still disturbed by her appearance) and then she takes her regular seat at the window – albeit with more than usual care, for her jeans are exceptionally snug. DS Leyton raises his mug to Skelgill in a celebratory gesture.

'Brainwave, Guv – this undercover job – stroke of genius how you've pulled that off.' He tries to drink but the liquid is too hot. 'And here's me thinking you've swanned off to the Ukraine 'cause you couldn't think of anything better.'

Skelgill's countenance presents conflicted emotions: a clear willingness to take the credit for the idea (but a certain embarrassment under the amused gaze of DS Jones) and yet consternation at DS Leyton's revealing remark. In the end he settles for a scowl.

'Ukraine.'

'Come again, Guv?'

'It's just Ukraine – not *the* Ukraine.' Skelgill glances at DS Jones, who is still smirking. 'You don't say *the* Poland, do you?'

DS Leyton is momentarily flummoxed.

'You say *the* Lakes, Guv.'

With this spanner thrown into the works Skelgill's attention reverts by default to DS Jones. Over the weekend, of her own accord, she has undergone a radical haircut and bleaching in the line of duty, and – while it must be said – she carries well the provocative look, it is an uncompromising departure from her usual serene appearance. She detects his scrutiny, and begins to shuffle her papers self-consciously. Watching on, DS Leyton assumes responsibility for rebooting the conversation.

'So – how did it go in Kyiv, then, Guv? From what I see on the news it's pretty hairy.'

'What?' Skelgill wrestles to free his thoughts. 'Uneventful, Leyton. We met Shevchenko and his sidekick – sorted out this plan – quick walk round while Jones was buying her outfit – no sooner we were there than it was time to fly home. These trips are not all they're bulled up to be.'

DS Leyton nods, though he appears rather unconvinced by this explanation. However, he turns to DS Jones and waves a hand in reference to her get-up.

'Well, if this is how the girls look, Kyiv must be one big disco.'

DS Jones glances over at him.

'I think it's fair to say they're a little less conservative than us Brits.'

'Well, you hoodwinked DI Smart.' DS Leyton turns back to Skelgill. 'He passed here a minute before you came back, Guvnor – he was rabbiting away about some... er – *young lady* you were making a fuss over in reception.'

Skelgill glowers. He knows "young lady" is unlikely to have been the phrase employed by DI Smart.

'Aye – and she fooled George, as well.'

'So we should have no bother with Wolfstein, Guv.'

Skelgill is startled by this suggestion.

'Hold your horses, Leyton – who said anything about Wolfstein?'

DS Leyton is taken aback by his superior's vehemence.

'But, Guv – I thought it was pretty obvious it must be him – that's why you've been sniffing around Blackbeck Castle – and getting me to research into him – and Pavlenko had the name of Wolfstein's gaff written on that photograph.'

Skelgill is again frowning.

'That might have said "black beck", Leyton – but there was nothing about the castle.'

DS Leyton seems alarmed.

'He's the only foreigner we've got in our sights, Guv.'

'Aye – but he's not Polish, is he?' Skelgill waves a dismissive hand. 'He might be eccentric but he's hardly gangmaster material.'

Now DS Leyton licks a finger and flicks through his notes.

'Actually, Guv – the boys have come up with a bit of biography on him.' He folds over a couple of pages. 'Far as we can gather – he comes from a wealthy German family that lived in what was Czechoslovakia – he was sent to school in England – but went back and studied at college in Prague. All the career references have him as an academic – but I reckon there's definitely something dodgy about him leaving his last job at the university.'

'How come?'

'If it ain't being lost in translation – they're being cagey about what they'll tell us – claiming the parties are bound by a compromise agreement – whatever that is when it's at home.'

Automatically, Skelgill and DS Leyton glance to their female colleague. (She has done all the courses – *and* paid attention.) She looks startled, as though they have caught her entertaining inappropriate thoughts that are readable on her face – but then she demonstrates her mind has at worst been multi-tasking.

'I think it's to preserve confidentiality – when someone leaves a job and they have information that might prejudice their former employer – especially if they go to work for a competitor.'

Skelgill ponders for a moment.

'What about vice versa?'

'I suppose it's possible, Guv. I guess there'd need to be something on both sides to reach a compromise in the first place.'

Left handed, Skelgill picks up his first mug of tea and swallows its remaining contents.

'Anyway, Leyton – I can't see Wolfstein turning up in person to meet Jones – he'd send the kung fu twins.'

'At least we'd know straightaway, Guv.' DS Jones gestures towards her boss's desktop telephone. 'Maybe Kyiv will be able to tell us what to expect – if Yashin has come up with the rendezvous.'

Skelgill turns to DS Leyton.

'What time's Shevchenko supposed to call?'

'He sent me an email at the crack of dawn, Guv – reckoned he'd phone about ten-thirty.' He checks his watch. 'Quarter of an hour – what are they, two hours ahead?'

DS Jones nods to confirm this fact.

DS Leyton looks hopefully towards Skelgill.

'Couple of things I can fill you in with in the meantime, Guv?'

Over the rim of his fresh mug, Skelgill nods his assent.

'First off – and this might be significant, Guv – Leonid Pavlenko's mobile.'

'Have we found it?'

DS Leyton shakes his head with slow reluctance.

'Nah, Guv – but we got a trace – it was switched on for a couple of hours near Coniston on the Thursday – eleven days ago.'

Skelgill stares blankly at his subordinate.

'Is that it?'

'That's it, Guv.'

'Remind me when he was reported missing?'

'Not till the Monday, Guv, this time last week.'

Skelgill remains pensive. DS Leyton continues.

'He was knocking around the Coniston area three days before he checked into the B&B at Keswick.'

Skelgill has his eyes screwed up; the action emphasizes the puffy bags beneath that indicate a deficit of sleep.

'A phone signal doesn't prove he was there, Leyton.'

DS Leyton holds out a palm in appeal.

'Surely, though, Guv – add that to the necklace, what the old geezer had hold of – plus "black beck" written on the photo – it's some coincidence, all together.'

However, Skelgill's doubts are now embellished with a series of deep furrows that line his brow.

'So why didn't he use the phone after Thursday?'

DS Leyton's expression becomes conspiratorial.

'Maybe he was mugged, Guv?'

'What – by a seventy-five-year-old tramp?'

'He might not have had a UK adaptor.' This is DS Jones that chips in. 'The phone could have run out of charge.'

Skelgill looks questioningly at DS Leyton.

'Right enough – I don't recall one being in his bag, Guv.'

DS Jones offers another suggestion.

'Perhaps he ran out of credit?'

Skelgill shrugs hopelessly; he knows this is a blind alley.

'There's half a dozen possible explanations.' He appears unwilling to iterate what these may be.

Now a silence descends. DS Leyton frowns and peruses his notes rather glumly. However, after a minute he perks up.

'We've got more on that Jed Tarr character, Guv.'

He waits for his superior to show some interest.

'Aye?'

'He's an ex-miner – worked at Haig colliery at Whitehaven until it closed after the miner's strike. Bit of a firebrand by all accounts. Did a six-month stretch for *grievous* – lorry driver tried to cross a picket line and he whacked him with an axe handle.'

Skelgill is making grotesque faces that suggest he is imagining some confrontation. This unfavourable reaction is not ameliorated by DS Leyton's supplementary information.

'Five years ago he got a caution for suspected involvement in a dog-fighting ring – there wasn't enough evidence to press charges but the fact he took the caution suggests he was up to no good. There's mention of badger baiting in the case reports.'

Skelgill grimaces.

'You wouldn't want to be a small mammal on his patch then, Leyton.'

'Not even a large one, Guv. There's a bunch of complaints from walkers and cavers about his aggressive behaviour – folks who've got perfect rights to be on the land – him carrying a shotgun and all.'

Skelgill folds his arms and slumps back in his chair.

'Trouble is, Leyton, so long as he's on the estate *he's* got a perfect right to tote a twelve-bore.'

DS Leyton is nodding – but now he has been reminded of another point.

'On the animal cruelty front, Guv – your farmer chum Arthur Hope left a voice message over the weekend.'

'Another killing?'

'Rustled, Guv.' He consults his notes. 'He said from Dunnerdale – "Herdwick tup" – I expect that makes sense to you?'

Skelgill is already nodding in a slightly superior way.

'A tup's a ram, Leyton – you can pay upwards of three thousand guineas for a show champion.'

DS Leyton raises his thick eyebrows and grins mischievously.

'Cor blimey, Guv – that's an expensive lamb chop.'

Skelgill frowns disapprovingly.

'Leyton – tups are not bred for eating.'

DS Leyton looks rather sheepish.

'Sorry, Guv.'

Skelgill shakes his head resignedly. He ponders this new information, his features undergoing more variations – but these freeze into an unreceptive scowl as his office door opens and the angular, sharp-suited figure of DI Alec Smart slides into the space beside DS Leyton's seat. His stoat-like eyes dart about, after each scan returning to dwell upon DS Jones, as though she is some favoured prey item.

'Just got wind of your jape, Skel.'

Skelgill takes a second to respond.

'It's no jape – it's dead serious.'

DI Smart seems not to detect the hostility in Skelgill's tone.

'The Chief just had a quiet word – asked me to put a couple of my lads on standby.' He casts about the room with a disparaging smile. 'Since your crew's a bit thin on the ground.'

Unsurprisingly, Skelgill is no more endeared by this observation.

'I think we'll cope, Smart.'

DI Smart brushes a sleeve of his jacket and glances down in an admiring way at his own outfit.

'Chief said you might need a tail – my lads are city boys, they're used to it – and we don't want our *next* Inspector coming to any harm.' He sneers fawningly at DS Jones and, without taking his eyes off her, places a patronising hand on DS Leyton's shoulder. 'No offence, mate.'

Skelgill's expression has darkened to the extent that it is a wonder there is no rumble of thunder. But at this juncture his telephone rings, and his sergeants both lean forward expectantly, knowing this will be the call they have awaited. Skelgill ignores DI Smart and picks up the receiver and, though he does not speak, he listens to the operator.

'Ask him to hold thirty seconds – I've got someone just leaving.'

While he shows no urgency, it must be evident even to the thick-skinned DI Alec Smart that Skelgill has supplied him with his marching orders. He takes a last lingering look at DS Jones, a wry smile curving his thin lips into a spare crescent, makes a telephone gesture to Skelgill with the thumb and little finger of one hand and, ignoring DS Leyton entirely, sidles out of the office leaving the door ajar. DS Leyton quickly reaches across and slaps it shut with a bang. Although there is clearly a desire among the small coterie to exchange some comradely disapproval in relation to DI Smart's uninvited intervention, there is no time – Skelgill presses a button on the telephone base and replaces the handset.

'Captain – I've got you on loudspeaker – Jones and Leyton are with me.'

Immediately the harsh eastern voice with its curious American drawl crackles into their midst.

'Crazy new look, Anya.'

Shevchenko has dispensed with introductions. DS Jones seems momentarily discomfited, as if he has inadvertently revealed some pet name of theirs. She replies with a tentative, 'Anya?'

'We have your internal passport – it will arrive by courier tomorrow morning – the name is Anya Davydenko – she is known to Irina Yanukovych – a contemporary from college.'

'And who's this Irina – ?' Skelgill sounds perplexed.

'Inspector – the woman in the photograph – Leonid Pavlenko's girl.'

'You've identified her?'

'Of course.' Captain Shevchenko sounds like he has known this fact all along.

'Is there anything you can tell us about her?'

'Is more difficult.'

'How come?'

'She is from Donetsk – and also Pavlenko – you know we have problems in the east – is not possible to investigate officially.'

'Aye – we've seen it on the news.'

'But it fits our story that the name of the new girl is familiar to Irina Yanukovych.'

'I get that.' Skelgill glances at DS Jones; he looks like he might be wondering if she can really play Anya Davydenko. He addresses the microphone. 'What about timings?'

'Is arranged.' Shevchenko pauses, though there is the sound of his breathing and he is probably lighting a cigarette. '*Anya*' (he persists with the alias) 'you need to be on the London train tomorrow – arrive at your city eight-fifteen evening time.'

The three British officers exchange amused glances at the description of the small provincial town of Penrith as a city. Shevchenko continues, a little stiltedly, as though he might be referring to some roughly prepared notes.

'Imagine you leave Kyiv last Saturday by car – Lviv, Poland – Wroclaw, Dresden, Germany – Cologne, Brussels, Belgium – Calais, France – to Dover by tomorrow morning. Then make own way – train to London – train from London.'

DS Jones is scribbling furiously. She leans closer to the telephone base unit.

'Should I catch it from London?'

Shevchenko laughs. 'Is not KGB. They only care if you arrive – not how you get there – but if you come to railway station in police car they might suspect.'

Now there is a polite chorus of chuckles.

'What if they ask how I got into Britain?'

'You say you are brought on Polish passport – but remember – you speak only little English – so do not understand too much – it will make simple for you. Is more important you look like you have long journey – not come straight from boudoir.'

DS Jones looks earnestly at Skelgill.

'Maybe I should sleep on the couch in my clothes tonight.'

Shevchenko replies in Ukrainian, and DS Jones's cheeks seem to colour – although she keeps a straight face and hurriedly continues with the conversation.

'What do you think they will ask me?'

'Who knows – you have met Yashin – he is man of few words – he would rather not talk with me at all.'

Now DS Leyton clears his throat by way of introduction.

'Captain – it's DS Leyton speaking – any idea who the geezer's going to be that's meeting DS Jones?'

Shevchenko's disembodied voice seems to take on a note of amusement.

'You are Cockney – you sound like *Eastenders* – BBC is always favourite of my mother.'

DS Leyton takes hold of the lapels of his jacket and, from a seated position, does an amusing rendition of a Cockney walk.

183

'Least you can understand me, squire – can't always say that for my colleagues.'

Skelgill interjects.

'Aye – we do that on purpose, Leyton – when you're talking tripe.'

For the benefit of Shevchenko, DS Jones pours a little oil on these troubled waters.

'We have our regional differences – just not quite on your scale.'

'In our regions they speak different languages – but answer to question is *no* – no idea. Although I expect will be Polish, as we have discussed previously.'

Skelgill is nodding.

'What chance they suspect something?'

'Then they will not come – is no point risk to be identified – if they come, you can believe they do not know.'

'We have CCTV at all of our railway stations – it's common knowledge.'

'But meeting prove nothing – you are going to record conversation?'

Skelgill hesitates. He glances with concern at DS Jones – their discussions to date have not found accord on the pros and cons of a wire.

'We might.'

Shevchenko apparently blows out a lungful of smoke. He sounds a little scathing.

'If I were meeting you – I would say, "Can I help?" – there is nothing given away.'

Again Skelgill looks anxiously at his female subordinate.

'We might recognise the person straight off – then the game's up.'

'But if you do not?'

There is a considerable pause before Skelgill replies.

'Then we take it to the next stage.'

There is silence from the loudspeaker, but after a few moments Shevchenko's voice comes back on the line.

'For me – the deeper you go the better.'

Skelgill is nodding grimly.

'We'll do our best – thanks for your help so far.'

'You're welcome – bud' laska.'

He now continues in Ukrainian – DS Jones appears to understand, though she seems embarrassed, and her reply is somewhat blurted.

'Spasybi, Juri.'

Skelgill glowers, but Shevchenko has a message for him.

'Inspector – Lieutenant Stransky send best regards – she say she sorry not to join you in banya – but maybe next time?'

Skelgill is temporarily tongue-tied, but in this small hiatus Shevchenko clears the line. He is left staring at a rather nonplussed DS Leyton.

'Guv – what's a *banya*?'

18. THIN AIR

As the 20:15 *Pendolino* from London Euston slides like a great unblinking reptile into Penrith North Lakes only a handful of citizens wait in the cool spring dusk. The Easter long-weekend is over, and few folk have cause to travel north from here on a Tuesday evening. It is that time of day when darkness has not quite taken hold and yet artificial light does little to enhance visibility. A brace of feral pigeons strut anxiously about the feet of a bearded and bush-hatted tramp who squats in the right angle of the Victorian stone building and the Elizabethan concrete platform. The birds dart to retrieve bread flakes exploding from an untidily devoured burger, retreating from each foray lest they become too tempting a target. Fellow passengers have spaced themselves judiciously away from this little pocket of activity; the scene could be a long museum plaza decorated with statues, and the birds litter caught by a wind devil – but now the slowing train draws the people like iron filings to a passing magnet, as they spy attractive vacant double-seats that might elude their possession. There is a moment's tension when the carriages come to a halt but no doors open, until an electronic signal disengages the locks. An orderly and roughly equal exchange of travellers then follows, although the rolling stock surely gains in testosterone.

Seen through the furtive eyes of the tramp, perhaps with a view to potential donations, disembarking are a local family – going by their accents – whose primary-age twin boys wear identical *London Eye* baseball caps and alternatively punch one another, a couple of dishevelled-looking businessmen, an elderly lady and gent – from the First Class section (rarely a good bet) – and, slowly approaching from one of the rear carriages, pulling an airline trolley-bag whose rattling wheels create a discernable Doppler effect, an attractive young woman who might be a foreign student (and hence unlikely to be in a position to offer charity).

The train pulls away and the new arrivals in their turn swing into the small sectioned-off concourse; only the nearest of the boys seems to notice the tramp, and he gets a whack in the ear for his trouble, the price of taking his eye off his opponent. "Pack 'eet, will thee!" emanates from the father, although with limited impact. The girl, meanwhile, seems less certain of her destination. She reaches the mahogany-and-glass partition and double doors and stops, and then she gazes rather wistfully at the overhead departures board. The tramp is now preoccupied with a milkshake; he has the lid off and is determinedly (and noisily) vacuuming up the last of the froth in the base of the cup.

'Do you need some directions?'

'Yes.'

'I'll show you.'

*

'Leyton – what do you mean *they're on the bus?*'

'Apparently they both got on the bus, Guv – Jones and the guy you saw.'

'I didn't see him, Leyton – he was out of my line of sight – he opened the station doors and spoke to her – he never came out on the platform.'

'Why did she go with him, Guv?'

'I guess she didn't recognise him.' Skelgill rubs his chin with one hand as he talks into his mobile. The removal of his false beard has left some sticky substance behind. 'She must have felt safe enough to go outside.'

'And on the bus, Guv – it's not like she's getting into some stranger's car – apparently there's a dozen or more people on board.'

'So where are Smart's crew now?'

'They're right behind it, Guv – I spoke to them under a minute ago – it's the Workington service, heading west on the A66.'

'Where are you?'

'Just coming off the M6, Guv – I'll be two ticks.'

'Make it one, Leyton – I could have done with you here before she went.'

'I know, Guv – but that express gets a shift on – I've been busting a gut and it still beat me – I didn't like to leave her at Oxenholme – I figured we needed to know she got on safely.'

Skelgill is still rubbing furiously.

'Aye.' He cannot question his colleague's concern.

'How will I recognise you, Guv?'

'Very funny, Leyton.'

Skelgill is waiting outside the railway station. He has an old sleeping bag draped over one arm, and several bulging plastic carrier bags grasped by the fingers of the same hand, albeit these contain lightweight items of outdoor clothing, chosen for their bulk. Directly in front there is a designated drop-off and pick-up zone, about a dozen restricted-use car parking spaces and, just a few yards further round as the traffic flows, a standing area reserved for buses. While DS Leyton was driving DS Jones to Kendal, to intercept and board the train one stop south, Skelgill had shambled the half mile from the local police station, having changed into his vagrant's outfit (employing to good effect, it must be said, clothes from his own wardrobe). DI Smart's team – whose charity Skelgill has reluctantly decided to accept (though he relayed this request through the Chief's office, and not directly to Smart) – a cocky DS and a loquacious DC who with their sharp suits and Mancunian accents might have been cloned from their immediate boss, were not then in place. However their detail was, on arrival, to keep their heads down and tail DS Jones if the need arose.

Through narrowed eyes in the growing darkness Skelgill stares at the ruins of Penrith Castle, illuminated little more than fifty yards away. Built six hundred years ago as a defence against raids by the Scots, its red sandstone matches that of the station – and, given that at one time it fell into the ownership of the Lancaster & Carlisle Railway Company, there is a temptation to speculate whether its depleted condition owes something to the construction of the railway offices. However, it seems unlikely that any such conundrum occupies Skelgill's thoughts at present – perhaps only that it is a castle, and a reminder of the temptation to draw a connection between the events he is investigating and the vaguely comparable edifice at Blackbeck.

'Need a lift, squire?'

Skelgill is disturbed from his reverie – DS Leyton has arrived, and calls out across the interior of his car through the open passenger window. Skelgill dumps his gear in the back seat, and clambers into the front.

'Where are they now?'

'Jones is still on the bus. The tail's right behind. They're just passing north of Keswick. Starsky and Hutch are radioing every time there's a stop – there's been two so far.'

Skelgill permits himself a wry grin at his colleague's description of DI Smart's team.

'Next stop'll be Cockermouth.'

'Want to catch 'em up, Guv?'

There is an eager note in DS Leyton's voice. Skelgill is nodding rather absently, and it is not entirely clear if this is in direct response to the question. DS Leyton, however, takes it as a *yes* and only the head restraint saves his boss from whiplash. Despite the jolt, Skelgill remains focused.

'What did they see?'

'Male, middle-aged, balding, stocky, about five-eight, smart-casual clothes – they just walked over to the bus beside one another   he was talking, DS Jones was nodding.'

'The Workington service is a shuttle – did he get off when it arrived?'

'They didn't say, Guv.'

'It connects with the train – that's why it didn't hang about.'

DS Leyton presses the tip of his tongue against his upper lip as he concentrates on the curves of the traffic island that crosses above the motorway. Once he has beaten the last set of amber lights he relaxes and speaks again.

'I'd better radio in about the trace, Guv – make sure it's still working – it was fine while she was on the train.'

Skelgill grimaces. He had implored DS Jones to wear a substantial transmitter, but time, technological resources and – it must be said – DS Jones herself were ranged against him. Her argument is that a gadget hidden in a bag, or concealed in her clothing, could be both easy to discover and perhaps difficult to keep on one's person. Moreover, he has been forced to concede that someone of Anya Davydenko's means would certainly not possess a trackable smartphone – and that, while a basic pay-as-you-go handset would be more realistic, to appear authentic it would present the problem of needing to be programmed with her contacts from home – and thus they have decided it would be simpler if she has no mobile at all. And while they have not anticipated "Anya's" credentials to be seriously tested, DS Jones has insisted that her disguise be convincing in every possible detail – thus she had even purchased locally branded underwear and toiletries in Kyiv, to cover the eventuality that her belongings be covertly examined.

Of course, their expectation – indeed Skelgill's plan as agreed with the Chief – was that DS Jones would simply draw out Yashin's Cumbrian contact by meeting him at the railway station. At this juncture an arrest might well ensue. Failing that, and provided DS Jones feels in no danger, she will go so far as to allow the person to sufficiently incriminate himself, provided she remains in public view (or, at least, confident that her colleagues know her whereabouts). In consequence, they have settled upon a tiny in-ear tracking device that emits a GPS location signal every two minutes. This technology is employed in the preservation of rare migratory birds that must run the gauntlet of Mediterranean marksmen. It can be turned off by the wearer (though not the bird) should they feel there is a risk of detection. Indeed Skelgill has been quick to highlight this weakness – that all a shooter need do is obtain a scanner and dinner is served! No doubt his acuity in this regard owes something to various clandestine methods he employs to locate specimen fish.

By now DS Leyton is making rapid progress westwards, and they are only a couple of miles short of Keswick as he calls HQ.

'It's in Keswick, Sarge – moving towards the town centre.' The DC responsible for monitoring the tracking device sounds a little apprehensive, as though he has an inkling this is not the plan.

'What?'

'Are you sure?'

Both officers exclaim in quick succession.

'That's what's come up on the screen, sir – last signal about thirty seconds ago.'

Skelgill reaches across and places a palm on DS Leyton's shoulder.

'Do a u-turn.'

'But, Guv?'

'Turn the car round, Leyton!'

DS Leyton's hesitancy is understandable; the exit for Keswick lies just ahead of them.

'I want my bike, Leyton – get a shift on – it's two minutes from here!'

By *bike*, Skelgill means his *Triumph* motorcycle – this much will be apparent to DS Leyton – and the sudden reality of being sprung into an emergency situation might explain Skelgill's thinking: on two wheels he will command the road in a way that even DS Leyton's driving cannot match. And his tone is uncompromising. As DS Leyton slews the car around, Skelgill terminates the radio connection with HQ and calls up DI Smart's team in the tailing car. He is answered by a laconic, "Yup."

'Stop the bus.'

'What's that, pal?'

The voice is that of the DS.

'Stop the bus, now!'

"Stop the bus, now!" is actually an abridged version of Skelgill's bellowed instruction, and if these events one day become the subject of a 'real crime' TV reconstruction, or even – heaven forbid – a detective series, then this particular scene shall be notable for its high percentage of bleeped-out adjectives and nouns, with up to three bleeps in succession, such is Skelgill's command of Anglo-Saxon. Notwithstanding, the choice of

words has the desired effect, for the next response comes somewhat meekly.

'We're just doing it, sir.'

There then follows a minute of radio silence, until the line crackles back into life. Now the unenviable job has evidently been delegated to the DC. His voice is trembling and breathless.

'She's not on it, sir – nor the bloke she met.'

'I know that you idiot.' (Again there will be considerable editing.) 'What did the driver say?'

'I can't believe it, sir – we stopped close behind both times and watched until the bus drove away – he said they got off at Threlkeld – and he thought it was odd – they went and stood in the bus shelter – it was only a yard from the door of the coach – that's why we didn't see them. Then a minute or so later we did notice a strange thing – it was a black Porsche Cayenne that had been parked just after the stop – it came steaming past us before we even got out of the village.'

'Did you get the number?'

'Didn't think to at the time, sir – but there was damage to the nearside.'

'Sorry.'

'*Sorry*, sir?'

'I'm just getting you to practise for when I see you.' Skelgill sounds rather like a Dickensian judge handing down a death sentence. 'Now get off the line and get back to Keswick as fast as your little Keystone Cops' machine will carry you – park up south of the junction on High Hill – stop that Porsche if it comes your way – preferably by the pair of you lying in the road!'

Skelgill has to brace against the dashboard as DS Leyton brings the car to a shuddering halt before his house. He bales out like a pilot abandoning a badly winged World War I biplane, but then he swings around on the door and leans back inside.

'Leyton – you take the Borrowdale road – lie up facing south, just after the mini-roundabout. He might not suspect he's being tailed – he could just be covering his tracks. Get back on to HQ to check the next signal – but before you do, call Whitehaven. Jones took that car's number last Wednesday – it's got to be the same one – she was going to forward it – if she did, find out who he is and where he might be heading.'

'Righto, Guv – what about you?'

'I'll blast into the town centre.'

'How will I contact you, Guv?'

'I'll call you in a few minutes – I can jam the phone into my helmet – not very hi-tech but it does the job.'

*

'Can you hear me, Leyton?'

'Just about, Guv – it sounds like you're in a hurricane.'

'Aye, well – I'm doing ninety-five.'

'Cor blimey – take it easy, squire.'

Skelgill evidently ignores this advice and drops a couple of gears to roar past a truck held up by a caravan.

'What's the latest?'

'There was another signal just after I left your gaff – centre of Keswick – possibly stationary – could be the traffic lights near the car park.'

'Where are the Manc no-marks?'

'They're in place, Guv – like you told 'em.'

'Did you get hold of Whitehaven?'

'They're checking their emails now, Guv – this time of night there's only one duty officer in the admin section.'

'Where are you?'

'Just getting into position, Guv – nothing passed me on the way in – how about you?'

'I'm about a minute behind – what about the transmitter?'

There now comes a delay before DS Leyton responds – as if he is hoping something will happen while he formulates a response.

'I'm waiting to hear, Guv – I'm keeping the radio channel clear – no report for a few minutes.'

'I want to know about every single bleep, Leyton.' Skelgill hisses the words between gritted teeth. 'Call them up.'

He has reached the eastern edge of Keswick, and is now obliged to decelerate – though his manoeuvres remain unpopular with those motorists he both overtakes and forces into evasive action. Despite the reduced wind noise, he cannot hear properly DS Leyton's two-way radio conversation with police HQ, and has to wait in frustration for his sergeant to return to the mobile phone line.

'Come on, Leyton.'

'Nothing for six minutes, Guv.'

Skelgill does not reply. The implications of this news must come as another strangling wrench of the icy dread that has gripped his insides since things began to go awry some fifteen minutes ago. Has the device failed? Has DS Jones turned it off? Has it been discovered and destroyed?

But then – respite of a kind.

'Leyton – I see the Porsche.'

'Jeez, Guv – where?'

'It's coming out of town – heading east on Penrith Road.'

'He must have turned round, Guv – I'm on my way.'

Again Skelgill is silent. Behind his visor his grey-green eyes stare icily. The car passes within touching distance of his right hand.

'Stay put, Leyton.'

'Guv – but – why?'

'There's no passenger.'

'What if she's in the back, Guv... or – ?' In scrabbling for an explanation DS Leyton arrives at a possibility he cannot contemplate.

'Leyton – head for the town centre – in case there's another signal from there.'

DS Leyton inhales to protest – he is torn between his instincts to join the chase and his superior's pragmatism.

'Are you following, Guv?'

'I'm just turning – I don't want to make it obvious.'

'Right, Guv. What about stopping it?'

There is a delay before Skelgill replies. He is concentrating on the Porsche, which is several cars ahead, and hemmed in itself by a couple more vehicles. It would be easy at this point for Skelgill to pull alongside, as a motorcyclist might slice through suburban traffic – but the car's windows are heavily tinted, and in the dark the reflection of streetlamps is all he is likely to see.

'Leyton – he's taking the Windermere road – I've not got enough battery to give you a running commentary – hang up the call – I'll phone you as soon as it's clear what his game is.'

'But, Guv –'

'Leyton – we haven't got the resources to cover all the options – he can't lose me on these roads.'

'Have you got plenty of petrol, Guv?'

'Hang up, Leyton.'

DS Leyton reluctantly does as he is bid and Skelgill's phone, safely though somewhat uncomfortably tucked into his helmet, lapses into resting mode. As the line of traffic that has turned south climbs out of Keswick and leaves the last habitation behind, it becomes evident that the Porsche driver is not going to settle for travelling in slow convoy. At the first opportunity he pulls out and overtakes the two cars ahead of him – notwithstanding the approach of a sharp left-hand bend. On this occasion the road remains clear, though Skelgill watches with consternation; he might not mind if the driver ploughs himself into another wall – but if DS Jones is with him...

And now he faces an additional conundrum. Keeping up with the car is not a problem – with nine hundred CCs throbbing between his legs, Skelgill has power to burn, and only on the motorway could the 4X4 outrun him. But it is more a matter of remaining inconspicuous. Though he has the cover of darkness, it is also his enemy, for a continuous single headlight in the rear-view mirror is far more distinctive than a pair.

Skelgill's response to the dilemma is characteristically counter-intuitive. Rather than hang back at the furthest possible distance, trying his best not to draw attention to himself, he does precisely the opposite. He clears the intervening traffic, switches on his full beam, and races up close behind his quarry. As Lakeland roads go the A591 from Keswick, at least as far as Grasmere, is generally a fast one – it bisects the dale that holds

Thirlmere reservoir (an unnatural lake and Skelgill's least favourite for angling), sweeps beneath the screes of Helvellyn, and even boasts a section of dual carriageway as it crosses the pass at Dunmail Raise, where a massive cairn of mythical origins rises between the divided lanes. But Skelgill has little time for his surroundings, rich though they may be in interest. Instead he appears intent upon intimidating the Porsche driver, and persistently tailgates him as they hurtle due south.

Skelgill's bravado elicits an intriguing though not entirely unpredictable response. His actions prove to be something of a red rag to the proverbial bull, who – rather than give way and let his pursuer past – accelerates violently at every opportunity and, where he must slow down, hogs the road such that he blocks the overtake. Skelgill plays along with this game of cat and mouse. He attempts passes and permits the car to thwart him, and allows the driver to believe he has superior acceleration each time they reach a short straight. When the Porsche speeds through Grasmere and subsequently Ambleside, ignoring the statutory limits, Skelgill drops off, as though he draws the line at such flagrant law breaking.

Given the Porsche driver's reaction, it may be surmised that Skelgill's tactic of hiding in plain sight is working. And surely any remaining flicker of doubt must be extinguished when the truck-and-trailer of car and bike part company at the junction marked Little Langdale. Unsurprisingly there is no indication from the Porsche as it slows to turn right – but Skelgill seems to be anticipating the manoeuvre. He undertakes the car, passing its damaged front wing, and raises his right hand in the traditional English archer's two-fingered salute. The driver blasts his horn – it would seem in anger rather than in comradely recognition of a road race well run – and the pair parts company.

For a few moments, at least.

Skelgill continues for just another hundred yards before he turns the *Triumph* around and draws to a halt. He kicks the gear up into neutral. Bending forward he tugs off his helmet and retrieves his mobile phone. Quickly he summons DS Leyton.

'Guv.' He sounds relieved, though somewhat wheezy.

'Leyton – he's taken the turn for Little Langdale.'

'We've got an ID on the car, Guv – keeper by the name of Peter Henry Rick – owns a building company – home address just outside of Gosforth, near Seascale.'

'What about Jones – the trace?'

'Nothing since those two from Keswick, Guv.' Now there is a discernable tremor in the sergeant's voice.

Skelgill hisses, though he does not speak.

'Want me to send a team round to his house, Guv? Won't take them long from the coast road.'

Skelgill ponders for maybe five seconds. Then his response is decisive.

'Hold off just now. I need to go before I lose him. I'll call you back.'

Skelgill waits neither for further questions, nor DS Leyton's words of caution. He ends the call and slips the handset into a breast pocket of his weatherbeaten *Barbour*. He hooks his left forearm through the helmet, switches off the lights of his bike, and shoots away, his hair streaming in the wind. He knows well the narrow lane that winds towards Little Langdale, and it is barely a minute before he begins to glimpse ahead the impatient red flash of brake lights, as the Porsche lumbers around one tight bend after another. Following in the darkness he will be virtually invisible to the driver – and for his part he employs engine braking to further conceal his presence. With his helmet off he can hear the car, too – its discs emit a high-pitched squeal each time they are rudely pressed into use. He seems unperturbed by the lack of illumination – the sky is cloudless and the waxing moon a sliver shy of full; it casts a wan light across the rising fellsides. And as for oncoming traffic he is trusting to luck and judgement: that at this hour there will be few if any travellers with cause to use such an obscure route.

After some ten minutes the Porsche passes the gated track that leads up to Blackbeck mines. Skelgill seems to take this as his cue to close the gap. Half a minute more and there looms a shadowy recess in the wooded roadside. It is the mouth of Blackbeck Castle's driveway. The car's brake lights flicker and the vehicle slows – but then it slides past the opening and swings round the next corner. Skelgill, tense and hunched over his handlebars, relaxes, stretching out his arms and flexing his stiffening back.

Thus the Porsche and its grumbling shadow pass through the scattered hamlet of Little Langdale. There is an occasional light in a cottage window, and half a dozen cars outside the pub – perhaps more than Skelgill might expect for a quarter to ten on a Tuesday night – but on the road the only sign of life is a dog fox that slinks towards the tarn, hurrying from Skelgill's unlit approach in search of moorhen chicks for supper.

Peter Henry Rick – if it is *he* driving – shows no inclination to take it easy. Indeed, as the landscape opens out on the approach to Wrynose Pass, and the absence of headlamps reveals a clear road ahead, he travels as fast as the terrain allows, alternately accelerating and braking as successive bends are negotiated. Skelgill is now able to hang well back and, on the sole occasion that a vehicle approaches from the west, he has ample warning to pull into a passing place, dismount, and pretend he is attending to some call of nature.

Skelgill takes care in descending the sharp diving switchbacks of Hard Knott Pass – a frost is not out of the question on such a night. He skims past the Roman fort, and as he spies the scattered lights of Eskdale he must call to mind that it is just six days since he and DS Jones came this way, in high spirits following their snack stop at Boot. Now the circumstances could hardly be more inauspicious. He grimaces – though it might be the cold that is taking its toll. Riding is a chilling experience at the best of times; the air temperature has fallen to low single figures and he is poorly kitted out for the job. But Gosforth lies just eight miles due west, so he has at least broken the back of the ordeal.

In fact it is a good mile short of the village – although well beyond the bend on which the Porsche formerly had its accident – that Peter Henry Rick turns abruptly into a driveway. Skelgill coasts to a halt behind the boundary wall and kills his engine. He drops his helmet upon the grass verge and scrambles for a clear view. The property is set back from the lane by some fifty yards. There is a large detached brick-built residence of modern design and a series of outbuildings to one side and beyond, where a floodlit compound holds stacks of construction materials and a yellow backhoe loader of an American make. The house itself is in darkness. Skelgill watches intently as the driver gets out and triggers with his movement a security light; he ducks lower, raising a crooked forearm to shield his pale brow from sight.

Instead of entering the house, as might be expected, the man strides across the crunching gravel of the drive and unlocks the door of the nearest outbuilding. There must be a staircase within, for a light now comes on in a first floor window, and there is a glimpse of his head and shoulders as he apparently takes some item from a shelf and sits down. After about thirty seconds more, the security light trips off. Skelgill decides to act. He kneels beside his motorcycle and tugs free from beneath the seat a tubular aluminium torch.

There is lawn on either side of the driveway and he chooses this for its forgiving nature underfoot. Commando fashion he runs along its margin until he reaches the point where the gravel opens out into a turning area. He has noted that the car itself did not set off the spotlight, and now he crouches and approaches gingerly, almost on all fours, keeping the vehicle directly between himself and the wall-mounted light fitting. Reaching his target, slowly he rises. Across the interior of the Porsche he can just discern that the office light is still on – although that the driver apparently did not lock the car suggests he might return at any moment. Now Skelgill raises his torch. Cupping the lens with one hand, he angles the powerful beam down through the smoked glass.

The back seat and rear compartment are both empty. Wherever DS Jones might be, she did not leave Keswick in this car.

Retracing his steps Skelgill returns to his bike. Squatting behind the boundary wall he takes out his mobile, only to silently curse his luck: on this occasion there really is no signal. Be careful of what you wish for. He taps out a text to DS Leyton nonetheless – perhaps hoping that the phone will be smart enough to despatch the message at the faintest hint of one bar. Hooking an arm through his helmet, he kicks the bike off its stand and, bending his back to the task, heaves its near quarter ton of metal onto the tarmac and begins to push. Only when he has rounded two bends, a good furlong from the entrance to the driveway, and separated by a thick belt of trees, does he relent and pause for breath.

Now he may depart without revealing his presence. He depresses the electric starter, but though the engine turns over a dozen times it does not fire. His eyes narrow. He throws a leg across the seat and sits astride the machine, flicking up the stand with his left heel. He adjusts the choke and squeezes the clutch and tries again. The battery is strong yet there is no ignition. He reaches down on his left side to turn the petrol tap to reserve – only to sit up with a look of consternation: in his haste to leave home he failed to notice that the switch was *already* set to reserve. He is out of fuel.

He kicks down the stand and dismounts, then he checks his mobile again – but still there is no signal. He wipes both hands hard across his face – it is a gesture of frustration, though he smears the perspiration that is a product of his efforts. He folds his arms and stares with a grimace at the bright moon. There is a service station just north of Gosforth on the main A595 coast road – maybe three miles from his present position – but at this time of night in such a rural district it is likely to be closed. His eyes begin to dart aimlessly about the heavens, drawn to those familiar constellations not outshone by the moon. But then a light of another kind offers a glimmer of hope. Slowly moving towards him, perhaps half a mile away, a single headlamp is winding down the lane.

Skelgill reaches for his torch. Such is the biker's code that no knight of the road could ever pass another in distress – it is an unwritten duty to help a fellow enthusiast. Here is a chance of the couple of pints of fuel that will get him to the nearest garage (he even carries a coiled length of syphon tubing for such purpose, and has obliged others on occasion). He steps into the road with his torch at his side, and prepares to flag down the approaching rider.

But when the dazzling light rounds the final bend and forces him to raise a shading hand in a salute, his shoulders sag. It is not a motorbike, but a Morris Minor shooting-brake, a timbered pre-63 registration with a split windshield and only one functioning headlamp, on main beam, at that. The car draws to a halt and its engine stalls. For some obscure reason, the wipers graunch back and forth across the dry screen. Skelgill has retreated to the verge, on the driver's side of the narrow lane.

'This is as far as it goes.'

'I beg your pardon, madam?'

That Skelgill uses the term *madam* reflects the fact that an elderly woman addresses him. She is wearing a dark headscarf from which spills a mass of unruly grey curls. She has a fawn mackintosh buttoned up around her throat. She squints at him from behind thick-lensed horn-rimmed spectacles, through a gap of a couple of inches between the glass and the top of the doorframe. Her accent is pukka RP.

'The window – it doesn't wind down any further – nor up, come to that – hasn't for the best part of thirty years – heater doesn't work either – and there's only a pouffe for the passenger seat – so don't expect any home comforts.'

Skelgill is nonplussed. He gestures rather pathetically across to his motorcycle.

'I've run out of fuel.'

The woman glares at him furiously.

'Well – what are you waiting for? Hop in, man – I keep a spare can for my *Kawasaki* – you may have that – though you shall have to walk back – I can't possibly drive – I've had four double whiskies.'

19. BECALMED

'It's like she vanished into thin air, Guv.'

Skelgill is bent over his desk; his hands wrung together, his funereal countenance is a mask of concern. It is now eight a.m. on Wednesday morning and there has been no sighting of DS Jones since she disembarked from the bus bound for Workington almost twelve hours ago. Skelgill has slept fitfully in his office, every so often waking and pacing to the control room where her tracking device is being monitored; but the last signal sounded in the centre of Keswick just before nine p.m.

He did not return to headquarters until almost two a.m. Having secured the precious gallon of petrol offered by the eccentric gentlewoman – establishing in the process that she does indeed own a *Kawasaki* (and that *four* whiskies was probably a conservative estimate on her part) – there was still much to do. He had trudged back to his bike, and subsequently returned the empty jerry can, and then he had driven the much quicker coastal route, filling up his tank at an all-night garage on the outskirts of Whitehaven. He had not revealed to the woman that he is a detective. Although it seems unlikely she would spread any such hot gossip – she had been entirely uninquiring of his presence in the vicinity – he does not want to take the chance of Peter Henry Rick hearing talk of a police officer stranded in the lane outside his property. With a similar aim in mind, and a restored mobile signal, he had called DS Leyton. As he had anticipated, his sergeant was champing at the bit to search the premises of Rick & Co – and thus he cautioned him against any such precipitous action.

Some time after midnight he had parked up in the deserted public lot in the centre of Keswick. With pubs and restaurants long closed and locals back to work after the Bank Holiday there was an unearthly sense of desolation. It was not only DS Jones that was gone – but it seemed *everyone* had gone. Skelgill might have believed he was walking in a dream, sole survivor in a scene from a horror movie just before the first zombie lurches into view. Despite the stark emptiness he had kept a low profile, sticking to the shadows and slipping through cobbled ginnels as he crisscrossed the old town. Quite what clue he was hoping to discover, perhaps even he did not know, but he had searched around, looking in shop doorways and windows, and in loading bays and gated yards. He had checked communal entrances to flats and the front gardens of nearby houses. He had shone his torch into almost every car and van he passed, and it was a wonder some householder, heading late to bed and drawing their curtains, had not spotted his suspicious behaviour and reported him as a sneak thief on the prowl. He had inspected the row of B&Bs where – in a fashion – these events had their origin just over a week earlier. He had stared pensively at the end property, *Grisedale Vista*, from where Leonid Pavlenko (erroneously called "Mr Leonard") was reported missing. All of the guesthouses were in darkness, but he could make out from street level that there was another of Mrs Robinson's notices in the front window. He scaled the steps to discover it stated, "Closed until Whitsun" – perhaps Easter had been a financial success (or maybe too much of a trial). He had paused to reinstate a gnome that was lying face down in a pool of water; it turned out to be the one with the fishing rod.

'We don't even know she got into that car, Leyton. She was last seen by the bus driver standing in the shelter.'

'But the transmitter, Guv – *that* went to Keswick.'

'Aye, the transmitter.'

DS Leyton's tiredness has translated into dark bags beneath his eyes. His heavy jowls seem more pronounced than usual, their contours raised by a day's unshaven growth. He watches his boss with a pained expression: one that tells he worries not only for DS Jones, but also that he shares Skelgill's agony. Skelgill has literally limped back into his office following a review with the Chief. She did of course show understanding (compassion would be too much to hope for), but in such circumstances there is no need to point an accusing finger – no matter that it was DI Smart's team that allowed DS Jones to disappear from under their noses – it is plain where the responsibility lies, and Skelgill is not shirking it. (DI Smart, on the other hand, is attending an unspecified "emergency" in Carlisle, along with others who can be spared.) However, the decision has been taken to restrict on a need-to-know basis news of DS Jones's predicament. The rationale for this is that a limited undercover operation was officially sanctioned, and DS Jones equipped accordingly – and in the absence of any definitive information concerning her whereabouts, or that her safety is threatened, there is a strategy, albeit tenuous, that says she will be best served if her superiors can hold their nerve. Skelgill has been given twenty-four hours before the lid must be lifted and all hell breaks loose.

'I can't see beyond pulling this Rick geezer in, Guv – I mean, what else can we do?'

Skelgill responds with a look of exasperation – though it is not aimed at his colleague, but the circumstances. He shakes his head and exhales deeply.

'Leyton – I know where you're coming from – but we've got nothing on him – not a shred of evidence.'

'But the car was at the bus stop, Guv – then he drove to Keswick.'

'Leyton – Smart's pair of goons can't even be certain that Rick is the guy she left the station with.'

'But if we pull him, Guv – we can find out what he was up to.'

'If we pull him, Leyton – and he *is* involved – the cat's out of the bag.'

DS Leyton furrows his brow.

'What are you saying, Guv – that we're stuck in a *Catch 22*?'

'Let's just assume Jones is fine – that she reckons everything's going to plan – she thinks the transmitter's working and that we know where she is.' Skelgill slaps his palms down upon the desk. 'If we jump in with our size twelves – blow her cover – alert them that they've been infiltrated – what are they going to do?'

'Well, Guv...'

'If we've stumbled on a people-trafficking operation – or worse – are they going to present themselves to George at the front desk and say it's a fair cop?'

Closing his eyes, DS Leyton scratches his head vigorously, as though he is trying to dislodge a particularly tenacious thought that might be useful at this moment.

'Guv – we don't have to reveal we're looking for DS Jones – we could say it's Anya Davydenko that we're trying to find.'

'That's as likely to have the same result, Leyton – they're going to ask themselves how come we fastened onto them so quickly.' Skelgill's features are grim. 'Then they might start asking *her*.'

A look of trepidation slowly takes hold of DS Leyton's countenance.

'It don't bear thinking about, Guv.'

'So don't think about it.'

With this retort Skelgill snaps unfairly at his sergeant – but the pressure is telling. DS Leyton, however, takes it on the chin.

'This Rick geezer, Guv – I get your drift – about how we can't be certain – but why else would he take that route – when he could have got home via Whitehaven in half the time?'

Skelgill nods. The inference is that the longer cross-country journey would minimise the chances of being spotted by a police patrol or inadvertently caught on camera. And there is also the possibility that another purpose lay behind Peter Henry Rick's choice – one that he abandoned for some reason. But such speculation does not take them any closer to identifying DS Jones's whereabouts. Skelgill grinds the heels of his hands into his eyes. Then he reaches for his cup – he is drinking black coffee from the machine this morning – but it is empty and he crushes and tosses it away in frustration.

'I'll fetch us some more in a mo, Guv.'

DS Leyton swallows the last of his own drink and rises and digs into his pocket for change; he is keeping pace with Skelgill, though he must be running short of suitable cash. Skelgill, however, does not offer to pay; his eyes are fixed on the bare desk before him. DS Leyton makes as if to leave the room, but then he hesitates, and raises a finger, as though a penny has dropped. He turns back to face Skelgill; now there is a note of enthusiasm in his voice.

'That's it, Guv – she is safe isn't she? So long as they think she's Anya Davydenko.'

Skelgill looks up; he glares through narrowed eyes.

'How do you work that out?'

DS Leyton seems taken aback by his superior's hostility; after all, this is the strategy he has borne from his meeting with the Chief. He takes half a pace back and holds out his palms in a gesture of appeal.

'They've gone to all this trouble to get her, Guv – she's the precious commodity – why would they want her to come to any harm?'

Skelgill continues to stare – but there is a wild look in his eyes – as if he is shocked that his sergeant is dangerously missing the point. It must be ten seconds before he fashions a reply.

'She's taken it too far.'

In his voice there is a strangled note that rings somewhere on the scale between frustration and despair. DS Leyton requires a moment to process the meaning of this statement.

'But she's a smart cookie, Guv – a whole lot smarter than me, that's for sure – she must have been confident in what she was doing – deciding to go along with it – she knew the tail were behind her, if she needed them to wade in.'

'Aye – and she's smart enough to know you don't go solo.'

Now it is DS Leyton's turn to harbour conflicting emotions. For Skelgill to make this assertion – he the undisputed champion, the number one exponent in the art of maverick detective work (only a tiny fraction of which is known to his superiors, and not a great deal more to his subordinates) – is a severe case of pots, kettles and the colour of soot. But his loyal sergeant – long suffering in turning a blind eye to his boss's unconventional tactics – is not going to take Skelgill to task, probably never, and certainly not at such a juncture. Instead, he punches a fist into the opposing palm.

'Think she's in Keswick, Guv?'

It takes Skelgill a moment to disembark from the train of thought that was rushing him to an unwelcome destination. But eventually he swivels in his chair and gestures to one of the maps on the wall behind.

'If that transmitter was deliberately switched off, how far could you get from the town centre in one minute fifty-nine seconds?'

DS Leyton looks baffled. But Skelgill waits patiently for his answer.

'In a car, Guv – up to a mile, if you got a clear run of the lights and traffic.'

Skelgill is nodding.

'That's anywhere in Keswick, then.' Scowling, he spins back around. 'Not to mention that you could just keep on driving.'

DS Leyton pulls the coins from his pocket and weighs them reflectively in the palm of his hand.

'If it were switched off, Guv – surely it's most likely that DS Jones did it.' Skelgill does not respond. But DS Leyton seems empowered to make a further suggestion. 'I was thinking, Guv – say it was interfering with a car radio – you know – like a mobile phone each time it talks to a mast – giving itself away.'

Skelgill stares – rather vacantly, it must be said, despite this being an idea of some merit.

'So why hasn't she turned it back on?'

DS Leyton looks a tad crestfallen. He shrugs and tugs alternately at the shoulders of his jacket.

'Maybe there's a problem with the device – like you said, what if she thinks it's working?'

Skelgill enters a few more moments' brooding silence.

'I hope she does.'

He says this with considerable emotion. It might seem a paradoxical statement – but DS Leyton appears to comprehend the point: provided DS Jones believes in a guardian angel, she will find the strength to see out her mission.

'Damn technology, eh Guv?'

DS Leyton slips out. It seems he wishes to give his superior a moment alone, and it is several minutes before he returns with their drinks, plus bars of chocolate.

'Cheers.'

'You're welcome, Guv.' DS Leyton deftly slits the packaging of his snack with a thumbnail. 'Not often I get one of these to myself – the kids are like gannets.'

Skelgill raises an eyebrow.

'Gannets only eat fish, Leyton.'

'Not London gannets, Guv – they'll eat anything – they're allnivorous.'

Now Skelgill can't resist a wry smile. He realises his sergeant is doing his best to sustain their morale, when really this ought to be his remit.

'I was thinking of going fishing later.'

DS Leyton glances up – but if he is surprised, or even shocked, then he does not show it – and in any event, Skelgill's response to an intractable predicament is never easy to forecast; he has learned that there are times when his boss is best left to his own devices.

'Really, Guv – what's good about now?'

'This warm weather, Leyton – you know fish are cold blooded?' (DS Leyton nods eagerly; Skelgill regards his enthusiasm with a doubting frown.) 'The higher the water temperature, the more they eat. Now they've finished spawning, pike'll even take a fly.'

20. MOON RISING

Esox lucius, the scientific name for the pike, is said to mean "pitiless water wolf" – though Skelgill's own pursuit of the creature's etymology (relentless, much like his pursuit of the creature itself) has revealed a more literal translation that he prefers: "great fish of the light".

As the sun sets and the full moon rises to take its place in the pearly evening sky, it is illumination that Skelgill seeks – and not his regular quarry, the spotted wolf that lurks below. He has paddled out, slipping across the silvery meniscus that is the surface of Bassenthwaite Lake, his bow wave creasing the perfect reflection of Skiddaw's great pyramid, its upper slopes aglow beneath the sun's dying rays. With no wind – no need for an anchor, and too early in the season for there to be large squadrons of midges – he is becalmed with his thoughts and the occasional plaintive birdcall.

Of course, he has a line out. To sit in the boat, empty handed, would not only make him feel – and even *look* – naked, but also it would deprive him of his powers. Like a crossword solver without a pen, a drummer without sticks, an artist without a brush, stripped of his fishing gear his imagination is emasculated. In common with the copper lightning conductor on a church tower, through his rod – and the taut filament of nylon that penetrates the skin of the great body of water – is his channel of communion with nature's latent forces. Thus he pays lip service to angling, and awaits inspiration to bite.

That he can be here at all owes much to DS Leyton. Skelgill's intimation that he might fish had been recognised as an act of bravado, a valiant effort to demonstrate (perhaps to himself) that he had not lost his nerve, that he believed the situation was under control; but it was a cry for help. Consequently, later in the day – the longest day, of blank news, of pacing, of coffee by the gallon – his trusty lieutenant had rekindled the idea, pointing out that, while there was little but to sit and wait for some form of contact from DS Jones, surely it would benefit Skelgill to get a break? In response to this incontestable reasoning, Skelgill had insisted that DS Leyton, too, must go home and attend to his family's routine – a sure fire way of taking one's mind off the nagging worry that returns like a recalcitrant toothache. Curiously (it seemed to Skelgill, largely unfamiliar with such bath-time bedlam) DS Leyton had eschewed this offer and proposed a small venture of his own.

In the absence of a tangible lead, it remains DS Leyton's assertion that Little Langdale is a hotspot of sorts as far as their investigation is concerned – and he persists with this view despite Skelgill's reluctance to draw conclusions from the events they have recorded. As he had reiterated to his boss, there is no denying that William Thymer – *Ticker* – had suspiciously drowned in the village tarn, with various signs of (as DS Leyton put it) "hocus-pocus" about his camp, and in his possession a distinctive charm that potentially linked him to the missing Leonid Pavlenko. Pavlenko, in turn, was almost certainly in the vicinity (at nearby Coniston, at least), and had a note on the back of his girlfriend's photograph that made reference to "black beck". They have evidence from Kyiv that this female, Irina Yanukovych, came to Cumbria, and there are further Eastern European connections in the area, including the Polish girl Eva who abruptly departed from the local inn having apparently tried to contact the police.

Thus DS Leyton's proposal had been to spend the evening quietly tucked away, incognito, in a corner of the Langdale Arms. As he pointed out, the landlord believes he is a visitor on a walking holiday, lodging nearby, and expressly partial to the establishment's renowned pies.

Skelgill had been sceptical. The idea that DS Leyton might hit upon some nugget of information, strike a rich seam of evidence that would lead them to DS Jones's whereabouts, had seemed to him a most unlikely prospect. But he could not argue with his sergeant's wish to do *something*. Rather than twiddle his thumbs (or dunk his kids) he could at least feel that he was making a positive contribution to the case. And with this sentiment, Skelgill could concur. He set aside his reservations and consented to the request – and now, at just past eight-thirty p.m., he receives a text message to confirm that his colleague is in situ. DS Leyton also reports that the pub is conveniently busy because there is an overflow of delegates from the latest conference being held at Blackbeck Castle.

Skelgill replaces his phone in one of the many pockets of his vest. It has the appearance of a field medic's garment, adorned as it is with various items of angling paraphernalia – disgorging forceps, line clippers, pliers and suchlike, spare flies and weights and lures, and iridescent imitation minnows that bristle with treble hooks. To accidentally sit upon Skelgill's carelessly discarded waistcoat could be the precursor to a trip to the nearest A&E department. He retrieves the line that has gone slack out in the water – a ledgering rig baited with a brandling – he is ostensibly fishing for perch, a less troublesome catch – though at this time the fish are not troubling the worm. And ideas are not troubling his brain.

That Skelgill is drawn to his stamping ground, however, suggests he has some solution – it is just not yet available to his conscious mind. The facts and inferences he has gathered – many of which seem at best vaguely connected – perhaps bear relationships that, once understood, will explain one another, rather like individual jigsaw pieces that, triggered by a moment of insight, suddenly begin to fall into place and reveal the bigger picture. To appreciate the true nature of a great wood, when all one sees is trees, it is necessary to find that forest giant – not always so obvious at its foot – that can be scaled to provide a revealing overview.

Conscious analysis does not come easily to Skelgill, nor anyway does it offer the processing power to deal with a multiplicity of variables. Moreover, though he would claim that the much-vaunted managerial skill of "T-CUP" (thinking clearly under pressure) numbers among his abilities, right now he is burdened by guilt over DS Jones's disappearance, which interrupts his deliberations at least every minute. And yet he and

DS Leyton, discussing this several times over during the day, have concluded there was little more they could have done. DS Jones had to be given sufficient leeway to 'play it by ear'. To penetrate the ring – to make a single arrest, even – she had to obtain evidence of a sufficient quality to demonstrate there was a crime afoot. Being offered directions at a railway station by a helpful stranger would receive short shrift from the Crown Prosecution Service, never mind a jury. Being accompanied to the correct bus, shown the right stop, being offered a lift – none of these actions are against the law – so it is easy to see why DS Jones played along (believing she was under the watchful eye of her colleagues). But, step by step, she had walked voluntarily into what was effectively her own abduction. Could they have foreseen this? Might they have anticipated a malfunction with the tracking device? On reflection, probably. But time and, above all, resources were limited. And now – with DI Smart's operation apparently cracking off (the "Carlisle emergency") – manpower is even more stretched. Indeed, the clandestine watch that was put on the premises of Rick & Co – to track his movements should he leave – had to be recalled when shifts changed over at six p.m. this evening.

One thing Skelgill can be sure about, however, is that the person who met DS Jones at Penrith railway station could not have suspected she was a police officer. As Captain Shevchenko had rightly asserted, they would simply not turn up. This knowledge also suggests that the use of first the bus and then the car – left at an isolated and darkened village stop – is simply a regular precaution to avoid being identified, and was not a conscious act to lose a tail. It does not, however, explain what occurred in Keswick, and how they lost trace of her altogether. And while Skelgill has been adamant the police should not jeopardise DS Jones's cover, he does not share DS Leyton's optimism that it will protect her indefinitely. In the meantime can he dare to believe that she is burrowing deeply enough to undermine the foundations of whatever illegal edifice has been built on their patch? That she is waiting for the right moment to make her move and get back in touch? With a second night upon them, he needs it to be soon.

His mobile rings.

Skelgill tears at the *Velcro* of his gilet. The number is unfamiliar, though at a glance it seems to comprise mostly threes and sevens.

'Skelgill.'

'Ah, Inspector – is it convenient? This is Rhian Roberts.'

He looks again briefly at the handset, a puzzled expression crossing his features.

'It's fine – madam.'

'I received a message that you need my help.'

Again Skelgill hesitates.

'Who from?'

The woman responds with an amused chuckle.

'Let's say it was an anonymous source. And so we have been conducting some... *investigations* of our own.'

In the background behind her Skelgill can hear the light chatter of voices and the odd clink and clatter of what could be teacups and saucers. He checks his watch – it is now after nine – late perhaps for her to be socialising.

'I see.'

He obviously doesn't, but she does not elaborate.

'You are outdoors?'

'I'm fishing – on Bass Lake.'

'Then you see the full moon?'

Skelgill turns to the southeast.

'Plain as day.'

'I mentioned that there are four great *sabbats* – tomorrow is Beltane – tonight is May Eve, Walpurgis Night.'

A look of alarm is gradually taking of hold of Skelgill's countenance.

'Tonight?'

'You understand what I am saying?'

Once more, he is slow to respond.

'Aye – I think I do.'

'I am preparing with my own coven at this moment – a full moon on such a night is exceptionally propitious.'

'Or not.' His voice is quiet, mechanical.

'Quite right, Inspector – there are those who would wish to subvert such incalculable energy.'

He stares unblinking across the pale surface of the lake. A mist is beginning to rise as the night air cools more quickly than the water. From a distant shore the ululating hoot of a tawny owl resonates with the insistent pinking of blackbirds. Skelgill is motionless; though upon close inspection the hairs on his bare forearms bristle in unison. His right hand, holding the mobile phone, has drifted away from his ear. Now the witch's disembodied voice seems to emanate from dusk's sharp ether.

'If you need to act, you might have only a few hours to do so. You know where to go. We shall be with you in spirit – I have placed your cause high upon our agenda. Now, she awaits.'

*

'Come on Merkel – pull your weight, man!'

Skelgill is jolted from his trance. He looks with some incredulity at his mobile phone, gripped tightly in the hand that has fallen to rest upon his lap. The screen is blank – in sleep mode. Then he swivels at the waist to face the source of the intrusion: a coxless four is crossing his bows some seventy-five yards off. In the gathering darkness it is difficult to make out much of the rowers – they do not appear to be wearing athletic kit – though their voices carry as if they are almost beside him. They appear oblivious to Skelgill's presence. They are sculling hard, and their occasional breathless conversation (in the most refined of accents) tells its own story: they are sixth-formers from Oakthwaite School – they have obviously sneaked out to the public bar at the coaching inn just beyond Peel Wyke, and have cut fine their homeward return.

'Quick hands, chaps – old Ravelston-Dykes will have our guts for garters if we're not back for lights-out!'

'Jenkins, I told you we should have drawn the line at two sherries!'

'That was you to blame, Merkel – come on man, *pull* – you Jerries are supposed to be team-players!'

At the behest of 'Jenkins' they fall silent and set to their task – at least they seem to know what they are doing, and swiftly they make progress towards the wooded banks where the great institution lies concealed from everyday sight.

But Skelgill has activated his phone. His features are cast into strong relief by its eerie blue glow. There is something vulpine about the light in his eyes, his teeth are bared and his breath comes quickly. He locates a number and brings the handset up to his ear.

'George?'

'Skelly?'

'Aye – can you nip into my office and do me a favour?'

'No bother – it's like the Marie Celeste in here – they're all up at Carlisle.'

'In the grey cabinet there's a file from the Oakthwaite case – it's all in order, Jones did it.' (For a second he hesitates, caught out by the memory.) 'There's a school roll, goes right back – there's a name I want you to check – look between 1970 and 1975 – send me a text.'

*

'Guv – how's it going caught a whopper?'

'Leyton – are you still in the pub?'

DS Leyton inhales, inured though he is to his boss's brusqueness.

'I am, Guv – it's gone a bit dead – that conference lot all cleared off half an hour ago.'

'Listen – we don't have the time to do this by the book – pay attention to what I need you to do.'

21. MAYDAY

All the while that Skelgill makes frenetic preparations with rope and harness, an ungodly chanting emanates from the gaping black chasm that is the splintered roof of Blackbeck mines' so-called 'Apse'. Kneeling, he works assiduously in the silvery light, every so often pausing beneath the moon to check his watch, which tells him midnight is fast approaching.

There is no wind and the sky remains clear, and a frost is beginning to sparkle on the bracken shoots that rise around him like hundreds of tiny serpents, cloned and frozen for the moment in their race towards the spangled firmament. But despite the cold, perspiration streams from Skelgill's brow – for the past two hours have seen him row, ride and run like the devil, beginning with a sprint across Bassenthwaite Lake that would have had the coxless four gaping in admiration. Making a cursory mooring and stowing his fishing tackle as best he could, he had leapt astride his trusty *Triumph* and roared off eastwards along the A66. Upon reaching his home, there arrived a requirement for 'thinking clearly under pressure' – like some frantic burglar he had ranged about his garage and shed and the back of his car, grabbing items of gear and jamming them into his largest rucksack – whether there was some method in the madness only he knew. Back on the road he had retraced his southward journey of yesterday eve, passing the shimmering lakes of Thirlmere, Grasmere, Rydal Water and the northern tip of Windermere, as he turned west into the mountains crowding Little Langdale.

Immediately beyond the locked track to the quarry he had been confronted by a small convoy, their dazzling halogens all but blinding him – it was the most he could do to stay on the road, ducking his head and holding a line against its tight curves as one oncoming vehicle after another swept past him in quick succession. But he had survived and continued, passing the driveway of Blackbeck Castle, to reach the spot where he had urged DS Jones to mount the verge nine days earlier. Opposite the boundary wall of Blackbeck estate, across the narrow lane, is a dense thicket of rhododendrons – it was into here that he had steered his motorcycle, comprehensively concealing its presence.

Thus the final leg of his nocturnal triathlon had begun – a lung-busting yomp up through the forest, following his nose and the gradient until he met the towering wall that circles the castle grounds. He glanced at the recessed grey gate without apparent inclination to stop – but a little further on he drew to a halt, pausing to tie to a twig a strip of pale cloth – torn from a shirt that had come to hand in his garage – thence to take a brief detour off the path. A couple of minutes later, onwards and upwards he had laboured, driving himself beneath the watchful face of the moon and the weight of his pack. Emerging from the edge of the forest he had struck directly at the shining lunar disc. Arriving at his present destination he had deposited his rucksack and jogged the two hundred and fifty yards to the cliff that overlooks the quarry. A minute later he had returned, his features grave.

And still from beneath echoes the ominous chanting. The collective gender of the irreligious choir is indeterminate – though surely both male and female – and there is a curious murmuring harmony that masks any single voice. The language, too, is impenetrable – as far as Skelgill is concerned it could be Latin or Greek or even ancient Cumbric but its sentiment is unmistakable, at once imploring and demanding, its rhythm reinforced by the low rumble of a base drum, an underlying pulse that seems every half minute or so to emanate from the very body of the earth, a four-note warpath riff with its relentless promise of crescendo.

Skelgill drops to a sitting position upon a patch of springy turf. He wriggles into his climbing harness, raising his hips and pulling the leg loops hard up into his groin – better suffer and adjust to the discomfort now than be half-castrated in mid air. He wrenches the waist strap tight before doubling it back through its buckle. His rope is prepared – this is a popular abseil and a sturdy iron ring bolted into an outcrop of slate has served generations of adventurers. He unclips the *Sheriff* from his belay loop and pairs it with the rope before locking them both into the karabiner. His fingers work overtime – and perhaps it is the mantra about *speed* and *haste* that plays upon his lips. Finally he shrugs his shoulders into the rucksack, rises to his feet, leans against the rope and edges towards the abyss.

However, rather than reverse over the rocky rim, he kneels and then inches forwards upon a jutting shard of slate, taking care not to dislodge any loose fragments that might reveal his presence. The floor of the cave is a good fifty feet below and this sinkhole perhaps fifteen feet in diameter. Peering down the shaft, for the first time he is able to see into the chamber. Almost directly beneath is the 'altar' slab and thrusting up towards him the crude 'reredos' – how ironic that he showed these spectacular monoliths to DS Jones – for she stands tied against the vertical rock, while another girl – a striking blonde whom Skelgill recognises from Leonid Pavlenko's photograph as Irina Yanukovych – lies similarly restrained, upon the plinth.

*

The dizzying rush of disbelief is a test of Skelgill's willpower – yet somehow he resists the urge to cry out or launch himself like a comic book superhero – or even to topple, disoriented by vertigo and the mesmeric chant that resonates about his bewildered brain. It is clear his heart is racing; his chest heaves with breaths hissed between bared teeth; his eyes dart about wildly as he strives to understand what is taking place.

But as he clings on he becomes accustomed to the gloom and begins to process the various components of the scene. In fact the darkness is not uniform. Set closely around the pair five candles make a regular pattern (the points of a pentagram?); they burn steadily in the still air. And the angled beam of the moon, a faint cylinder of light defined by the aperture and the millions of tiny water droplets suspended in the moist ether, strikes the shattered rocks and lays down a circular pool of light that bathes the prone girl – up to her shoulders – and creeps closer to cover both her and DS Jones in their entirety.

What is shocking to behold is that the two girls are dressed in white gossamer – little more than tightly wrapped sarongs that expose the thighs and much of the breasts – and it is plain, even at this distance, that they are otherwise naked. As the incessant chanting is punctuated by the tantalisingly climactic throb of the drum, the females appear both alert and yet curiously passive.

Skelgill edges around the rim of the chasm, so that the upright rock is between him and DS Jones. He can no longer see the two girls, but his view into the cave lengthens. Outside the ring of light cast by the candles and the spotlight of the moon there is near darkness, but he can just discern a semi-circle of hooded figures. As he watches, their line divides and one of their number comes forwards leading a tethered animal – a Herdwick ram. In what seems like slow motion – but must only take half a dozen seconds – another person follows and draws a ceremonial sword – and as the relentless chanting increases in ferocity and tempo the sheep is slaughtered – the head is hacked off and the body cavity split asunder.

It is not clear if the girls witness this act of butchery – or indeed if they are looking at all – but now the 'executioner' approaches them bearing a chalice; it drips black with blood. Skelgill scrambles back to his original position – he watches with a morbid fascination as the figure anoints the girls in turn – marking a counter-clockwise swastika upon the exposed flesh of the left breast above the heart. The prone Irina Yanukovych is plainly trembling, but DS Jones holds her nerve, though she closes her eyes while the symbol is daubed.

Then abruptly the drum signals a change and the monotonous chant assumes a slower tempo. The black coven – for of course that is what they must be – has crowded around the altar – but now the leader holds up the chalice and walks through the throng, who turn and follow. They disappear from Skelgill's line of vision – and, though the incantation continues, its volume diminishes.

He checks his watch – and this might provide the explanation – for it is eight minutes to midnight – and below he can see that the patch of moonlight has extended across the body of Irina Yanukovych and is now falling upon the bare feet of DS Jones. Perhaps the coven is undertaking its final vile preparation before returning to the altar at the witching hour.

Skelgill must act.

He shrugs the coil of rope from his shoulder and tosses it into the aperture. He watches through narrowed eyes as it snakes down into the void. He knows its length and that it will comfortably reach the ground. It falls directly behind the shard to which DS Jones is secured. There is a space of about eight feet at which he can aim between the rock and the pool of water that extends into the invisible depths of the cavern. Now he takes up the slack and begins to back over the edge. There is always a point in abseiling when trust must be transferred to some higher power (even if that be the manufacturers of the rope or of the expansion bolts that hold the anchor point in place) – it is a point of no return – but Skelgill shows no hesitation as he dips his backside and then pushes off, simultaneously reducing the friction on his belay device so that he drops well beneath the overhang and the attendant risk of a crack to the skull. Smoothly, he descends the shaft, taking just ten seconds to touch down gently upon the rough-hewn stone floor. He has no stopper knot on the rope and briskly hauls the running end free of his harness.

He casts about. The chanting – certainly now coming from somewhere beyond the exit to this great chamber – has taken on a more urgent note, more strained, more frenzied; but it sounds as though they have been left alone – and why should the coven worry? For there is only one way out – and they have numbers and, as Skelgill's reconnaissance has already determined, a guard patrolling the quarry. Cautiously he rounds the immense upright and vaults onto the flat 'altar' slab. He moves nimbly and before she can react he has his hand pressed firmly over DS Jones's mouth. There is sudden fear and alarm in her eyes – but Skelgill hisses into her ear and she realises it is he.

'Keep dead quiet.'

DS Jones nods.

The other girl appears petrified; Skelgill kneels and whispers to her, too. She seems to grasp she is to be silent, though she recoils when he reaches over his shoulder and pulls a glinting blade from his backpack. Swiftly he cuts the bonds that fasten her wrists and ankles. Then he rises and releases DS Jones. She sways forwards as the binding that pinned her drops away, and Skelgill has to support her weight, wrapping his arms about her body. He can feel that she is cold, chilled and damp and her nipples press through the fabric of the flimsy sacrificial garment.

'Are you okay?'

His words again are whispered directly into her ear.

'They've given us something, Guv – to subdue us – I feel numb.'

Skelgill grimaces, though in their embrace she does not see his concern.

'Getting worse or better?'

'Better, I think, Guv.'

Skelgill steps away. Keeping a grip of her elbows he helps her down off the horizontal slab, which is about three feet higher than ground level. He leads her to the rear of the vertical shard. She walks sluggishly, and he gathers in the dangling rope and feeds it into her hands for support. Then he darts back and similarly assists Irina Yanukovych. It is hard to tell if she is more or less affected by the drug – in the gloom she regards him languidly, but she manages to walk unaided and, albeit unsteadily, to join DS Jones in hanging on to the rope.

Skelgill rips off his rucksack and tips out its remaining contents. There is a second harness and various lengths of rope and sundry gadgets. He has little more than darkness in which to work, which is perhaps just as well for now he guides one after the other of the Ukrainian girl's bare feet into the leg loops of the apparatus and slides it up to her waist, doing his best to tuck in the sarong to preserve some sort of modesty. Then he stoops and grabs a handful of climbing paraphernalia – these are ascenders, devices for climbing a rope, he clips them on and secures them to the harness. He looks at DS Jones and mouths an instruction.

'She's got to climb.'

DS Jones whispers to the girl, who nods and speaks in turn into DS Jones's ear.

'She's done it before, Guv – national service.'

'Tell her to go.'

The girl, despite her obvious lethargy, understands what she must do – and though fear has the power to immobilise, now it drives flight. Slowly – painfully slowly to Skelgill's anxious eyes – she begins to scale the rope.

He unbuckles his own harness and lets it drop to the ground. He kneels and, carefully holding the leg loops in position, he presents it to DS Jones. She steps into the loops and allows him to raise the gear to her waist. Again there is an awkward intimate moment, but the exigency means decorum must be set aside. Indeed, Irina Yanukovych is getting the hang of it and is already above head height. Skelgill reaches to rig up the remaining ascenders for his colleague.

'Remember your training.'

His words are a command – he refers to a course he runs for police recruits, the basic escape from a mineshaft or pothole, accomplished with more rudimentary hand-tied *Prusik* loops – but DS Jones nods as though it were a question.

'Yes, Guv – *but what about you*?'

Skelgill glances anxiously over his shoulder – for DS Jones almost cries out these last words. It has dawned upon her that he has forfeited his own means of escape.

'I didn't bank on there being three of us – my mistake.' He grins ingenuously. 'Now shift.'

'But, Guv – what will you do?'

'Improvise.'

'But –'

He grabs her face between his hands and speaks with renewed urgency, almost spitting the words. 'Listen to me. From the top you might have ten minutes' head start. Get the moon at your back and run if you can. When you meet the wall turn left. Stay on the path. After half a mile look for a strip of cloth on a branch. Untie it. It marks the way to the bottom of the mine – in the gully where it's boarded up – remember?' (She nods once.) 'There's a bin bag under a pile of bracken, to the left of the tunnel entrance. It's got warm clothes, energy drinks, mint cake – and my phone – if you can get a signal.'

He stoops to pick up the rope, and then from behind he reaches around her waist to secure the running end. This could be a hug of sorts – but the action is swift and he steps away and delivers her a stinging slap across the buttock.

'Up you go, lass.'

His unexpected prompt sees DS Jones respond accordingly. He moves aside to give her space – there is the splash of water as he inadvertently treads in the shallow margins of the pool. She begins to ascend – and immediately it becomes clear what he has done with the rope: as she goes up, so it does too – and within thirty seconds there is no loose end that could be shaken by a pursuer attempting to foil the escape.

But Skelgill is well and truly stranded.

All the while from afar the quietened chanting has floated reassuringly – if it ever could be such – telling Skelgill that the coven has been otherwise occupied. But now that changes. The drumbeat drops in tempo, and it is apparent that the coven is making its ponderous return to the Apse. Skelgill must be cognisant of the danger – for he stoops to fumble for his knife – though he has eyes only for the moonlit shaft above, and the two spectral figures that slither towards safety, silhouetted against the midnight blue of the sky. Already they are well out of reach, halfway to heaven, and another minute will see their bare soles kick to salvation.

In the black hell beneath, Skelgill turns to face his foes. The incantation, at first growing in volume as the group approaches the altar stones, suddenly dies away. There is a deathly silence, not a breath, not a cry of alarm – only the cold drip of water behind him. Then comes the shuffling of feet. Darker than the darkness twelve figures slowly materialise, ranged six on either side of the great upright, the void beneath their monk-hoods blacker than coal. And from behind the monolith a thirteenth slowly emerges – the butcher with the sword – the *Magistra* it would seem – for embroidered on the cloak Skelgill can discern the glinting motif of an inverted pentagram incorporating a ram's head. And grasped in one fist – now raised aloft – is the real thing, blind eyes opaque in the moonlight, tongue lolling, blood congealed about the severed neck. If the coven has been thwarted in its despicable act...

*

Though no person moves, gradually the chant resumes – no drum now, just an alien phrase of five syllables, stressed on the last and repeated. There has been no debate, no recriminations over the missing girls, no discussion about what to do next – it is as though the coven operates as one mind, a sinister subterranean predator that has seamlessly transferred the focus of its hypnotic powers to its new quarry.

The *Magistra* levels the sword to point directly at Skelgill. He stands rooted at the edge of the black pool, arms akimbo, his expression impassive. He might be at bay but he appears determined to reveal neither confidence nor fear; he knows that every second's procrastination increases the chances of the girls' escape.

The stand off seems interminable.

And then he makes a move – a small step... *backwards*.

Some members of the coven respond, and in a minor way break ranks – the incantation for just a moment loses its unity – as if certain voices reveal a tremor of jubilation; and then the chant resumes its harmony, its vigour renewed and its volume raised.

Skelgill takes another step; the water rises over his boots and up to his shins. His eyes are fixed upon the sword, unblinking.

And then – another step – and another. The water reaches his knees – his thighs – and engulfs his waist. But rather than raise his arms he holds them stiffly – and now his hands are beneath the surface.

He is a good twenty feet out in the pool, and still, slowly, he backs away – seemingly mesmerised, moving like an automaton that is commanded by the will of the coven.

The deeper water must be freezing, placing Skelgill at risk of succumbing to cold shock – and indeed as the rising tide reaches his chest his lips part and his breathing starts to become more urgent, deep and rasping.

At thirty-five feet from the shore Skelgill's shoulders submerge. His face is little more than a pale oval in the darkness that thickens beyond him. The chanting has become more frenzied and disorderly, as though its exponents are excited by the impact of their magic; rogue shrieks of triumph punctuate the rhythm of the incantation.

As if swayed by the collective hysteria, and sensing the moment, the *Magistra* raises the sword – and then makes as if to cast it point first at Skelgill.

Skelgill's head disappears beneath the surface.

There are a few bubbles.

Then nothing more.

The coven is silent.

After perhaps five minutes the *Magistra* turns and walks through the line of hooded figures. The assembly, resuming its chant, falls in and follows.

22. RECKONING

As the stream reputed to be the source of the Black Beck trickles from the rudely barricaded mine entrance, DS Jones and Irina Yanukovych huddle like itinerant beggars against the rock wall of the narrow canyon. They have unearthed the concealed bin-liner and now each wears a baggy fleecy and what might be ski-pants (though they exhibit signs of having been pressed into use for fishing); items that Skelgill had hurriedly selected – presumably with DS Jones and himself in mind. The Ukrainian girl is hungrily devouring a bar of Kendal mint cake – probably for the first time in her life – and DS Jones has an open bottle of juice in one hand and Skelgill's mobile phone in the other.

Their frame of mind is hard to discern. From high the full moon illuminates two blonde crowns – their eyes are hidden in shadow beneath their brows. The impression is of a kind of exhaustion – no surprise given their harrowing experience, the tranquillising effects of the narcotic, and the physically demanding escape. But if they rest in reverie like climbers who have successfully scaled their target peak, they must know the task is but half complete; once recovered they must press on – and, as Skelgill is wont to point out, most mountain accidents occur on the descent.

And there is no phone signal.

DS Jones waves the handset in the prescribed figure-of-eight pattern – but even if there were a signal in this part of the Langdales, the rock walls of the gully in which they hide would shield its reach; they might as well be in a cave. She glances at the girl beside her – they are not so different – in age and physique and appearance – though she cannot fail to have noticed that Irina Yanukovych was beginning to flag as they traversed the steep wooded hillside from the point marked by Skelgill's coded signal. Now they must surely fly – for this cannot be the most expedient of sanctuaries – if pursuers approach, they are cornered with nowhere to run. But Skelgill made no suggestion for what to do next. DS Jones is checked by indecision.

Then comes a sound.

The girls hear it simultaneously, and Irina Yanukovych instinctively grabs DS Jones by the wrist. They stiffen, listening intently. Crouching together in the moonlight, they could be a pair of ancient forest inhabitants, caught out up to mischief when they ought to be safe with their kin.

It comes again – and again – and again – growing in intensity, though regular, perhaps every two seconds – a disturbing noise, a short rasping hiss, as if a creature is suffering some kind of maltreatment.

Though they turn their heads from side to side it is plain that they cannot identify its source – yet it is closing in upon them – it seems to be in the air – like some winged demon that circles above, nearing with each pass.

DS Jones prises herself free from her panicked companion. She scrambles to her feet and stumbles to Skelgill's hidden cache. Amongst its remaining contents is an axe. She steps in front of the other girl – now cowering in terror – pluckily facing down the gully towards the black shadow of the forest.

'*Here*!'

The strangled cry comes from behind. She spins around – her face a mask of shock – for the voice is harsh and anguished... yet terrifyingly familiar.

Skelgill.

Panting like a dog – his features drawn into a fearful grimace, his hair plastered across his forehead, his skin smeared with blood and clay, his shirt soaked and torn – he clatters against the planks that bar the entrance and stretches imploringly through the gaps like a desperate refugee, as though at his back is some great dread – a tsunami – a volcanic eruption – the devil himself.

'*The axe*!'

Again his hoarse cry implores his colleague to act – but DS Jones drops the axe and hurls herself at the partition, first grabbing his hands and then forcing upon him a desperate embrace, their bodies separated by the rough barrier.

'Guv – Guv – what happened – what happened – it's all right.'

In contrast to her vigorous greeting, her voice is soothing – and the contact she initiates seems to quell Skelgill's disquiet. He does not resist her attention, though his breath comes hard and fast, and anguish haunts his eyes.

'The girl – how much – English – does she – understand?'

Between gasps he blurts out the disjointed question.

'Not so much, Guv.'

'He's – in there.'

'Who, Guv?'

'Her boyfriend – I won't – say his name.'

But DS Jones mouths the word.

'Pavlenko?'

Staring, Skelgill nods.

'I had to swim for it – through a sump – that pool's an offshoot – of the beck – I nearly – didn't make it – *aargh*!' He suddenly cries out as if there is a stabbing pain in his temple. He closes his eyes and pulls a face in revulsion at the image that must be conjured. 'There's a body – jammed in the sump – my lungs were – bursting – I just pulled it free in time – I felt his – missing tooth.'

Again Skelgill makes an agonised groan. DS Jones reaches up and, much as he had clasped her face – just a short while ago – she now does the same to him. And again it is as if her touch conducts away some of the dread – for his eyes now recover their focus, and his jaw takes on a determined set.

'The axe.'

'Sure, Guv.'

She retrieves the tool – a hefty hatchet, a good two pounds or more – and slips it through the bars of what is about to be a short-lived prison.

'Stand back.'

She does as he bids – and he wastes no time in smashing the barrier, hacking at a plank at its middle, and then attacking the intersections where cross-members are nailed. He yells with some abandon, as if it helps to release the tension of his ordeal. But he only goes so far as create the necessary gap to squeeze through. DS Jones steps forwards – but now he pins her arms to her sides. He glances at Irina Yanukovych; she shivers anxiously.

'You pair feeling better?'

DS Jones nods decisively.

'I think the fresh air's helped – and the mint cake.'

Skelgill forces a grin.

'You need to go – it's not safe to stay here.'

Now a look of alarm returns to DS Jones's features.

'But, Guv – what *now*?' She registers that his command excludes himself.

Skelgill turns away; there is a resolute look in his eyes. After a moment, he speaks over his shoulder. He has chosen to ignore her question.

'No phone signal?'

'No, Guv.'

'Come on – bring the bag.'

He leads the way out of the moonlit gully, its steep sides velvety black, the beck at its centre a silvery ribbon. At the mouth of the cleft he stops and turns and puts out his right arm like a traffic policeman.

'Stay dead level on the contour. You'll pass Ticker's camp among some pines – then just after that there's a cliff with a waterfall. Follow the beck all the way to the culvert. There's a grassy area with a standing stone – *Meg's Hat*. Just bunk down there – keep warm – don't show yourselves to the road – even if you hear a car passing. I'll know where to find you. Go.'

DS Jones inhales to reply, her face questioning – but Skelgill strides away, axe at the ready. Though his features have lost their horror-struck cast, it is apparent that he still bears a certain burden. While he has spoken of the discovery of the corpse of Leonid Pavlenko, what he has not said is that older remains lie in the submerged tunnel through which he escaped.

*

From his vantage point on the cliff above the quarry, Skelgill can see the coven, dark shapes, still hooded, outlined against the paler slate of the bedrock. Its members stand in a loose assembly of individual clusters – they do not appear to be listening to a single voice. The *Magistra* is apparent in one such clique – the metallic embroidery upon the cloak glints beneath the stars. This person seems shorter now – perhaps because alongside is a much taller figure, bending to confer – and with these two is the 'guard', whom Skelgill spied earlier. His wiry form and paramilitary garb, and the casual manner in which he drapes his broken shotgun over his right forearm, tell Skelgill a good deal. He knows this man: Jed Tarr, gamekeeper to Blackbeck estate. The pair of German Shepherds he holds on the leash merely confirms the identification.

And between the gathering and the cliff are parked vehicles that also come in for Skelgill's scrutiny. For a start there is a black Porsche Cayenne with damage to its nearside front wing. Beside it is a short wheelbase Defender, Coniston Green, if his eyes are not tricked by the moonlight. Others include a new plate Range Rover, an Audi estate painted with the livery of a well-known local firm of land agents, a matching pair of popular marque fleet cars – also new – a small white van of the type employed by tradesmen, and three more modest motors, making ten in all. Skelgill nods pensively. Certain of these are familiar for obvious reasons – and some he has seen parked outside the Langdale Arms. Together they comprise the convoy that almost ran him off the road.

But now there is the sound of another vehicle.

As Skelgill's ears prick up, so too do those of the coven – and it is evident from their reaction that this is an unexpected arrival. The figures turn as one towards the track that leads up to the disused workings – and, for the first time, a single voice is raised sufficiently for Skelgill to make out the words.

'I thought the gate was supposed to be locked?'

It is a male that speaks – the tall figure beside the *Magistra* – and the question, uttered rather accusingly, is directed towards

Jed Tarr. Skelgill at once recognises the privately educated tones as those of the landowner.

Tarr does not reply, for he is now regarding the bright beam that has swung like a searchlight into the quarry, illuminating its shattered cliffs, to home in upon the gathering beneath Skelgill. Tarr would wish to shield his eyes, but with the gun over one wrist and the dogs restrained about the other all he can do is dip his head and squint into the oncoming headlamps. Members of the coven raise their cloaked sleeves against the blindness. Skelgill, in his lofty eyrie, is not troubled – indeed he can see the nature of what approaches. It is a tractor with a bulldozer attachment, and – going by the splintered timber rattling in the toothed bucket – it has accounted for the locked gate. But of equal significance is what follows – a second convoy – this time consisting of farmers' pick-up trucks. These vehicles fan out, forming an arc perhaps a cricket pitch short of Tarr, who stands his ground before the uninvited visitors. The coven members, on the other hand, have backed off and converged into a tighter group, brooding and silent.

Leaving their lights blazing and engines running, the shadowy occupants of the pick-ups begin to disembark, though most – having noted the shotgun – stand prudently for cover behind their open doors. But not so the pair from the tractor. The driver – a big man – lowers himself from the cab with practised ease; the passenger – clearly unfamiliar with the arrangement of footholds – makes a less dignified landing. Then together they begin to advance upon Tarr.

'Reet – is it thee who's bin killing t'yowes?'

If he has not already recognised the powerful – if a little bowed – frame silhouetted by the array of headlights, Skelgill instantly knows this voice as belonging to retired hill farmer, Arthur Hope. And, though an armed adversary confronts the man, he demonstrates little regard for his own safety. Beside him the second figure is more wary. Short, stocky – and, frankly, somewhat overweight – and now placing a restraining hand on the farmer – and moving ahead alone – taking charge as the only professional trained to deal with such a situation – is the unmistakable form of DS Leyton.

'Put the gun down.'

If Arthur Hope's tone of voice sounded typically blunt, then DS Leyton's carries a note of threat – one that belies the easy-going character who is always ready to cheer up his colleagues and fetch unlimited rounds of tea when times get tough around the office. He repeats the words and takes another pace forwards.

'Tarr – put the gun down.'

Skelgill has risen to his feet. He may wonder what thoughts are running through Jed Tarr's mind at this moment. That he is a hard case is not in doubt. Just meeting him confirms that fact – not to mention the disreputable CV that DS Leyton's team has unearthed. He will not shirk at using violence. But will he be computing the odds? The gun is a traditional side-by-side affair. He might have more ammunition in his pockets, but two shots are all he has in hand. And, if he has counted, he and the coven behind him – for what it might be worth in a fight – are lined up against a menacing Londoner and fifteen aggrieved Cumbrian farmers – with whose precious livestock (indeed very livelihoods) he and his coterie have taken severe liberties. Discounting the belligerent Cockney, whom he could shoot, who on earth would sensibly take on fifteen aggrieved Cumbrian farmers? (Ask the 1972 All Blacks.)

But Tarr finds himself between a rock and a hard place.

His paymasters are behind him and an uncertain fate stands ahead.

As DS Leyton takes another step towards him, now approaching within to six feet, Tarr is prompted by his limited instincts.

The gun is still broken and – since he holds the dogs – his left hand is not free to snap up the barrel in the normal rapid manner a shooter would employ as he raises it to fire. Thus the action becomes more ungainly, one of leverage against the forearm – and in this moment Skelgill yells out.

'Leyton!'

His cry causes a split second of distraction. Tarr turns his head to see where the voice has come from, still trying to close the gun. He finally succeeds – but only as Skelgill hurls the axe – and perhaps this is what his warning to his colleague meant.

In a *Western* of old, or perhaps a *Bond* movie of today, such an act would see the hatchet bury itself between the shoulder blades of the villain and terminate his role. But, accurate with his left arm though Skelgill might be, such an outcome would be too much to ask for.

However, there is a melodramatic outcome of sorts – for the spinning axe at least finds its target. It strikes Tarr on the back of a leg with the full force of its steel head – and instantly it takes him down onto one knee with a sharp cry of pain.

DS Leyton might give the appearance of being athletically challenged, but in this moment he lowers a shoulder and there is a blur as he barges Tarr completely off his feet. The gun discharges with a flash of orange and a colossal bang that reverberates about the rocky amphitheatre – but DS Leyton is not hit and the weapon clatters onto the stony ground as he brings his bulk to bear upon his foe. The dogs – watchful thus far – suddenly join the fray – but only by enthusiastically biting the ankles of their hissing and spitting and kicking keeper.

A second later Arthur Hope lumbers into action, and there is the thwack of solid thudding punches and corresponding groans. From behind this little stramash the line of farmers makes its charge. The coven now cowers yet closer together – the smaller members retreating to the back of the group. Skelgill watches, inhaling through bared teeth, a look of trepidation taking over his countenance; a citizens' arrest of uncertain protocol is about to be enacted.

And then he sees – with perhaps a tinge of regret – a superior resolution as far as the law of the land is concerned – for into the mine swings another vehicle – and another, and two more – and to Skelgill's relief they flicker with the reassuringly familiar blue lights of the emergency services.

*

By the time Skelgill has retrieved his rope from the iron anchor above the Apse and lowered himself by means of the *Dülfersitz*, the traditional gearless abseil, some sort of order has been established in the quarry below. He jogs across the bedrock.

Jed Tarr is handcuffed and lying face down.

DS Leyton has the gun safely in his possession.

Arthur Hope holds the two Alsatians on their leashes. (They recognise Skelgill and seem pleased to see him.)

The coven is being processed by the police – several of its male members are noticeably bruised and bleeding, and looking none too well for their introduction to the shepherding community. However, sympathy does not seem to be going about in large supply; most of the officers are local men, and like Skelgill they are well acquainted with their farming brethren. Skelgill makes a point of thanking each of the latter in person.

But he keeps his words of gratitude brief, for there is a more pressing matter. He detaches himself from the main throng and strides across to a uniformed constable who stands to attention beside a squad car.

'Dodd.'

'Sir – glad you're alright.'

'I need your car, Dodd.'

'Sir?'

'I've got to find DS Jones.'

'We've got her, sir – she's at the Langdale Arms with a WPC and the other girl. A paramedic has stayed just to check they're okay.'

'What?'

'The tracker, sir – that's how come we're all here, sir.'

'You mean Leyton didn't call you?'

'No, sir.'

Skelgill is nonplussed. PC Dodd continues.

'The tracker began flashing, sir – about a quarter-to-eleven. It was moving south from Keswick – heading down this way. We tried to call you but there was no reply.'

'Aye – I was on my bike – then I lost the signal.'

'And we lost the tracker, too, sir – at about eleven-thirty p.m. – but then it came back on again just after midnight – we found her where you'd told her to hide, sir.'

Skelgill's brow is furrowed and for a few moments he stands in pensive silence. The eager constable begins to look concerned – perhaps he has upset the plans of this infamously enigmatic officer?

'She was in Keswick, you say?'

'That's right, sir – the signal started up more or less exactly at the point of the last trace on Tuesday night.'

Skelgill is nodding to himself.

'Good job, Dodd.'

Now PC Dodd – who is no fool – is looking at Skelgill with a certain mixture of fascination and admiration. He risks interrupting his superior's thoughts.

'Sir?'

'Aye?'

'How did you know – to come here, sir?'

Skelgill manufactures a wry grin.

'Let's say I got my own signal.'

PC Dodd understands this is not to be questioned further. He nods obediently. However, in the avoidance of doubt, Skelgill adds a rider.

'But if anyone asks – let's say I received yours.'

'I understand, sir.'

Now Skelgill revises his plan of taking the car – instead he strides across to the milling group of police and farmers. They have the recumbent coven members lined against the rock wall – most are huddled in their cloaks, a couple still hooded – but as Skelgill ranges along their line, like a witness at an identity parade, he finds familiar faces, some glowering, others frightened: Dr Wolfstein; Peter Henry Rick; the publican from the Langdale Arms and the two portly sales reps he and DS Jones had seen there; Reginald Pope of *Pope & Parish* land agents; then several he does not know, two of them elderly females; and finally – still hooded, but distinctive for the embroidered cloak – the *Magistra*.

Skelgill stands motionless for a moment. The person does not respond, but there is perhaps the hint of a flinch, as if it is apparent what is coming. He reaches down and flips back the hood.

Mrs Robinson.

"The leader is always female, Inspector."

23. LOCK-IN

'Guv – I just found the pies.'

'It's a reet proper lock-in, marra.'

Skelgill sounds buoyant; it must be adrenaline that refuses to abandon his bloodstream.

'I've turned a blind eye to enough of 'em, Guv – 'bout time I had one of my own.'

DS Leyton resumes his seat at the hearth. Skelgill has kindled a crackling blaze, and the aroma of wood smoke fills the air. They have hauled close a sofa – on which lounge he and DS Jones – and an easy chair for DS Leyton. The men have pints of ale standing upon a low oak table, but DS Jones – who has been advised to avoid alcohol – nurses a mug of hot chocolate and has her feet tucked beneath her. The WPC has escorted Irina Yanukovych to hospital for a check-up. It is just after two a.m. and they have the Langdale Arms at their disposal.

'Where are they then?'

'In the oven, Guv – take half an hour – I thought it would be quicker than microwaving them individually.'

'How many?'

'About a dozen, Guv.'

'Nice one, Leyton.'

DS Leyton grins and raises his glass.

'Cheers, Guv.'

Skelgill reciprocates, and smacks his lips after a long draught.

'He might be a crook – but he keeps a decent pint.'

'Fancy him being Polish, eh, Guv? He covered that one up – what does it say over the door – Graham Parker?'

'Maybe he covered it up too well.'

Skelgill's remark hints at some suspicion hitherto unshared. DS Leyton shrugs and examines the clarity of his best bitter against the flames of the fire.

'He had me fooled, Guv – then again, I struggle to tell a Brummie from a Scouser – you northerners all sound the same to me.'

Skelgill is about to reprimand his colleague for taking such a dire liberty with England's geography and dialects – but there is a sharp electronic alert and DS Jones reaches for Skelgill's phone. The pub's *Wi-Fi* is providing access to real-time updates that are being posted by various teams of officers, hurriedly mobilised in the wake of the arrests – for perhaps DS Jones's most significant revelation has been that other girls are likely being held at locations throughout the county. Now she scrolls through the latest news as her colleagues look on.

'This is about him, Guv – the publican.' She scans the contents of the message. 'Real name Chechlacz. Admits to being Yashin's direct contact. Claims his family moved from Poland to Wolverhampton when he was a teenager. Spent twenty years working in the licensed trade in the West Midlands. Moved to Prague in 2010 – ran a nightclub there until about six months ago.'

DS Leyton holds out an upturned palm.

'There you go, Guv – that's your Wolfstein connection – they must have had some dodgy business going on in Prague.'

Skelgill is nodding, though he holds his peace. Now DS Leyton addresses DS Jones.

'So, if he's the middleman – Chechlacz – how come he didn't meet you at the station?'

She shakes her head.

'I don't know – I suppose he had to be at work here – with it being evening.'

DS Leyton nods equably.

'What did the Rick geezer say to you?'

'He said, "Come this way" a few times – but otherwise not a lot – and remember I was pretending not to speak English – so there was virtually no conversation.'

'And you weren't worried – when you got off the bus and into his motor?'

Again she shakes her head.

'I knew DI Smart's team would be right behind.'

DS Leyton flashes an alarmed glance at Skelgill, who is staring doggedly into the flames. It is evident that DS Jones does not yet know the full story. She follows her fellow sergeant's gaze and looks inquiringly at Skelgill. After a moment he folds his arms and turns to speak to her.

'The numskulls tailed the bus towards Cockermouth.'

It takes DS Jones a second or two to process the implications of this detail.

'But you were *tracking* me.'

Skelgill remains silent, and though he nods it falls to DS Leyton to elucidate.

'As far as Keswick, girl – then the signal stopped.'

Now DS Jones sucks in her cheeks, emphasising her prominent cheekbones. She gives a vexed shake of the head.

'She tricked me – I saw no reason to be cautious – the guy dropped me off right outside the B&B – she was waiting at the door – she didn't look a threat and I was excited – that they'd taken me to the place that Pavlenko had disappeared from – I knew I was onto something. She showed me to what was to be my room – there's a complete bedsit in the basement – she said she'd bring me some tea – but, the next thing, I realised I was locked in.'

'I said to the Guvnor, you vanished into thin air – didn't I, Guv?'

Skelgill nods reluctantly.

'But you knew I was there – *didn't you?*'

What begins as a confident assertion ends on a note of rising apprehension. DS Leyton remains discomfited, while Skelgill appears torn about this matter. But DS Jones has a supplementary question.

'But I saw you, Guv – about midnight?'

Now it is Skelgill's turn to look alarmed.

'What do you mean?'

'There's a narrow skylight high up on the wall of the room – I saw you poking about outside the guest house – you did something with a gnome – I wondered if you were hiding a camera.'

Skelgill is genuinely shaken – to think he was just feet away from her! He shifts uncomfortably in his seat. It takes him a few moments to respond – as if he is harbouring second thoughts about relating the details of her disappearance.

'Thing is Jones – you were effectively underground – the transmitter couldn't get through – neither from that cellar – nor the caves at Blackbeck.'

At this juncture DS Jones would seem entitled to express dissatisfaction with the performance of the insurance policy that was supposed to have underwritten her risky escapade. However, with the dawning realisation that they had lost track of her comes another revelation.

'Guv – when you appeared in the cave – I'd only been there maybe ten or fifteen minutes.'

She evidently feels no requirement to iterate in full the implications of her observation, but – like PC Dodd an hour or so ago – she has deduced that Skelgill was somehow ahead of the game. DS Leyton, of course, has an even sharper perspective – having been directed earlier still by Skelgill to mobilise what local troops Arthur Hope could muster.

Skelgill continues to sit with folded arms. Now he manufactures an expression patently designed to reassure his colleagues that whatever it was he did was above board.

'I worked it out – with a bit of help.'

'What kind of help, Guv?'

DS Leyton is intrigued, but Skelgill only taps his temple with an index finger. His manner is rather condescending, in that it might imply he believes such an approach could be a novelty to his subordinate. However, he deigns to elaborate.

'I was considering, why would Wolfstein choose to settle in the Lakes? Then it suddenly struck me – that he could have gone to school round here. On Bass Lake, these sixth-formers came sculling past me – one of them was a German – though you wouldn't have known it. I got George to check the

Oakthwaite files – and sure enough Wolfstein was there – in the Seventies.'

Skelgill is again staring into the fire. From either side of him, sergeants Leyton and Jones trade glances – although if there is a message implicit in their exchange it is difficult to discern, other than it suggests a certain recurring bafflement at their superior's methods. In the meantime, he continues.

'Remember, Leyton – you told us that Blackbeck Castle – at about the same time – had been used by some kind of New Age sect?' (DS Leyton nods in confirmation.) 'I thought – what if that was when this black magic business started – if he'd been involved as a young man – then the coven kept going and he stayed in touch? One day he inherits the family fortune – it coincides with him needing to get out of Prague – the castle comes on the market and his old acquaintance Reginald Pope is on hand to sort him out a good deal.'

DS Leyton looks substantially satisfied with this explanation.

'I always said there was something dodgy about Blackbeck, Guv.'

Skelgill rewards his sergeant with a generous tip of the head.

'Old Ticker – he must have got wind of what they were up to – creeping about the woods – seeing stuff he shouldn't have.'

'Such as them doing away with Pavlenko, Guv?'

Skelgill nods, his features grim.

'Even if they only suspected, Leyton – that Ticker knew – he had to follow suit.'

DS Leyton shakes his head with a certain reluctant admiration.

'They did a good job of making it look like an accident, Guv.'

'Aye, well – he was superstitious – he was easy meat.'

Skelgill glances across towards the bar – the press article about William Thymer remains pinned to the noticeboard. He frowns – perhaps considering the possibility that he and DS Jones inadvertently drew the publican's attention to the old tramp. Although their interest had been entirely casual, to someone cognisant of Leonid Pavlenko's fate it might have appeared quite the opposite.

DS Jones is contemplatively swirling the last of her milky drink around her mug.

'That medical report, Guv – about the exceptional level of CRH hormone in his bloodstream.' (Her colleagues each turn to regard her with a look of curiosity.) 'We were inclined to put it down to depression – and write off the death as suicide – but the autopsy stated it could also be caused by a sudden trauma.'

Skelgill has first hand knowledge of how such an experience might play out. The involuntary contraction of his features has DS Leyton is watching him anxiously.

'Reckon they just put the fear of God into him, Guv?'

Skelgill emits a short, mildly hysterical laugh,

'I wouldn't put it quite like that, Leyton.'

DS Leyton takes a couple of gulps of beer, as though he is in sudden need of fortification.

'Guv – you don't think there's anything in this black magic malarkey – do you?'

In DS Leyton's question there is a certain naivety that suggests if his boss answers in the affirmative he is quite willing to go along with this greater authority. Skelgill's reply, after some consideration, is however somewhat ambiguous.

'I do recall a time when I believed in the Tooth Fairy – and sure enough it worked – a shilling in the morning.'

Skelgill tosses off the last of his ale and rises and strides across to the bar. He pulls himself a fresh measure – rather inexpertly, it must be said, too much brawn and too little patience, yielding a good third of a pint of froth. From beneath the counter he fishes out a clean glass and dispenses another, making a better job of it. Then he carries both back to the table. To DS Leyton's evident surprise, Skelgill presents him with the more professional of the brace.

'Oh – right, cheers, Guv...'

Skelgill senses his sergeant's hesitation.

'What's up?'

'Well, Guv – I was just thinking – about driving back.'

Still standing, Skelgill spreads out his arms to indicate their surroundings.

'Leyton – it's past two in the morning – this is an inn with rooms – we've nicked all the guests – who's going anywhere on a night like this?'

DS Leyton appears a little flustered, but nonetheless he makes a kind of compliant nodding gesture with the whole upper half of his body.

'Right, Guv – I suppose I'd better drop the missus a text – in case she wakes up and wonders where I am.'

Skelgill shrugs and slides between the furniture to resume his seat, as DS Leyton bends forwards with a grunt to retrieve his phone from his back pocket. DS Jones meanwhile is distracted by a new alert.

'Wow – listen to this, Guv – they've found Eva – the Polish barmaid – *and* her replacement – both of them were locked in a strong-room in Jed Tarr's cottage.'

DS Leyton lets out an exclamation of disapproval. He glowers fiercely, as if he now considers he went too easy on the man. DS Jones continues.

'Except it describes them both as Ukrainian nationals.' She lifts a hand in the direction of the bar. 'Remember, Guv – when I said that second girl had answered me in Ukrainian?'

Skelgill's features carry a knowing expression.

'That's what they'd do, isn't it? Make them pretend they're Polish – removes any suspicion in public – but once they've got a Ukrainian girl here she's completely at their mercy – tell her if she runs away the police will lock her up as an *illegal*.'

DS Leyton absently taps the edge of his handset upon the surface of the table.

'So where do you reckon they were holding Pavlenko's girl?'

He looks to DS Jones to supply the answer, but it is Skelgill that interjects.

'In the castle, Leyton. Like Rapunzel in the tower.'

As Skelgill adds this cryptic rider his eyes glaze over and he appears to be launched into an involuntary daydream. Whether he relives his surreal nocturnal experience, or the unsatisfactory relating of a doctored version of it to the Chief (in what proved a vain attempt to raise a search warrant), it would be impossible to know – but the trance ends with a sudden jolt that could be an imagined response to being shot at by Jed Tarr or equally to his very real dismissal by the Chief with a flea in his ear.

In any event, DS Jones has an immediate query.

'I thought the towers were blanks, Guv – follies?'

Skelgill recovers his wits – and, indeed, frowns in an avuncular though censorious manner: that DS Jones had accepted Dr Wolfstein's statement about the construction at face value.

'Wait till we find the way in.'

DS Leyton has not been apprised of such matters.

'What is this, Guv? It's all news to me.'

Skelgill glances at each of his colleagues in turn.

'Think about it – they've been using the abandoned mines for some of their ceremonies – they've got a private gate that virtually leads to the lower entrance – Tarr was a miner, Rick is a builder – I tell you there's a tunnel in the castle grounds that leads into one of the towers. That's where they kept Irina Yanukovych. Our boys will find it in the morning – mark my words.'

DS Leyton seems content with this explanation, but it highlights for him an associated conundrum.

'I get the castle bit, Guv – and being next to the mines and all that – but I can't believe it's not Wolfstein who's the brains behind the business – I mean, that woman – I know she was a bit of a stickler round her little B&B – but the head honcho of a witches' coven?'

Skelgill glances casually at DS Jones.

'I did some research, Leyton – evidently the leader is normally female.'

DS Jones nods obediently, and DS Leyton shrugs in acquiescence – but he is still troubled by some of the loose ends.

'Fair enough, Guv – but then why did she draw our attention in the first place – by reporting Pavlenko missing? That seems bonkers to me.'

Skelgill turns to his sergeant; he seems to be trying to decide what kind of expression he should use – patronising, reprimanding, exasperated – but in the end he settles for a smile.

'Because he never went missing, Leyton – not from Keswick, anyway.'

'Come again, Guv?'

'He came straight to Blackbeck – and never got away.'

DS Leyton remains nonplussed.

'What are you saying, Guv?'

'That the girl got a message to him – so he turned up at the castle – perhaps he called at the front gates – maybe they caught him later – in the forest – or trespassing in the grounds.'

'But Keswick, Guv – what was that all about?'

Skelgill takes a drink of his beer and relaxes into the soft cushions of the sofa. His characteristic brusqueness appears to have deserted him, and patiently he begins to enlighten his sergeant.

'Think about it, Leyton. We'll know soon enough how he died – the same trick they used on Ticker and thought they were pulling on me – maybe something more direct? But assume he was killed on the Thursday, shortly after the last signal from his mobile. Now I don't know if he managed to dump the handset – like he might have done with the charm that Ticker found – perhaps hoping it would leave a clue to his whereabouts – or if they got it and destroyed it – but either way they'd be worried that he could be traced to Blackbeck Castle, or nearby. So they hatch a plan. Three days later he checks into a B&B in Keswick, twenty-odd miles away, no apparent connection. That completely lifts any suspicion from Blackbeck – we've no reason to doubt the landlady's word – and his bag's there to prove it. She even gets the name wrong – perhaps to suggest his behaviour was shifty – which fits with him disappearing without being seen by her or the other guests. She also told us he'd got a *Bartholomew* map of Derwentwater – to put us off the scent – but, you know Leyton, no such map exists.'

DS Leyton is alternately nodding and shaking his head, a look of some awe in his eyes.

'Cor blimey, Guv – it's the perfect alibi – if a dead man can have an alibi.' (His colleagues chuckle.) 'But you know what I mean, Guv? We'd never in a million years suspect the landlady of making the whole thing up – she was so efficient you'd have her down as your ideal witness.'

Skelgill scowls.

'Except she wasn't efficient enough for you, Leyton – they might have known about the passport, but that hidden photograph blew the whole thing apart – if we didn't twig at the time. And you discovered the phone call between the guest house and here at the pub.'

DS Leyton is unaccustomed to such unstinting praise, especially from Skelgill, and in the presence of another officer. Rather self-consciously he picks up his first unfinished beer and gazes down into the glass.

'Just me and my big nose, Guv – sometimes I've got no idea where it's going but I follow it all the same.'

Skelgill grins.

'Steady on Leyton, that's my speciality.'

'Maybe I'm learning from you at last, Guv?'

'You just stick to violent thugs, Leyton.'

DS Leyton shrugs. They have not spoken too much about this incident – though it will no doubt make its way into police folklore in the days to come, and DS Leyton will surely be recognised for his bravery.

'It was you that got him with the axe, Guv.'

'I was aiming at you, Leyton – for being so stupid.'

Now they all share in a round of relieved laughter. Skelgill silently raises a glass to his colleague, but DS Leyton continues to look uncomfortable beneath the burden of credit.

'It was you that cracked it, Guv – you sussed out what was going on tonight – beats me how you did that.'

Skelgill grins.

'That's partly down to you, too, Leyton – insisting I should go fishing.' Skelgill swallows some more beer. 'The clue was right under my nose – or in front of my eyes, at least.'

'What – the public schoolboys, rowing?'

Skelgill shakes his head.

'Know what day it is today, Leyton?'

DS Leyton looks at his watch.

'Thursday, Guv – oh, you mean the date – it's May Day.'

'And last night was May Eve.' Skelgill waves a hand about the pub. 'This crowd call it Beltane.'

'I've heard of that, Guv.'

'It's a big night if your business happens to be black magic – especially when there's a full moon.'

DS Leyton nods, and now he becomes rather pensive and glances anxiously at DS Jones; she is clearly flagging, and has settled back into the comfort of the sofa, her eyelids beginning to droop.

'What do you reckon they were up to, Guv?'

Skelgill, too, glances at DS Jones. Mildly, she returns his gaze – though his concern suggests an aversion to visiting this subject in her presence. He turns back to DS Leyton.

'We'll find out soon enough, Leyton – once we start throwing a few charges at them – I'd say we're working on the spectrum between kidnap and murder, with plenty in between.'

Indeed, DS Jones seems to flinch at this analysis, and DS Leyton is quick to offer a distraction of sorts.

'Not to mention killing all those sheep, Guv.'

Skelgill raises an eyebrow – but DS Leyton's response is an ironic chuckle.

'Just as well our boys turned up when they did, Guv. Your farmer pal and his mates were getting right stuck in.'

Skelgill pulls a regretful face, though on which side the regret lies it is hard to tell.

'Leyton – how come our mob managed to put in such a big appearance – I thought they were all supposed to be drafted onto Smart's heist up at Carlisle?'

Now DS Leyton raises a finger as if he has been meaning to mention this matter.

'Turns out DI Smart was working on duff gen, Guv – the snout's taken the money and done a runner – so it was all called off about ten p.m.' He grins conspiratorially. 'The laugh is, Guv

– a report came in from a member of the public of some geezers rustling a vanload of sheep up near Wigton – the Chief sent DI Smart as he was nearest – now the joke going round among the lads is he's the man if there's a ram raid.'

Skelgill chuckles – and DS Jones, too, is roused to join in. This is not an entirely new pun in Cumbrian police circles – but nonetheless it has ample life in its old legs as far as the unpopular DI Smart is concerned.

DS Leyton is still holding his phone, though he has not yet contrived to send the text to his better half – but now it rings. He accepts the call and listens to a lengthy explanation, his own contributions being largely along the lines of "Cor blimey" and "Struth". His colleagues wait with growing interest for the conversation of sorts to end.

'I better get back to HQ, Guv.'

'Why – what's up?'

'We've found *six* more girls, Guv. All locked in. Rick's place, in an outbuilding – that estate agent geezer, his gaff – those two sales reps – and even at both of the elderly ladies' cottages.

Skelgill is nodding. A look of some triumph is spreading across his countenance. He stands up.

'You're right, Leyton – we need to get onto this.'

'Nah, Guv.' DS Leyton springs to his feet and places a hand on his superior's upper arm. Then he indicates with a concerned bow of the head towards DS Jones, partly shielded behind Skelgill. 'I can deal with this – they're only looking for one extra bod to lend a hand – one of us that's been directly on the case – you pick it up in the morning.'

'It *is* the morning, Leyton.'

'Guv – I've not even finished one pint – I'll be fine to drive up.'

Skelgill bites the side of a cheek. He ponders for a moment or two.

'What about the pies?'

'I'll take a couple with me, Guv – whack 'em in the microwave when I get there.'

'Tell you what, Leyton – take the lot. I owe you.'

*

'Guv, what made you risk coming into the cave?'

Skelgill stirs from his present reverie. They have each relaxed into facing ends of the accommodating country style sofa. The blaze in the hearth, too, has settled, there is the calming hiss of unseasoned timber and the occasional shift of a log with its attendant flurry of sparks. The lights are turned down low, and the warm glow of the fire cocoons them from the shadowy darkness of the old timbered room. A glinting brown bottle and a pair of half-filled liqueur glasses rest upon the table. He lifts his gaze from the grate to meet that of his colleague.

'What else could I have done?'

'Called for help.'

Skelgill shakes his head decisively.

'There was no time – thanks to Smart and his latest useless supergrass we had no boots on the ground – and the Chief already thought I was crackers – she wasn't interested.'

'But even if you'd shouted down that you were the police.'

Skelgill looks perplexed, as if this idea never crossed his mind.

'Aye, and then what? They'd have just cleared off in their cars – taken you who knows where.'

'But once they knew you were onto them, Guv? Surely they'd have just abandoned us in the cave – I'm certain nobody recognised me – I only actually met Rick and Mrs Robinson – after that it was all in near darkness.'

Skelgill looks doubtful.

'Jones, I don't get the feeling they would have taken to kindly to leaving witnesses of any sort.' He leans back against the cushions and sends a sigh towards the ceiling, as a smoker would exhale a column of smoke. 'I couldn't even be sure I'd get away. There was no means of knowing whether Tarr was the only security they'd got. Or how prepared they'd have been to come after me.'

'It was dangerous, Guv.'

'Aye, happen it was – but once I saw you – like *that* – how could I have left you?'

Though she still snuggles in Skelgill's oversized clothes he casts a hand at her – and she understands he refers to the revealing white robe she had worn. She sees that there is a strained look in his eyes as he regards her curled form. She raises herself to free her legs from beneath her, and now stretches her toes out towards him.

'It was Mrs Robinson that got me dressed, Guv – she tricked me with a laced drink – and I just kind of felt myself doing what she wanted.'

Skelgill has been holding her gaze – but his expression becomes increasingly pained and he turns to stare into the depths of the fire.

'I know it doesn't look good, Guv – these revolting characters keeping these girls locked up like slaves.'

Skelgill is grimly shaking his head.

'Nobody touched me, Guv.'

She bends forwards, demonstrating her athletic flexibility, and grabs his nearest hand as it rests on his thigh. They remain like this for some moments. Skelgill clears his throat.

'I put you in too much danger – I'd never have forgiven myself if any of those –'

'Guv.' She cuts him off. 'It's all worked out – everything's fine... except there is one thing.'

Skelgill seems unable to look at her.

'Aye?'

'You gave DS Leyton all the pies.'

He grins archly and casts about their empty surroundings.

'It's one less temptation, Jones.'

'And one fewer distraction, Guv.'

***

Next in the series...

NO BARS HOLD

Summoned to an isolated maximum-security hospital, DI Skelgill inadvertently catches the eye of a notorious female serial killer. Does she read his censorious thoughts? Is this the trigger that turns a routine investigation into a rollercoaster of murder, mayhem, escapes and hostage taking?

And what of the establishment? Are these crises purely coincidental, or is some conspiracy afoot? Could it be blackmail, corruption, a power struggle... or something altogether more sinister?

In this, the sixth stand-alone Inspector Skelgill mystery, search teams comb the moorland for clues, while the maverick Cumbrian detective finds his mental sinews stretched to their very limit.

'Murder in the Mind' by Bruce Beckham is available from Amazon

FREE BOOKS, NEW RELEASES, THE BEAUTIFUL LAKES ... AND MOUNTAINS OF CAKES

Sign up for Bruce Beckham's author newsletter

Thank you for getting this far!

If you have enjoyed your encounter with DI Skelgill there's a growing series of whodunits set in England's rugged and beautiful Lake District to get your teeth into.

My newsletter often features one of the back catalogue to download for free, along with details of new releases and special offers.

No Skelgill mystery would be complete without a café stop or two, and each month there's a traditional Cumbrian recipe – tried and tested by yours truly (aka *Bruce Bake 'em*).

To sign up, this is the link:

https://mailchi.mp/acd032704a3f/newsletter-sign-up

Your email address will be safely stored in the USA by Mailchimp, and will be used for no other purpose. You can unsubscribe at any time simply by clicking the link at the foot of the newsletter.

Thank you, again – best wishes and happy reading!

Bruce Beckham

Printed in Great Britain
by Amazon